MW01227450

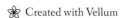 Created with Vellum

JESSE D'ANGELO

LADY OF THE LAKE

NEW
RULE
media

This is for all you lovers out there.

CHAPTER ONE
PRESENT DAY

"AM I A BAD PERSON?"

Charlie put the empty shot glass down on the bar as his companion quietly took a sip from his draft beer. A third round of tears welled up in Charlie's already bloodshot eyes as the portly, middle-aged man shook his head in disgust, looking into the dirty mirror behind the array of bottles.

"Am I a bad person, Bobby? I mean, I fucked up. I know I fucked up... We've just been growing apart, y'know?" Charlie choked back a sob. "Relationships get stale, people make mistakes... But she's... She's not even gonna give me another chance! Wants a divorce. Just like that..."

The other man nodded his head, gingerly taking another sip of beer. Charlie's suit was a mess, his tie pulled loose and top button undone. The handful of other patrons in the dim bar didn't look too much better off. A collection of mostly old men adorned the worn out barstools. Some drank to forget. Some just forgot to stop drinking.

"It's just... All gone. I mean, she's gonna take the *kids*..." Charlie looked over at his companion for support and the man simply nodded his head again. "Am I a bad person, Bobby? Am I? Cheating on my wife... *Am I a bad person?*"

"Look, Charlie. I've known you all of an hour, and I can tell you're not a bad person. You just fucked up, bro." The other man who Charlie called Bobby spoke softly, not lifting his head. He was significantly younger than Charlie, about thirty, yet his hair was thinning on top, which gave him the look of a much older man. His high forehead sloped into an angular profile, like an old Roman statue. He was saying what Charlie wanted to hear, and the shattered man knew it.

"You're so full of shit, you know that?" Charlie caught sight of the bartender as he walked by, waving a desperate hand out to him. "Hey Ted, another bourbon, huh?"

"I think you've had enough, Charlie. You have a ride home?" This barkeep knew Charlie all too well, and recognized he'd reached the point where his eyeballs were starting to float around on his red face.

"I... Hey! I'm fine, I just — " Charlie began to protest.

"I'll drive him home," The man who called himself Bobby offered. This seemed to satisfy the bartender, who kept on walking, collecting used glasses onto a tray.

Charlie looked over at his new friend. The young man had intense blue eyes, electric blue, and despite his small stature, a wiry physique hid beneath his baggy jeans and grey hoodie sweater.

"Thanks, man," Charlie offered, gazing back at himself in that dirty mirror. He cracked again, fresh tears flowing as he buried his head in his hands. "I'm a bad man, I know it! What am I gonna do, Bobby?"

Charlie sobbed as the other man sat there and watched, unsure of what to do. He had seen what other people do to console each other in times of emotional crisis, so he

2

imitated that behavior. The man who called himself Bobby put his hand on Charlie's back, gently giving him a few pats.

"You just fucked up, Charlie. That's all. You just need to sleep it off, give your wife some time... It'll be all right." Charlie looked up from his hands, his face a red, pulpy mess. His companion was clearly giving him stock advice and he knew it. Charlie's head fell back down into his hands, sobbing again but this time, interlaced with laughter.

"You're so full of shit, Bobby!" Charlie cried and laughed, snorting back mucus. The man he called Bobby chuckled with him in order to play along.

CHARLIE STUMBLED out of the bar and into the brisk late night, half supported by his new friend. In the parking lot, all of nine cars remained, and the surfaces were still glistening from a recent rain. Tall firs and cedar trees surrounded the area, and behind them, an overcast, starless night. The neon sign over the door advertised "Barley," the Y flickering and coming close to dying out altogether. Charlie moaned and howled *It's the Same Old Song* by the Four Tops, his tone shifting between sharp and flat as the younger man helped steady him.

"Come on, Charlie. Over here." The young man led Charlie over to a 2003 faded sky blue Chevy Express cargo van with no rear windows.

"Is this you?" Charlie slurred out, regarding the old van.

"Mm hm. Here, hold on a second." The man called Bobby leaned Charlie up against a sedan parked beside him as he fished through his pocket for his keys.

Charlie garbled the lyrics to the classic tune, his tone wavering from sharp to flat, as his friend produced the keys

3

to his vehicle, quickly looking all around them as he unlocked and opened the back door.

"Okay, here we go, Charlie. Come on."

Charlie's young friend crossed back over to him, helping him to his steady feet. Charlie clasped the young man's shoulder, smiling at him as they inched closer to the van's rear doors.

"Mmmm, you're all right Bobby. Thanks man."

"Hey, no problem. Now here, stand right there and check this out." The younger man positioned Charlie in front of the fold-out doors, and he could see the back of the van was completely empty and hollowed out. Sheets of clear plastic had been meticulously lined over everything, taped down and cocooning the entire interior of the vehicle. Charlie had just enough time to think this was a curious looking interior for a van, before he felt the pain of a sharp, muffled blow.

Everything went black.

A short baton was in the younger man's hand, and Charlie fell forward onto the plastic in the tailgate of the van, a small fracture in his left lobe. He landed just as the younger man had planned it, and all that remained was throwing Charlie's legs inside and calmly closing the doors behind him. The young, balding man took another casual glance around the dim parking lot and headed over to the driver's door. Hopping inside, he started the engine and pulled off into the country night.

THE VAN ROLLED down Interstate 87 at a steady sixty-seven miles per hour. The young man guided his machine through the wet night, periodically checking the back to make sure his cargo was still secure and unconscious. It had rained earlier, and knowing upstate New York, it could start up again at any time. But he liked the rain. It made everything clean and it relaxed him when his nerves scratched at the inside of his skull. But now he felt good. Content. He'd accomplished his task and his body was relaxed with satisfaction.

Gliding off the highway and onto a smaller country road, he crossed into Putnam County. A new road stretched ahead, one with no streetlights, no reflectors on the ground or guard rails. A true country lane, leading ever deeper into the early morning hours. The drive took nearly two hours, but he didn't mind. There was cool moisture in the air and the motion of the van was soothing. His work was not yet done, but he knew that soon he would be home and she would be happy with him.

THE HEADLIGHTS of the van swept over the modest two-story house in the rural countryside, slowing to a halt in the driveway. The engine cut and the young man got out. Black night surrounded him. In the distance were the outlines of other houses, but all were unlit silhouettes. It was nearly 4 a.m., and none of his few neighbors were awake. Stepping through muddy earth, he made his way to the back of the van and opened the doors.

Charlie lay there, beginning to wake up.

"Nnnng... Hey..." Charlie groaned as the man he called Bobby pulled him out by his shoes, gently sitting him up on the edge of the tailgate. A trickle of blood ran down the side of Charlie's head, and his eyes fluttered open to try and take in his surroundings.

"Are we... Home...?"

"Yeah, Charlie. We're home." The young man reached under Charlie's arms, scooping him up and helping him to his feet. Charlie's arm was up on his shoulder, and his new friend was taking the majority of his weight. Closing the doors of the van, the man called Bobby slowly began walking Charlie around the left side of the house, Charlie's feet barely dragging on the ground.

"Mmm, wait... Where are my keys? Gotta find my keys..."

Charlie reached for his keys with his one free hand as his friend carried him around the house, through the shadows and around to the back. Nestled in a patch of wet shrubbery was an old work shed, handmade and sturdy. The young man leaned Charlie against the wall, produced his own set of keys and opened the creaky door to the work shed.

"Here we go, Charlie. Come on."

Charlie found himself floating inside, into an unknown place. A place where the walls were lined with tools, some familiar and some completely alien. His friend pulled a chain dangling from above and a single light bulb came on, illuminating the small space. A workshop of some sort, Charlie figured, but he was too far gone to think clearly. A chair sat in the center of the room. Covered in plastic. With a gentle thud, Charlie came down onto the chair and his friend crossed over to a work bench lined with tools. He picked up a yellow raincoat from the bench and slipped into it, fastening the buttons. Charlie looked around, struggling to keep his eyes open.

"Hey, B-Bobby...? Where...?"

The other man turned back to face him, his face devoid of any emotion. In his right hand he held a wooden hammer. In his left hand, he held a large wood-carving chisel.

"Actually Charlie, my name is Zevon."

Before Charlie could think or say anything else, the young man moved with practiced, smooth speed. The point of the chisel came up to the crown of Charlie's head. The hammer came down on the chisel. A sharp *crack* came from Charlie's skull as the tool drove down deep into his brain. His eyeballs filled up with dark blood and his body spasmed in shock. He died on plastic sheeting.

"Sorry, buddy."

THE DOOR of the work shed creaked open and the man who called himself Zevon came out. His blood-spattered rain coat stripped off, he was down to his jeans and wife-beater, wiry muscles flexing beneath a layer of sweat. His hands clenched on the handles of a wheelbarrow. Loaded with a large burlap bag and a two-gallon plastic jug filled with blood, Zevon pushed the wheelbarrow out onto the damp lawn. Pushing his cargo further around to the back of the house, he navigated through the muddy grass towards a large, empty, black area. His eyes soon adjusted to the darkness and he found his way down the familiar path, to the place he'd been coming to for years...

The lake.

It was a large, expansive body of water, country houses lining its edges. The waters were calm, motionless and glassy, black with no moonlight to reflect on this cloudy night. Zevon pushed the wheelbarrow to the long, wooden pier, hearing the wheels thump as he moved it along the boards over the black waters. A smile on his face, he called out into the darkness of the lake like a husband coming home from work.

"It's me!"

Zevon reached the end of the pier, where a floating wooden platform was tied in place. With a practiced hand, he lifted up the bloody burlap sack from the wheelbarrow, dumping it out onto the floating platform. Beside it he placed the large jug of blood. He untied the platform from its dock, pushing it into the cold lake and allowing it to drift to the end of its tether. There it sat in the murk, waiting.

"He was a cheater." Zevon smiled as he stepped back.

"I hope you're hungry."

CHAPTER TWO
PRESENT DAY

AFTER A WEEK OF PACKING, cleaning, organizing and lugging her belongings into the moving van and the back of her pickup, Claire Carpenter's apartment was nearly empty. All that remained was the bed, the coffee table with one chair, a few cardboard boxes, two large suitcases, one small suitcase, and her cat, Fleetwood Mac, aka Fleetwood, aka Puffy Pants. The kitty travel case sat beside the food and water bowl, and those would be among the last things to go. Claire knelt down and poured one final bowl of food for Fleetwood, mixing in a dose of Clonidine which would mellow her nerves for the long ride ahead.

The long haired blonde cat strode over to the food with a feminine confidence and ate with authority. Claire stroked her back as she ate, smiling with warmth.

"Good girl, Puffy," she whispered. Claire stood back up, looking around, her chest cavity beginning to feel just as hollow as the emptying apartment. She was a beautiful woman of 32, slender and fit, polished and well dressed, but in a seemingly effortless way. Her eyes were a hazel-jade green and her skin was smooth caramel thanks to her black father and white mother. Her hair was golden and naturally curly, falling to her shoulders, and her perfectly chiseled, runway model face required no makeup. Most days she wouldn't wear any, and if she did, it would be a simple lip gloss and a little mascara. She didn't like to overdo it and didn't crave attention.

Moving from room to room, she felt a chill and rubbed her left arm. Each room save for the living room was now cleared out. The drawers and cabinets in the bathroom were empty. She had remembered to pack the loofah from the shower, she'd swept up the floors and taken out the garbage. There were a few nail holes left in the walls that required spackling, but the next tenant was just going to have to deal with that, she decided.

She stopped in her bedroom.

The bed and box spring sat alone on the floor, naked as the sheets, blankets and pillows had already been packed away. She approached the window, looking out at what had been her favorite view, the always vibrant and animated streets of Williamsburg, Brooklyn below. People buzzed about on their own personal missions, cars drove up and down, beeped, screeched, crashed and skidded. He favorite coffee shop was right where she could see it, as was the bakery where she got the best pumpernickel bagels known to man. The view faced the West, and at night she could see a perfect sunset casting the whole scene in glowing shades of orange and red.

She would never see her favorite view again.

Two clean cut, strong moving men crossed into the room, wearing identical shirts reading "Miller's Movers" and Claire snapped out of her trance.

"Time to move the bed out, Dr. Carpenter," one of them said as they each took a side.

"Right, right." Claire moved out of the way as they lifted the mattress, turned it sideways and carried it out the door. In a minute they'd be back for the box spring, so Claire got back to work. She knelt down to pick up a box and the top was open. Peeking out was a framed diploma reading, "Claire Carpenter, Doctor of Veterinary Medicine." She traced her fingers across the frame. This was still who she was. She held on to that knowledge and it gave her strength.

Claire closed up the box and carried it downstairs, loading it into the cab of her 2015 jade-green Toyota Tacoma. She went up and down several more times, bringing out the rest of it. After finishing her food and special prescription, Fleetwood was pleasantly stoned, blissfully splayed out on the floor. Claire scooped her up, gingerly sliding her into her travel cage and locking it. She rinsed out her food and water bowl, bringing it all down to the truck. The moving guys had finished with all the big stuff and had pleasantly waved goodbye, heading down the road to where they would rendezvous later.

Claire trotted back up the stairs to take one last look around. Empty. Not one box left. Later on she would discover that she had forgotten the ice cube tray in the freezer, but that wasn't exactly of much consequence. Walking through the apartment, she knew there was no turning back. New York City was over. A paler complexion of skin circled the base of her left ring finger, and she rubbed it unconsciously, feeling the absence. Yes, this place was over, too many memories.

Oh, come on, Claire, her friends would say. *You don't have to move out of the city! Just move to another place, go across town. You're a young, independent woman in New*

York! Why would you want to give that up to go live in Hicksville again?

The decision had not been an easy one. But not only did the apartment remind her of him, Ken... *Oh, Ken...* But the whole city did as well. Every street, every bakery. They had the same group of friends and colleagues, had the same hobbies, loved the same restaurants. If she stayed, she would surely bump into him from time to time, and she would know that the people she confided in still talked to him as well.

Confrontations were not her strong suit and her instinct was always to run and hide. But on a deeper level, the speed of the city, the hustle and hassle, were aspects she'd mistakenly thought she'd like when she first came. But there was too much concrete, neon and car horns. Not enough quiet and green. She missed the country. It was time to move on and she was making the right decision, she told herself.

"Goodbye," she said and headed outside, dropping her keys into the landlord's mail slot and trotting back down the stairs. She opened the driver's door of her pickup, giving one final look around the streets. She took a deep breath of that Brooklyn air. She could smell the bagels from here.

Letting out a sigh, she hopped in the truck and closed the door. Starting the engine, Claire Carpenter took off down the road toward her new life back in her old home town of White Feather, NY.

ZEVON LANG WAS a scrawny weakling of fifteen back in 2005. He sat in the passenger seat of his father's sky blue Chevy Express cargo van as they glided down New York's interstate 684 to their new home. Zevon's shaggy head of tawny hair did not yet exhibit any signs of male pattern baldness, nor did the muscles on his frame give any indication of the sinewy steel cables they would become.

His piercing blue eyes seemed even bigger on his head at this age as he stared off into the passing countryside. He wore a chain as a necklace, a black leather strap around his left wrist mounted by a cheap digital watch, and a black t-shirt to top off the look. His mind wandered as they drove, not distracted by music or any kind of conversation with his father.

Charles Lang drove just above the speed limit, checking the mirrors every few seconds and not saying a word. He wouldn't know what to say anyhow. He'd never had any luck connecting with the boy, not that anyone else ever had. He'd been to see three different therapists and one psychiatrist, and they had all been short-lived. Zevon wouldn't open up to any of them and refused to continue treatment. They all agreed that he had a depressive personality with acute self esteem issues, and words like "bi-polar" and "disturbed" had been brought up. When he was ten, he'd begun cutting himself, and when he stopped that, his next habit had been banging his head into the wall.

During a meltdown at his last school, Zevon had thrown a science book at his teacher, breaking the man's glasses. Every bridge had been burned. Now, whatever words passed between him and his son were strictly utilitarian; it had been a long ride and there was nothing left to say. The van was packed up with the last of their belongings and he was ready to start this new life from scratch, just him and the boy.

At least, that's what he told himself.

His employers, Corrado Medical Supply Services, had offered him a raise and the lofty title of assistant manager if he transferred to their distribution plant upstate, in White Feather, NY. New job, new town, new home and a new van (well, it was a 2003 with 35,000 miles on it, but that was nothing). Getting away from the big city would be just what they needed, he thought. A picturesque location straight off a greeting card, a house right on a lake.

Zevon would love it.

Of course, that's also just what he told himself. Zevon had never really fit in anywhere. He had trouble making friends, listened to that horrible heavy metal music (or whatever sub-genre Zevon claimed it was), didn't like sports and was painfully shy. Charles had tried putting him on a kids' softball team, but that was like pouring oil into water. He'd tried sitting him down and watching games together — Baseball, Football, Basketball... Nothing. Zevon couldn't care less. He would just draw his little pictures, whittle away at pieces of wood and watch movies alone. Well, they were moving to the country now, he thought. Plenty of wood for him to whittle.

───────

"ALMOST THERE, Z. YOU EXCITED?"

"Sure."

The exchange of words was a massive challenge for them both. Charles shifted in his seat, wiping the perspiration off of his balding head. He tried to think of what to say next. Seconds passed that felt like hours.

"Yup, right up this road, that's it. Moving van should be just a couple hours behind us." Zevon nodded his shaggy head as his father spoke. The trees and rolling hills of Putnam County did entrance him, and he figured there was no reason to hate the town of White Feather any more than the last place. No reason to like it any more either.

The van rolled on down the country road, its blue finish not yet faded, its bumpers and sides not yet adorned with the Knicks and scratches that would one day provide its great personality. The tires bumped on the uneven road as father and son rounded tight corners, up and down small hills, deeper and deeper into a maze of green. Houses were sparse and quaint. There were no traffic lights, no street lamps and no reflective markers. At night, this road was dark and perilous, just a black void populated by the sounds of small birds and insects.

───────

THE VAN PULLED around a corner and reached a clearing that opened up onto the front lawn of a modest-sized two-story house. Charles eased on the brake and brought them to a stop in front of their new home.

"And here we go! Made it!"

Cutting the engine, Charles hopped out of the van and promptly gave a good stretch, yawning and moaning with his aching body. Zevon got out in no rush, looking around. It was the first time he'd seen the place. It looked like a solid, simple American house; two stories, white with blue trim, flanked by Balsam Firs and Eastern Red Cedars on either side. It was at least a hundred yards before the property of the first neighbor began and Zevon noted that the entire yard was enveloped in foliage. A house plopped down in the middle of the woods, surrounded by green.

"Not bad, huh? C'mon, get your bags! Let's go inside!" Charles Lang shook out his cramped left foot as he fished out his new front door key. He was eager to get inside and make sure all the utilities were on and ready to go. Especially the water. If the toilet didn't flush, the real estate agent would be hearing from him.

As Charles climbed the front steps up onto the porch, Zevon continued to look around. He saw a bright-green frog jump away, so he followed it. The creature found its way to a little creek on the left side of the property, and Zevon watched it for a minute. He picked up a large stick and twirled it around, stepping on stones to cross the small stream. The place felt peaceful, warm and welcoming.

Very un-Metal, he thought.

Zevon followed the water as it trickled down the stream, around the side of the house. He passed a large, vacant space where one day he would erect a tool shed in which he could work on his projects. The space opened up into a vast backyard. Bright, emerald grass sloped downward at a modest angle, leading him like a magnet to the centerpiece of the property, the lake. His father had told him there was a lake behind the house, but he wasn't expecting such an impressive and beautiful body of water. A simple dock led out from the shore about twenty yards in, where awaited a small, floating platform tethered to a post.

The water rippled peacefully with the mild wind, a sparkling blue-green. The outer rim of the lake was lined with trees and shrubbery, and mixed in at periodic points were other houses. Neighbors all the way across the lake. Zevon could make out one man on the far side mowing his lawn, but the figure was barely more than a dot to the naked eye. He could barely even hear the sound of the lawn-mower. This was a peaceful place, Zevon thought.

Something almost sensual about it drew him in with a whisper and he wanted nothing more than to walk into that warm water and melt into a state of peace. Very un-Metal indeed.

"Lake Yakonkwe," his father called out from behind. "Old Mohawk Indian word, I think. Beautiful, right?"

"Yeah."

"Come on in, bud. Come help me with these boxes."

Zevon spoke in a tone so soft, his father could never hear: "Sure, Dad. Be right there." Zevon turned from the lake and went back to help his old man with the boxes.

CHAPTER FOUR
PRESENT DAY

WINTER HAD COME.

Zevon awakened to a frigid room, but it did not bother him. He was a machine. A quick trip to the bathroom to brush his teeth and take care of other personal business, and he was immediately downstairs for his morning workout. To get the blood pumping, he went to a beat-up old boom box and popped in one of his cherished old CD's, *The Crimson Idol* by W.A.S.P.

His favorite track, *Invisible Boy* charged him up as he launched into four sets of thirty push-ups. Four sets of ten wide grip pull-ups. Crunches and planks for the midsection. Looking into the mirror in his den, he crossed over to where he kept his weights and started in on the main workout. Blackie Lawless screamed and cried for him alone. It was a Monday, which meant super-sets of chest and back.

He looked back into the mirror to monitor his progress. And to check his hair. It was thinning at an accelerated rate, he'd decided. It was no longer just a receding hairline leading up into a widow's peak, but a large clearing was expanding in the back as well. He could always shave it all down, but that's what hipster douchebags do, he thought. All that truly mattered was that he was strong and lean, able to do his work and provide for the one person who had always been there for him. He shot a glance out the window to the lake, knowing she was out there, but also seeing that cover of ice over the water, frost on the trees, grass and windshields of cars. It was winter time, and she didn't come out in the winter time.

This was his time get stronger, get faster, to hone his craft and skills. He turned back to the weights, laying back and starting his first light set of bench presses. He would then go straight to single arm rows for his back, then back and forth, back and forth, at ever increasing weight intervals. He went on to repeat this pattern with three more exercises for the chest and back before moving over to the heavy punching bag in the corner of the room.

With speed, snap and torque, Zevon pounded and peppered the bag; his pumped muscles sparkling with sweat. The bag heaved and swayed to and fro, Zevon using quick, balanced footwork to move in and out, striking his target like a jaguar in the jungle. He would go for three minutes, then rest for thirty seconds, then repeat five times until he was gasping for air and drenched with sweat. He glanced back out the window once again.

The lake.

BUNDLED up in sweats and a warm hat, Zevon finished his workout by running his usual long route around the perimeter of the lake. The temperature was in the low forties, but the wind seemed to slice like a blade through his clothes and he'd swear each gust brought it down to nearly zero. But no matter, he pushed onward, rounding the trail and admiring the scenic view of the lake. His lake. It was the end of February, the ice was only an inch or two thick on the surface, and beneath its translucent veil, life still loomed beneath.

Soon winter would be over.

He made his way around, waving at Mr. Hollis as he passed by, avoiding eye contact with Mrs. Jones and admiring the birds and squirrels as they danced around, minding their own business. His next-door neighbor, Murray Siedelmann, waved from his porch as Zevon sped past. Murray was a widower, and had once been a high school English teacher before age got the better of him. Now he spent his days watching Court TV, practicing his baking skills and talking to his granddaughter on Skype.

"Hey, Murray!"

"Morning, Zevon," the old man said as he sipped his coffee. Zevon would complete four laps around the lake, as was his morning ritual. Except after leg day, sometimes. He finished his final lap, arriving at his back yard, taking deep gulps of freezing air. The work shed stood at his left, locked up tight. The lake stretched out to his right, and he took a few steps out onto his dock, gazing out at it. His stomach growled for breakfast.

FIVE SCRAMBLED EGG WHITES, sprouted-wheat toast with coconut oil instead of butter, a banana and a cup of black coffee was Zevon's favorite, or rather, the only thing he ever made for breakfast. A quick shower was next, followed by some work he'd been putting off. He got dressed in his bedroom, the walls not decorated, save for a calendar of wildlife photos. A few photos remained on the walls of the house, showcasing his mother with him as a baby, their grandparents and extended family. There were a few empty spaces on the walls with the outlines of where frames once sat, and those were the photos of his father that had been moved down to a cardboard box in the basement.

ZEVON UNLATCHED the padlock on the door of his work shed and stepped inside. He pulled the chain on the hanging light bulb, and it illuminated a clean, organized work space. The chair in the center was no longer draped in plastic sheeting and covered with blood. The tools lined the walls and were laid out in meticulous fashion on the large work table. Zevon crossed to a small CD player boom-box at the end of the table, large stacks of old CD's piled around it. He hadn't caught on to digital media yet and that was fine with him.

The new wave of modern Heavy Metal also hadn't clicked with him and he cringed whenever he heard what passed for Metal these days. Classic Metal only, please. He rummaged through the CD's and settled on some appropriately aggressive work music. Sepultura. He popped in the CD and let the pulsing old-school Heavy Metal drive of "Arise" accelerate the rhythm of his heartbeat. Nodding his head in sync, he removed his winter coat and sat down, eyeballing the selection of work in front of him.

Three wooden animal sculptures and a mailbox sign with a family name for the McCulloughs. The sculptures were almost finished, so he began with them. A brown bear, a wolf and an owl. A chip carving knife finished off the details of the eyes and some fine-grit sandpaper smoothed them all off to a nice finish. He lovingly wiped them all off with a clean rag, then brushed on a light stain and left them to dry.

Then he got on to the mailbox sign. The name McCullough was already stenciled on and the first gouges were made, but it was nowhere near done. Letting out a sigh, Zevon cracked his neck, chose a half-inch #7 gouge, and went in to work. Tapping away with his rubber mallet, he followed the lines he'd stenciled out and set the family name into relief.

Alternating between the #7 gouge and the half-inch chisel, he roughed out all the major shapes on the two-foot long cedar board of wood. He added flourishes, like the twisting of leaves and vines, beveled the edges and worked on the fine details. By the time he'd finished, the Sepultura CD had long since played its final track and the clock had advanced ahead by three hours.

Zevon hadn't even noticed. So intensely focused on the task at hand, he had a very hard time leaving something unfinished once he'd started. He looked over at the clock and stretched his arms out wide. Nearly 2 p.m. Time to go to town and drop this stuff off. And eat.

ZEVON'S FADED-BLUE Chevy van rumbled into downtown White Feather, with all its quaint and familiar people and places. Whether it was a large town or a small city, was hard to say. Though it had the small town feel of something out of a Norman Rockwell painting, there were over six thousand residents, three movie theaters, a community college with a decent football field, two high schools with even nicer football fields and all the comforts and amenities of a modern day city. Touch screens for digital signatures on the cash registers. High speed WIFI in all the cafes. Cars that closed their own trunks for you, for the people too lazy to be bothered to close their own trunks.

Zevon kept his head down and ignored all of these modern distractions. He didn't need any of it. It was all fodder and filler, useless nonsense to make you soft, weak, dependent. His routine was to go about his business, run his errands, make as little small talk as he could get away with and go back to his house by the lake. The van's gas tank was almost empty, so the first order of business was to fill it up at MapCo.

After that, it was over to Annie's Gifts, where Annie always greeted him with a smile and paid him cash for his wooden sculptures. She looked over the bear, wolf and owl with satisfaction, knowing they were perfect for her clientele. She happily paid Zevon $100 for each sculpture, then put a $250 price tag on them once he'd left and displayed them on a shelf.

He then drove across the bridge to the McCullough house, where Mrs. McCullough bounced up and down with excitement when she saw the sign he'd made. She gladly handed him the $400 she owed, and eyeballing his sculpted, chiseled physique, secretly wanted to hire him for much more lurid services.

She was an attractive woman, only a few years older than him, and Zevon noticed the way her large cleavage pressed against her shirt with each breath. He wanted to touch, oh god did he. But he had sworn loyalty to someone else, so his thoughts about Mrs. McCullough would have to wait until he was alone later in the bathroom.

Zevon thanked her politely for her business. He carried the sign outside for her and hung it from the hooks below their ornate mailbox, where it hung with regal poise. He thanked her again and jumped back into the van, sailing off back toward his house. It was late in the afternoon and he didn't feel like cooking lunch at home.

He stopped at Uncle Larry's for some Southern-fried catfish, collard greens and baked beans. Fried catfish wasn't the healthiest choice, he knew that, but it was so damn tasty, and he'd done well today. Two jobs finished and paid for; he deserved a reward. And he knew he'd burn off those calories anyway.

Tomorrow was leg day.

TWO WEEKS HAD PASSED since the start of school in early September, and Zevon still felt very much like the new kid at Hamilton High. He had been an outsider everywhere he'd been before, and this new place was no different. It was clean, vibrant and fresh. The kids were good looking, friendly, peppy and colorful. There was a successful football team, a drama club and a school paper.

There was an assortment of clubs and groups for every type of kid; there was the math club, several bands, the black history club, the young Feminists, speech and debate, you name it. But Zevon had determined there was no club for him. People had called him anti-social before, but he disagreed. He was not against being social, he'd say.

He just sucked at it.

Zevon got off the school bus with the other sophomores and middle school kids, pulling up his drooping black pants as he shuffled slowly towards the looming main building ahead. The mop of hair on his head was tussled, and he'd made some attempt to dress in a way he thought would be seen as cool. All black, save for a gray shirt with a Pantera logo on it.

Leather bracelets and pewter rings decorated his wrists and hands. He slouched as he walked forward, watching the cooler, older kids arrive in their nice cars, talking and laughing with all their nice friends. None of them saw him glide through the cracks in the crowd, and if they did, they would just look away.

Some of the students did take notice of him, however. This was a small enough town and most everyone had been there since middle school. Everyone knew each other, so when this unfamiliar little kid clad in black showed up at the start of the semester, some did take notice. Eyes did study him and judge as he slouched by. Boys would whisper words like "wimp" and "goth," while girls would whisper words like "creepy."

They noticed that he never interacted with anyone and was not assimilating into any of the known cliques. They noticed him scribbling in his sketch pad, and if someone was to steal a glance over his shoulder, they would mostly see art inspired by the Heavy Metal album covers he loved. Dark demons, swords dripping with blood, illegible band logos and other morbid fare adorned his private pages in glorious grayscale.

Tom Kepper joked around with his friends in the parking lot before the first bell rang as Zevon navigated through the bustle. Tom was a year older, and everything Zevon was not. He was tall, handsome, well groomed and well liked. He wore a hockey jersey, as did many in his group. Tom's hair was black and slicked back, his muscles well developed from years of playing hockey in the local under-18 leagues.

He secretly considered himself the leader of his group

of friends, and why shouldn't he? He was handsome and popular, dating one of the prettiest and most popular girls in school, a winning athlete, and it didn't hurt that his father was a Police Lieutenant there in White Feather. Who else could be considered their leader?

Eddie Deacon was the biggest and clearly the most obnoxious jock of the bunch. With a buzzed head of blonde hair, he didn't let his acne or bad teeth hinder his self confidence one bit. His family was rich, his body was strong, and it didn't matter if he was a straight-C student, because he knew a UFC championship belt would surely be in his future. When Eddie laughed, he was heard in the next county over, and he laughed quite a bit.

Finishing up a particularly tasteless impersonation of how one of the girls in their class might perform oral sex, Eddie let out one of his trumpeting cackles and the group followed along with him. Eddie's eyes suddenly locked in on Zevon moving through the crowd and followed him like a laser.

"Who's the new kid?" Eddie chuckled.

"Some kind of goth-punk, or whatever," Tom snickered. The group of friends watched Zevon as he went by, smiling and scanning for flaws to exploit. One of the other boys, Jared Marsh, spoke up with a raspy smoker's voice.

"I think his name is like, Xenon, or something," Jared said. The group laughed in a mixture of confusion and disbelief.

"Whaaaat?" Tom's voice went up high and his eyebrows wrinkled up.

"Fuck kind of name is that?" Eddie bellowed.

"I don't know! Xenon, Xerox... Something like that!"

Kathy, a beautiful red-haired model to be, and Tom's girlfriend-du-jour, pranced up to him and jumped into his arms. "Hey baby," Tom chuckled and gave her a kiss. Eddie's eyes remained locked on Zevon, a deranged smile frozen on his face.

"Freeeeaaak! Freak-freak-freak-freak-freak!"

Eddie's voice was loud enough that Zevon heard him and didn't need to wonder who he was talking about. He knew the feeling of eyes on the back of his head, and knew that if he heard that word in the distance, someone was surely talking about him.

He kept his head down, moving through the gateway and into the front quad, where he would be taught lessons that would surely prepare him for adult life.

CHAPTER SIX
2005

"MR. LUTZ! Xenon's drawing demons in class again!"

Tom Kepper leaned over and swiped the sketch pad from off Zevon's desk before he knew what was happening. Rick Lutz turned from his white board, where he was struggling to help these savages learn the periodic table, and turned his attention to the budding drama at the back of the room. Zevon stood up, furious, as Tom held up his art for Eddie and Jared to see.

"Give that back!" Zevon lunged forward, reaching out, but not bold enough to put his hands on the bigger, stronger boy.

"Xenon, do you worship the devil or something?" Tom laughed and the whole class followed, all eyes on the weirdo from Mars. "I mean, look at this stuff!"

Tom held up the book so everyone could see the sketch of an undead monster snarling, blood dripping from its fanged jaws. Zevon pressed forward, reaching for the book, but Tom put his hand on the boy's bony chest and easily kept him at arms length.

"Mr. Kepper," Rick Lutz said, sauntering between the desks of giggling adolescents. "I'll take that."

"You are a freaky-deek, Xenon!" Eddie belted.

"Stop calling me that!"

"Yeah, Eddie," Tom chortled. "He doesn't like it!"

"Mr. Kepper!"

Rick Lutz, a former paratrooper in the Israeli military, boasting a left arm burned from fingers to shoulder from an incident he would never talk about, was having none of this foolishness. He stopped in front of Tom's desk and held his hand out for the book.

"I'll take that."

Tom sighed, handing the sketch pad over to Mr. Lutz. The teacher glanced at the drawing, then moved his gaze to the frail boy panting before him.

"See," Tom said. "Xenon's not paying attention in class! All he cares about is *death metal*! He's just sooo hardcore!"

This elicited more laughter, and Zevon could feel all eyes on him like microscopes, analyzing him like a strange bacterial life form. Lutz held up his hand and the group quieted down.

"I guess you were paying much closer attention to the lesson, Mr. Kepper. Perhaps you can tell me how many electrons are in an atom of sodium?" Lutz awaited an answer, but Tom's guilty smile turned his face beet red.

"Umm... Ahh..."

"That's what I thought, Mr. Kepper," Lutz said. "Maybe from now on, you should pay more attention to your own work and less on your classmates? Unless you'd like to repeat this class yet again next semester?"

The class murmured as Tom was dealt the verbal blow. Tom sunk in his chair, embarrassed, yet still smiling.

"And it's not nice calling people names," Lutz added. "If I were you, I'd apologize. Unless of course, you can tell me the atomic number of Xenon? Since you like that word so much."

"Okay okay," Tom started. "Sorry... *Zero*."

The class reacted with hoots and hollers, and Zevon snarled through his teeth, getting up in Tom's face.

"Fuck you, asshole!"

Tom was up on his feet in an instant, looking down into the wild eyes of the smaller boy as he seethed. Mr. Lutz was standing between them before anything more could happen.

"Try it, pussy! Try it!" Tom was supremely confident.

"That's enough! I said enough!" Rick Lutz looked at Zevon, pointing to the other side of the room. "You, go sit over there." Zevon reached out for his sketch pad.

"Can I have my..."

"You'll get it back after class, Mr. Lang," Lutz said with calm authority. He glanced back down at the pencil illustration as he made his way back to the whiteboard. "Nice cross-hatching, by the way... And you, Mr. Kepper. You can report to the principal's office."

ZEVON SAT at a table at the high school quad, sketching in his book. It was a warm, sunny day, and everyone took advantage of it. Stoners and slackers played hackey-sack and practiced tricks on their skate boards. Bookworms sat in the sun and studied. Friends ran and fro, laughing and gossiping.

Weeks had passed and Zevon was still no closer to fitting in anywhere. Mostly it was cackling and giggling behind his back, sometimes an overt comment about his frail body and sometimes a creative jab about his name.

He figured if he even tried to explain to anyone that his mother had named him after her favorite singer, Warren Zevon, that would only make things worse. Named after a dead singer they'd never heard of from a bygone era of cheesy old music, big hair and bell bottoms? No thanks, he thought. Better that they think of him as some strange breed of space alien.

Zevon's pencil whipped across the surface of his 5.5 by 8.5-inch sketch pad, sloppily fleshing out curves and creating depth. His muse, this time not a demon or violent scene from a Heavy Metal album, twirled in the quad across from him, wearing dark purple spandex pants with a yellow flower print.

Her name was Stephanie Mayben, a young vixen with flowing mahogany hair, supple curves and sex in her eyes. For the fifteen year old Zevon, she had become nearly all he thought about. In a sketch pad that was mostly full of horrific scenes, demons, weapons and Heavy Metal logos, suddenly there was a flowing still-life of a young beauty in the sun. The Metal Gods would forgive him, he thought.

Sex was a big part of Metal, and this young girl *was* sex, personified. Whatever personal history, hopes or dreams, morality or personality she may have had, young Zevon certainly had no clue and had no intention of trying to find out. Watching from afar and fantasizing was the farthest he would allow himself to go.

Sneaking up behind the artist, Tom, Eddie and Jared peered over his shoulder as the drawing slowly came to life. Tom held his finger up to his lips as the others chuckled. From several feet behind Zevon, they could just barely make out the illustration in progress. Impressive work for someone his age, but the older boys could never admit that or risk losing face.

They had already marked little Xerox as a freak and a loser, so nothing he did could earn him a credit. Instead, they just snickered at him, watching him draw. Tom recognized the girl in the drawing and looked up, following Zevon's gaze across the lawn, his eyes landing on Stephanie.

"I think little Zero has a crush!" Jared rasped.

Tom's eyes went wide in a flash of devious brilliance. "Oh my god, I have an idea..." Tom whispered.

———

ZEVON SAT on an overturned log in his front lawn. The sun shone down on him as he whittled away at a long tree branch, intent on turning it into an ornate wizard's staff. His father was inside watching the game. Whichever game it was, Zevon didn't care; it was just "the game."

All he knew was that his detailing work was on point, and this mighty staff would surely be worthy of banishing the Balrog back to the depths of Hell. His attention was suddenly broken as a light, airy voice called out to him from the street.

"Hey! You're Zevon, right?"

It was a girl of sixteen, sitting on her bicycle, smiling at him. *A girl.* He recognized her from school as Becky Reiner, one of the popular kids. She had bright red hair and freckles, a tall and skinny figure with a smile on her face. Tight blue jeans and a vintage t-shirt showed off her lean figure. Zevon swallowed hard, unsure what to say.

"Um... Yeah?"

Brilliant, he thought. Becky rolled from the street across his lawn, approaching him with a warm smile. He stood up, sweaty, his hair disheveled. His shoulders slouched, ready for her to slap him or hurl some cold insult. He braced for the worst as Becky reached down into her purse.

"We have Chem together, right?" She asked.

"Um yeah, yeah." Zevon replied rigidly.

"Mr. Lutz is such a tool!"

"Uh, y-yeah."

"Well, sorry to bother you, but I just came to pass this along..." Becky pulled from her purse an envelope, holding it out to Zevon. "Steph asked me to give this to you. She'd do it herself, but she's kind of shy."

Zevon's eyes went wide as he reached out for the letter, taking it into his hands. He didn't know what to say, so he just stayed quiet, staring blankly at the young girl. Becky smiled again and hopped back up onto the seat of the bike, peddling away.

"Hope to see you there!" She called out as she dissolved into the landscape. Zevon was left standing in shock. Stephanie Mayben had sent someone to give a letter... to *him*?

The front of the envelope had a simple "You're invited" scribbled on the front. Dumbfounded, he opened up the envelope, pulled out the paper and began to read.

His eyes went wide as he reached the end.

CHAPTER SEVEN
PRESENT DAY

CLAIRE RECLINED ON HER PARENTS' well-worn, cozy sofa, eating her favorite pecan-caramel swirl ice cream while her father watched football from his recliner. Puffy Pants played with her mother's cat, China, while a gray and white terrier named Bosco chewed on his favorite rag doll at the foot of the couch.

It had been too long since Claire had been home, and the familiar sights, sounds and smells let her sink into a contented tranquility. Her mother was in the kitchen, washing the dishes, and the smell of veggie lasagna and creamed spinach still permeated the air.

"*Oh!*" Steve Carpenter reacted as one man wearing spandex pants and a shiny helmet tackled another man wearing spandex pants and a shiny helmet. Steve was a husky, strong black man of sixty-three. He always made a point to emphasize the word *black*, as he was of Jamaican descent, not an African-American, thank you very much.

His face was still strikingly handsome at this age, and his eyeglasses gave him a look of distinguished, intelligent authority. He was nearly one hundred pounds over the lean fighting weight of his younger days, but Steve was still a sexy beast according to his wife.

Brenda Carpenter walked into the room drying a dish with a towel, a petite, Southern blonde who wouldn't look out of place in a Hobbit's shire. Two years her husband's junior, with pale skin, a plump body, rosy cheeks, green eyes and a beaming smile, Brenda glowed as she took in the sight of father and daughter lounging together in their living room again. She giggled and spoke with a sweet, butterscotch accent, a transplant from Nashville over thirty years ago, when she was first swept off her feet by her soon-to-be husband during their time in nursing school together.

"Who's winnin', hon? The Barbarians or The Macho Men?" Brenda couldn't stand football, but she did enjoy rubbing that fact in her husband's face.

"The Titans are winning, *my darling*," Steve said. "You should like them. They're from Tennessee."

"Ooh! Go, Tennessee!" She turned her attention to Claire. "You want some more ice cream, baby?"

"Mom, stop trying to fatten me up."

"Yeah, *mom!*" Steve jested. "She has to look good for the boys!"

"Oh please, as if..." Claire rolled her eyes and scooped more ice cream into her mouth with a chuckle. Two cans of Coke sat beside her, both half full. She picked one up and took a sip. Why she could never just finish one can before starting the other, she didn't know. But it was her way, and she didn't care.

The game on TV went to commercial and Steve lurched forward, standing up from his chair with a histrionic groan. He rubbed his right knee and limped off to the kitchen.

"How's the knee doing, Dad?"

"Oh, you know. Crap." Steve reached the doorway to the kitchen, where Brenda stood blocking him, drying dishes. "Excuse me, *my darling.*"

"Oh, I'm sorry. Did you want to get in here, *my love?*"

"Yes, I would. I would like to get myself a cold beer."

"Oh, would you now?"

"Yes, I would."

Claire laughed at her parents as they continued to flirt, Brenda holding back a blushing smile as she blocked Steve's passage. He chuckled and kissed her on the lips, following the warm gesture with a sharp smack on her backside.

"Now get out of my way, woman."

Brenda hooted and laughed, stepping aside for him as he crossed to the fridge. Steve grabbed a cold Heineken and used his favorite football helmet-bottle opener to pop the top. He slid open the garbage pail and tossed the cap in, taking an icy gulp.

"Ahhhh, yeah..."

The dishes were all clean and Steve noted that the lid on the bottle of the dish soap was open. He reached over and closed it, knowing full well the reaction it would elicit. Brenda rolled her eyes.

"Y'see? He's doin' that just to piss me off," Brenda said.

"*What?* What'd I do?"

"Why do you have to close the cap on the soap? Just leave it open!" Brenda reached over and popped the cap open once again. Steve shook his head, taking a sip of beer.

"Baby, your mother is insane."

"You're the one who has to have the cap closed! It's OCD! It's not gonna hurt the soap to keep the cap open, my darling!"

"They wouldn't have put a cap on it if it wasn't meant to be closed, *my love!*"

Claire laughed, shaking her head and taking another scoop of pecan-caramel swirl. Nothing had changed.

"Dish soap doesn't go bad! Just leave it open!"

"Oh, you pain in my ass! What if... What if something falls into the top, like some dirt or something?"

"How is dirt gonna fall into —?"

"Baby, come here. Hold on, you got something on your face..." Steve leaned in close, reaching out for his wife's face. She laughed, pulling away as he comically began to swat at the air in front of her, making slapping sounds with his mouth. *"Psh! Psh! Psh!* Hold on, don't move! You got something on your face!"

"You guys are too much," Claire said as Fleetwood Mac jumped up into her lap, demanding attention. She stroked her feline friend, happy and content. She was home again, back in White Feather. Her parents were joking and bickering as they always had. The cozy living room had not changed, still sporting the same family photos, the same old couch and the same old carpet that now desperately needed to be replaced. Tonight, she would sleep in her old bedroom again.

Brenda and Steve stopped swatting at each other, embracing warmly and smiling. Steve gave her another kiss as they swayed side to side as if to music.

"You know you love me," Brenda said.

"I don't know why I love you, but I doooo..." Steve sang the lyrics to the old Clarence 'Frogman' Henry song. Brenda laughed, throwing her head back like a little girl, still taken by her youthful crush. She slapped his butt as they continued to dance.

"You guys are weird," Claire rolled her eyes. "I don't know if I can make it through two more weeks in this house with you guys. I'm ready to move into my new condo tonight!"

"Oh, I forgot to tell you, sweetie," Brenda said. "We're keeping you this time. We cancelled out your lease. You're staying here forever and ever..."

"Great, thanks Mom," Claire smiled, petting her cat and sinking deeper into the pillows of the old couch.

ZEVON MUST HAVE READ that letter about seventy times.

The edges of the paper had become oily from his sweaty hands as his eyes hungrily took in the text. The last time he'd received a party invitation was in the third grade, and the card had Cookie Monster printed on the front. But now this, an invite to a real high school party, a secret gathering of the cool crowd around a bonfire out in the woods? And penned in the feminine hand of a goddess like Stephanie Mayben? But that was only the beginning.

As he read on, Steph unraveled her true feelings and young Zevon melted into his shoes. Phrases like, "I really hope to see you there. Everyone else is so boring, but you're different. You're special" and "I've seen you watching me, and I've been watching you too" rang out in his head like church bells. The letter climaxed with, "I have to admit, I have a bit of a crush on you. Maybe we can meet up at the party and go somewhere private to talk, just the two of us?"

He had held it up to his nose. It even carried the aroma of a young woman's lust. It couldn't be, but it was. Any doubts simply floated away with a whiff of that sweet fragrance. His fears and anxieties were ever-present, pounding in his chest like a bass drum, but this was something that couldn't be denied, an opportunity he couldn't squander. The thought of kissing those soft, pink lips, or gliding his hands across her smooth, silky skin got him higher than any drug. The bulge in his pants begged to be let loose. He read through the letter again, then checked the clock. It was time.

Young Zevon loped down the stairs dressed for his big night out. A long sleeved button-up shirt hung from his narrow shoulders instead of just a black Metal-band t-shirt, and some attempt had been made to tidy up the hornet's nest of hair on his head. He wore a slightly nicer than usual pair of jeans and his black and white Adidas. He'd chosen a couple of studded-leather bracelets and his favorite rings, and looked like a proper Metal-head kid going out for a fancy night.

He crossed into the living room with trepidation as his father watched a football game from the edge of the couch. Charles Lang sipped from his can of Pabst Blue Ribbon and his muscles tensed with each feat of athleticism on the screen, as if he himself were remotely controlling the players.

"Dad?"

Zevon's voice sounded even younger than his fifteen years. Charles turned his head slightly towards his son while still managing to keep his eyes locked on the screen.

"Yeah, Z." He was on autopilot.

"Um, I'm going to that party now."

His father nodded his head in approval, shooting the quickest of glances at him before zeroing back in on the game.

"Okay, great. Have a good time," Charles offered. *It was about time the kid started going out*, he thought. Time to make some new friends, get out of the house once in a while.

"Okay. Thanks." Zevon hoped his father would say more, but he wasn't quite sure what. He feigned a smile and slouched back the other way as Charles took another swig of brew.

"Don't stay out too late," Charles figured he ought to throw in there.

"Okay, Dad," Zevon said as he closed the door behind him.

———

A LARGE BONFIRE raged out in the woods that night, and a throng of high schoolers danced, drank, laughed and hid from society. They were snuggly nestled in a womb of trees, grass, dirt and roots, and a full moon shone above. The temperature was a pleasant fifty-five degrees and between the large central fire, plenty of beer and a few hoodies, the cool crowd couldn't have been more comfortable or at ease.

An alien life form timidly approached the clearing through the narrow trail, emerging from the cover of the trees and into the moonlight. It had a spindly form with a big head and bug eyes, and it called itself Zevon. Stopping before anyone could see him, Zevon noted that if there was a moment to turn back, this would be it. He had not yet reached the crowd, nobody had seen him and no damage had been done.

The flowing and slick, polished lyrics of Andre 3000 from Outkast pumped through the speakers and it offended his ears. He recognized everyone from school, and knowing he'd have to take the plunge sooner or later, he willed his feet into motion.

Moving through the crowd, some of the familiar faces recognized him, some smiling politely, some not reacting at all, and a few wondering *who invited the freak?* He noticed Eddie Deacon drinking shots over by an old elm tree, and Tom Kepper making out with Kathy close by. His eyes found Becky Reiner flirting with a big jock and she noticed the little alien as he crept past. Going over to Tom and Eddie, she whispered something to them, piquing their attention and bringing them to their feet.

Zevon continued to walk, bouncing his head to the music and pretending to enjoy himself. He found a table with kegs of beer and several coolers with cans of beer, and although not a fan of alcohol, this was what people did. Reaching down into the icy cooler, he pulled out a can of Coors and cracked it open.

Hesitating, he took a sip, wincing almost instantly. The taste reminded him of cold piss, not that he'd ever drank cold piss. But he forced himself to take another sip, turning around to take in the party, bobbing his head like he was supposed to do. A young man he recognized from Algebra as Eric Maron passed by, saw Zevon and gave him a polite smile.

"Hey, man!" Eric nodded his head and gave Zevon a tap on his shoulder. Zevon allowed a slight smile to crack and he returned the sentiment.

"Hey," Zevon said. And Eric moved on. Zevon figured Eric must be his best friend in this new place. He took another sip of beer, forcing himself to like it. He felt himself loosen up slightly, both from the effects of beer and the fleeting social interaction. *This isn't so bad,* he thought. Someone could say something to him and he could say something in response, no problem. They all spoke the same language, were all made from the same stuff and all had feelings, right? And Zevon reminded himself that somewhere at this gathering was a girl who actually liked him, saw him for what he was and wanted to see him. He had a very special feeling about this night and his confidence began to surge.

Scanning through the crowd with laser-beam eyes, Zevon searched for the one who had invited him there. Within a minute, he had locked on target, his sensors recognized the curvature of her hair, the glow of her skin, the silky swoon of her voice as she laughed. Stephanie Mayben was standing near a smaller fire further into the clearing, talking with her friends Laura Clay and Cheryl Adams, and drinking from a bottle of Heineken.

Whatever confidence had grown in Zevon suddenly flushed back down his left pant leg as his eyes drank her in, marveling as she somehow moved in slow motion while everyone else was at normal speed. He desperately reached down to his pants pocket, feeling the letter he'd brought with him, reminding himself it was real.

He took several deep breaths, building his confidence back up. She likes me, he thought. She likes me and she wants me. He took another sip of what he'd heard referred to as liquid courage and summoned his legs into motion.

"Oh oh oh! Here we go!" Eddie's eyes were wide as he called his friends to attention. Tom, Kathy, Becky, Jared and a few others in the periphery focused their attention to the approach Zevon Lang was making. Their eyes moved from Zevon to Stephanie and back, excitedly watching the spectacle unfold.

"Oh my god! I can't believe it! This is gonna be great," Tom practically squealed, holding Kathy tighter. Becky jumped up and down, her smile beaming. They all snuck in closer as Zevon took step after step closer to his muse.

The young alien walked through a cloud of pot smoke, letting out a small cough as he crossed into the forbidden zone. There she was, Stephanie Mayben, standing with her two friends Laura and Cheryl. *Charlie's Angels*, as the cool crowd called them. He had entered their little circle of private space and their eyes all turned to meet him with confusion.

"Uh... Hi, Steph! Hi!" Zevon's best line.

"...Hi."

Steph stood frozen, waiting for him to say more. Laura and Cheryl exchanged glances at each other, trying to suppress the uncomfortable laughter that desperately wanted to come out.

"Hi, you guys," Zevon addressed the two other girls who politely nodded. Five seconds of silence stretched on for what seemed like five minutes. Zevon was starting to sweat, his hands fidgeting. His inexperience was palpable.

"You're in my History class, right? Third period?" Steph offered, figuring that was a fair place to start with this curious character.

"Yeah! Mr. Jarvis!"

"...Zevon?" It took her a second.

"Yeah, right!" She said his name! "Um, so... So..." Zevon thought he might finally understand what a panic attack was. The three girls shared a look, losing their patience but trying not to be rude.

"So uh, what's up?" Steph asked, cutting to the chase.

"Well, I uh... I thought... Y-You know..." Zevon smiled.

"Ummmmm..." Steph was perplexed. Laura and Cheryl stood at attention, eyes wide. Zevon stammered, not sure how to express what he needed to say.

"Well I thought... M-Maybe you want to get out of here? Go somewhere private?" Zevon was proud for getting it out, beaming at her, his eyes big and blue.

———

"OH NO HE ISN'T! No he is *not!*" Tom watched the spectacle unfold with more enthusiasm than if it had been the Super Bowl.

"*Ohmygod ohmygod ohmygod! Ohmygod ohmygod ohmygod!*" Was all Eddie could say as his eyes bugged out of his head.

"Oh dude, this could be bad! Where's Cyrus?" Tom asked.

"He's around somewhere! Oh shit!" Jared replied.

———

ZEVON TREMBLED, awaiting a reply. Steph shifted uncomfortably, and the glance she shared with her two friends told her they didn't know what to make of this either.

"I'm sorry," she said, trying to be polite. "I'm just hanging out with my friends right now. What's this about?"

"Y-You said you think I'm cute, a-and you want to go somewhere private and spend some time with me..." Zevon's eyes begged her to remember the words she'd written.

"*Ewwwwwwwww!*" Laura and Cheryl punctuated the moment for dramatic effect. Stephanie held her hands up, frustrated with her rude friends.

"Stop it guys, come on! Zevon, what are you talking about?" Her eyes were curious as she looked at him. She could see him trembling, all too familiar with the tell-tale

49

signs of young boys infatuated with her. This was nothing new.

Confused, Zevon pulled the letter from his pocket, as if he were about to enter it into evidence. He held it out for her to see, hands shaking.

"Y-You wrote me this letter. A-And you said..."

"Why the hell would Steph write a letter to *you*, dork?" Laura chided with a sneer.

"Laura, stop it!" Stephanie snapped. She stepped away from her two friends, reaching out for Zevon's shoulder and leading him away to spare him further indignity. They walked to a more private spot and she held onto his shoulder like a caring older sister. Zevon stood trembling, letter in hand. Steph reached out and took the letter, examining it.

"Y-You..."

"Zevon, I'm sorry," Steph said, letting out a sigh. She looked past him at Tom and his friends, laughing at Zevon in the background. It didn't take her too long to figure it out. "I didn't write you this letter. I think someone was just playing a mean joke."

Zevon felt like a balloon after taking a jab from a needle, rapidly deflating. She kept her hand on his shoulder, steadying him. He looked up into her eyes and saw compassion and sympathy. In the periphery, he heard laughing and instantly knew who it was. Tom Kepper. *Bastard.* The realization of what had truly happened slowly rolled over him like a wave of cold vomit.

"B-But why...?"

"People can be assholes, dude." Steph said. "Mean assholes. Try not to let them get to you. You seem like a cool kid, and I'm flattered that you like me. I really am. A lot of girls are gonna be into you, I know it."

"Really...?"

"Sure! Big blue eyes, cool name... Zevon! You just hold your head high, dude. Don't listen to those assholes!" Steph continued letting Zevon down as gently as possible.

The scene was drawing attention and a large shape moved through the crowd, displacing the high schoolers like a whale moving through the ocean. Zevon turned to see what everybody was looking at and found himself staring at the imposing figure of Cyrus Kushan, former student of Hamilton High and current boyfriend of Stephanie Mayben. His hair was black and greasy, his chest and shoulders well built and accented by tattoos designed to make him appear even more imposing.

Zevon took a step back, observing as Cyrus and his two friends, Aaron Bell and Scott Desjarlais, strode into the scene. Cyrus had graduated three years ago, but had decided to pass on college in favor of educating himself in the fine art of doing nothing. At six foot three, he towered over Steph as he came up beside her for a grabby hug.

"What's up, babe?" Cyrus's voice was appropriately deep, thick and masculine, making Zevon shrink a little more.

"Hey, Cy." Steph smiled, uncomfortable. Cyrus looked down at the timid little weirdo, standing with a half crumpled letter in his hand.

"Who the hell is this?" Cyrus growled.

"He's just a friend from class, babe. This is Zevon..."

Cyrus took a step toward Zevon and the whole crowd watched, frozen. Zevon looked around for help, but there was none. His eyes found Becky Reiner standing with Tom, Eddie, Jordan and the others, all smiling. Her cheeks were flushed red from laughing so hard and her grin was clearly at his expense. He turned back to Cyrus, a grown man over a foot taller than he, beer and vodka on his breath. Zevon tried to retreat with grace.

"L-Look, I think there's been some misund-" He started.

"You trying to come-on to my girl? I think it's time for you to leave, little man." Cyrus took a slow, menacing step forward and Zevon continued to withdraw.

"Babe, please leave him alone." Stephanie begged.

"I'm sorry, I just... I-I thought..." Zevon's eyes were glassy, fighting off tears.

"Just get him out of here, Cyrus!" Cheryl snapped.

"Yeah," Laura added for punctuation. Aaron and Scott flanked Zevon as Cyrus pushed forward, losing patience.

"Time for you to go, little creep." Cyrus lunged forward, grabbing Zevon's left arm and whipping him around like a rag doll. "Scott, give me a hand!"

Scott jumped at Cyrus's order, grabbing Zevon by his other arm and leg, the two of them lifting him up into the air. Applause broke through the crowd as they carried Zevon back through the clearing, wriggling like a worm on a hook. His equilibrium gone, everything became like a strange dream as he was jostled around in mid-air. A carnival funhouse where jeering faces stretched in warped mirrors and music distorted into atonal stings.

"Cyrus, stop it!" Stephanie cried, a lone voice in a stormy sea of hostiles. The mob left her behind in its dust.

Some of the crowd followed as he was carried out, the group led by Tom and his posse. Zevon tried in vain to jerk free from Cyrus and Scott, but his skinny arms were useless. The iron grip of the two older boys pinched into his skin, the pressure building into an unbearable pain.

He noted that the path moving beneath had transitioned from dirt back into paved sidewalk, and in a minute they were back out on the dark country road where many of the party goers had parked their cars.

"Here ya go, loser," Cyrus chuckled as he and Scott dumped Zevon onto the paved road. "Now go put on some black lipstick and jerk off to The Cure, or something." Cyrus and Scott slapped hands as they turned to walk away, leaving Zevon clutching his ribs and freshly scraped elbow.

"Nnng, fuck you guys..." Zevon groaned under his breath.

"That's what you get for dating these high school girls, bro," Aaron added as the three of them headed back in for more beer. Tom, Eddie and the others laughed and shook their heads at him, pleased with their masterful trickery.

Zevon watched them all leave him behind and a burning rage ignited behind his eyes. Pulling himself up to his feet, the anger began to boil and red hot tears ran down his face. He saw a rock on the ground the size of a nectarine, grabbed it without thinking and launched it with all his might at the focus of his hatred.

"Fuck you!"

The words burned the back of his throat as the rock raced through the air, finding its mark and clipping the left side of Cyrus's head. The lumbering brute staggered.

Everyone around him stopped.

His hand went up to his head and came down with blood-red fingertips. A stream of hot blood flowed down his neck from a small wound above his ear and Zevon instantly knew he had made a huge mistake. Cyrus turned with menace in his eyes to face a now shivering Zevon. All eyes turned to stare, mouths hanging open in disbelief.

"You little mother..." Cyrus growled as he stomped back out into the moonlit street. Aaron and Scott followed as Zevon shrunk in fear, stuttering and unable to get the words out of his mouth to plead for mercy. But begging wouldn't have done him any good, as Cyrus's left hand grabbed his shoulder, and the right punched deep into his gut with a forceful *whoosh*. The wind blasted out of Zevon, bringing him straight to his knees. Cyrus pulled him back up and delivered two more hard blows to his face, busting his nose in a spray of blood.

Tom stood in disbelief and somewhere in the back of his mind he registered someone saying, "Tom, call your dad! They're gonna kill him!" But Tom was frozen, his eyes gaping and his mouth hanging open. He had never imagined his little prank escalating to this, but there before him were Cyrus, Aaron and Scott taking turns punching the fifteen year old outcast, bloodying his face to a pulp.

Scott launched a booted kick up into the boy's ribcage, breaking two of his ribs and sending him to the ground. Once down, they took turns kicking him until he just lay there, caked in blood and mud.

Cyrus checked the wound on the side of his head again, catching his breath. At his feet, Zevon lay a mess of lacerations, bruises and broken bones.

"You got anything else to say now?" Cyrus barked at him. "Huh, do ya? *Bitch?*" There was no reply from Zevon, who was unable to do anything but cry and experience this uncanny pain. Cyrus decided to hammer home the point and make sure he was understood. "I can't hear you, *motherfucker!*"

"N-No..." Zevon managed to gargle out, his words mingled with bloody saliva.

"Then get the fuck on out of here, bitch! Go on!" Cyrus punctuated his statement with a final kick to Zevon's leg, and the young man pulled himself up to his knees. He brought out his right foot, wobbling as he eased some weight onto it. Then his left came under him, his body on fire and his balance gone. He stumbled and tripped backward, his face swollen, his bottom lip split, nose broken, cuts above his left eyebrow and right cheek.

"He said fuck off!" Aaron added. "That's right!"

Zevon peered around at the group of onlookers, just in case any of them would do or say anything to help him, but of course, none did. Tom Kepper stood rigid, as did Becky Reiner and all the others. Some were still laughing. In the crowd, Zevon caught sight of Stephanie's face, looking out at him with helpless sympathy.

There was nothing she could do.

Turning and staggering off on rubber legs, Zevon plunged into the night, blood pumping from cuts on his face and hands, heading for home. He tripped to the pavement, skinning the palms of his hands as he broke his fall, then wavered back to unsteady feet and continued on down the road.

THE LAST FIGHT Zevon had been in was back in the third grade, and to the best of his recollection, it was over which sneakers were better, Nikes or Adidas. A few ineffective blows had been thrown between him and little Jason Norris, and his biggest injury had come from scraping his elbow as they'd both tripped clumsily to the ground.

But now at fifteen years-old, having just faced Cyrus and his posse, Zevon stumbled through the dark, suburban woods, dripping blood. His body was running on fumes, wanting nothing more than to pass out and let unconsciousness turn that pain switch off. But he had to get home and his subconscious would not let him simply pass out in the middle of some dark country road.

Fire tore through his rib cage and his head throbbed like a balloon. His eyes burned with tears of rage as the thick blood streamed down his face, seeped from the cuts on his hands and had already dried on his skinned knees. As his weak legs carried him onto a familiar street with only moonlight to guide him, he could see his house in the distance.

Gasping for air, pain ripping his insides with every

breath, he limped across the threshold of his own front lawn. Whatever toughness it took to drive him that distance suddenly melted away and the restraint needed to keep from breaking down failed him at once.

Zevon burst into tears, but they were like no tears he'd ever known. They were a grotesque blurring of physical pain, the emotional anguish of betrayal and heartbreak, and the exaltation of getting back alive. Sobbing and snorting mucus, covered in his own bodily fluids and White Feather's finest dirt and grime, the teenager limped across the front yard, reaching out for the door knob. But just before he could open the door, he stopped. Inside, he could hear the sound of the muffled TV. Panic set in; he did not want his father to see him this way.

The boy limped around to where he would have a better view of the den through the side window. Being careful not to make a sound, he reached the window, peeking in. There sat his father, still cheering on his team, surrounded by a collection of beer cans. Zevon had never felt more of a disconnect with his father than at that moment. They were separated by a window pane and seemingly thousands of miles of understanding and experience.

Much like the lion enclosure at the zoo, you could jump in over the fence, but the lion would never understand. Zevon knew the same to be true here; he could turn that door knob and walk inside, but what could he possibly say to his father? He knew the old man would be concerned, sympathetic, insist on taking him the emergency room and be a caring parent.

But he also knew there would be disappointment in his eyes, frustration that his misfit son had struck out so badly and couldn't fit in anywhere. So Zevon turned from the window and walked down along the left side of the house instead of going to the front door.

He limped into the back yard, looking out at lake Yakonkwe with its soothing water lapping at the shore. His feet sank into the sandy soil and he allowed himself to fall to his knees into the water. Sobbing and feeling utterly alone, he reached into the cool September water, lifting a cupped hand to his head and letting it run through his wounds.

Beaten and bloodied, he feebly dipped both hands into the black, shimmering water, rubbing it all over his head and arms. The thick blood continued to run like cranberry sauce, dripping into the lake along with his tears.

"Please, God. Please," Zevon whispered, not praying for anything in particular, just praying please. *Please.* His body was failing, his head swollen and bleeding from a probable concussion. He had reached his physical limit.

His subconscious decided to take over and turn off the power switch, Zevon's eyes flickered in his head and darkness finally took him. He fell over with a cold splash, unconscious on the edge where the water met the sand. With every pull of the water, more of Zevon's blood drifted into the heart of the lake.

———————

HOURS PASSED.

It was the dead of the night. A couple of hours earlier, it would have been considered late night. A couple of hours later, it would have been called early morning. This was the darkest, deepest moment of the night. Even the insects were quiet and the only living being awake was the baker over at House of Bread downtown, getting up to get their day started making croissants and breakfast egg muffins.

All lights were off in the surrounding houses, the wind stopped blowing and the surface of the lake was like a still sheet of glass. It was the black of night, the dead of night, where real life and the dream world blended together.

Charles Lang was inside, fast asleep on the couch. Zevon remained in his blacked-out state, half submerged in the lake's embrace, the blood finally clotted on his multiple head wounds.

A slight trickle danced on the lake's surface, a small displacement of water lapping across Zevon's face. More ripples soon came, delicately approaching the youth, originating from several feet out in the water.

A dark shape approached him, floating through the cold blackness. The moonlight fell upon this shape, revealing a smooth, curved form, flowing lines and graceful movement. It was the unmistakable shape of a woman, submerged from the waist down, drifting his way. Her silhouette glided up behind the injured youth, curiously looking him up and down.

"Hello?"

The woman's voice was deep, smooth and sultry, yet somehow child-like. Zevon stirred. A feminine hand reached out, brushing slender fingers through his bloody hair.

"You're alive?"

Her voice found Zevon's ears and he stirred again. Heavy eyelids began to struggle open and his bleary eyes drifted across the dark figure before him. Someone was there, he knew that, and he also realized that he was laying half in the lake, in the middle of the night, freezing.

Summoning his weak frame into motion, he pushed himself up off the sand, getting his knees back under him and sitting upright.

"Ohhhhhh…" His head was throbbing, his body shivering. His hand reached up to his head, appraising the damage. The woman remained in shadow, floating in the water a few feet away. Seeming pleased to see him alive, she drifted a bit closer.

"Are you going to take care of me now?" She spoke the question with an honest, childlike innocence.

Zevon could not answer.

He did his best to take in his surroundings and try to figure out what was happening. This female was indeed there with him, talking to him. Her drift slowed to a halt mere inches from him and the moonlight brought her into much better focus, to his utter shock.

She was gorgeous on a level he could only have imagined in a dream. An adult, surely, of no distinguishable age, but also timelessly young. Flowing, wavy-golden hair framed an angelic face with the biggest crystal-blue eyes he'd ever seen. A shimmering, translucent gown clung to a full-figured, voluptuous body.

Her breasts offered themselves outward, straining against the paper-thin material, glistening with beads of water. She was the most beautiful woman he had ever seen. The ultimate image of femininity, carved from marble by an unnamed, ancient Greek master, and left for only him to find.

She was a glamorous force of nature.

"Oh my God, y-you're so… So…"

Zevon's adolescent heart began pounding with lustful force as he slowly regained his senses. *I must be dreaming*, he thought. This mystery lady reached out a perfectly-sculpted hand, caressing the wounds on his head with soothing care.

"You're hurt," she said. Zevon stared at her, dumbfounded as she tended to his wounds. His blood on her fingers, she gently touched her lips to taste it.

"This can't be real... Wh-who are you?" The awestruck Zevon found his voice.

She looked at him, gently caressing him with her eyes.

"I've been here all alone, for so long," She whispered. "But now you're here." Her voice was like a scoop of vanilla ice cream with a shot of spiced rum.

"What's your name?" Zevon asked. He waited a moment but got no answer. "I-I'm Zevon."

"Zeeeevoooon," She repeated, stroking his hair, glancing up at the house behind them. "You live in that house with your parents?"

"Just my dad. My mom died..." The angelic lady stroked his face with sympathy as he trembled from the cold.

"Ohhh... I'll take care of you," she cooed. "Will you take care of me?" Zevon trembled, feeling her soft silkiness pressed up against his body. The unmistakable feeling of lust surged through his loins and his erection strained against his pants.

"Okay, I'm losing it," He whispered more to himself than her. Pulling herself in even closer to him, her breasts rubbed against his left shoulder and arm, and he could feel her body's soft heat.

"Will you take care of me?" She repeated again.

"Jesus! Take care of you?" Zevon laughed in delirious disbelief. "I don't even... Do you even have a *name*? Like..." The lady just smiled again and shrugged playfully.

"I don't know," she said.

"You don't know."

"Will you take care of me?"

She nuzzled her pretty face into his neck, smelling him,

massaging his aching body. Zevon was melting despite the cold, September morning air.

"U-Uh, okay sure," He surrendered. *None of this is real anyway*, he figured. "What exactly is it you want me to do...?"

"Oh, Zevon," The mystery woman hugged him and beamed the biggest, most genuine smile he'd ever hoped to see, her teeth perfectly white and sparkling.

"What? What do you want?" His eyes locked onto hers.

"I'm hungry, Zevon," she said in blunt frankness. "And I can't leave the lake. I need you to bring me food."

She drifted around to face him, her crystal-blue eyes aligning with his electric-blue eyes, her hands cradling his face like a child. "In return, I'll always be faithful and loyal to you. I'll give you strength. I'll always take care of you."

CHAPTER TEN
PRESENT DAY

IT WAS the start of March, and the air was growing warmer. Zevon noticed the icicles dripping and thin sheets of ice cracking beneath his boots as he walked. Puddles of liquid water were forming and the hope of Spring was on the horizon. His heavy winter coat, hat and gloves had been closeted in favor of a lighter leather jacket and beanie.

All around him, he could see the signs of Winter dying and that was just fine with him. These frigid months were always the emptiest and loneliest for him. When he looked out at the lake, it was still frozen, but the ice was thinning and beginning to crack.

Zevon continued on with his mundane daily activities. He cooked and ate his meals, went for his morning run and lifted weights five to six days a week. He read books and watched soul-sucking network television. Rom-Coms were his favorites. Sappy studio films with handsome men and pretty girls, always falling in love, always happy endings.

They would meet, there would be a spark, there would be some inevitable drama, usually revolving on a large deceit by one of the parties, then after an apology and large romantic overture at the end, they would kiss and realize how in love they were. The sun would set, upbeat music would play and it would leave the viewer feeling that this could be you too. Zevon felt encouraged and longed for that kind of romance.

In his lonely moments, he would masturbate. He tried not to. He knew it was base and filthy and vile. *She* wouldn't like it. But he wanted those things he saw in the movies. The taste of soft lips, the feel of a warm body. He would go into the bathroom and draw a bath. Lock the door, cover the window and the mirror with towels... Just in case someone was watching or listening. He would ease into the hot bath and think about the women he'd seen in the movies, or the women out on the streets.

He tended to his collection of pets.

They were all tiny critters he had found around the lake who now resided in aquariums and terrariums in the den. He had a few fish, three small frogs, a praying mantis, a tarantula, a northern red-belly snake named Lemmy and his favorite, a large bull frog he'd named Roland.

"How you doin' today, Roland? Huh?" Zevon looked through the glass at the amphibian. The frog looked back at him, its throat pulsating. His little friend. Whether or not Roland shared the sentiment, he had no idea.

Zevon chopped wood out on the big stump in the back yard, readying his raw material of choice for his work. He swung the axe with force, the echo of each strike bouncing across the lake where neighbors would hear it on the far side.

The snow was receding faster than his hair line. Birds chirped as they sensed life returning to the land. Zevon carried the chopped wood over to his work shed, bringing some inside and leaving some outside by the door, under a blue tarp.

He looked out to the lake again, anxious. The ice no longer stretched all the way to the shore, but came to an end five feet shy of the sand. A person could walk in, dive under the ice and swim beneath if they wanted to. If they were insane and didn't care about their own life. Zevon walked up to the lake, kicking a pebble into the water's edge.

"You there?"

Zevon spoke to the lake, awaiting a response. He meandered to the dock, stepping up onto it, his boots clip-clopping on the boards as he casually strolled out. He stopped, looking all around at the cracks in the ice and the empty gaps at the edges where water lapped at the earth.

He waited, but empty moments passed and the only answer he got was a knife of frigid wind that seemed to slash through all of his clothes, even the ringlets and stitches of his boots. He took another few steps out, right to the end of the dock where the floating platform awaited, still held in place by the ice.

"Hey, it's me," Zevon timidly called out just a little louder this time. "You there?" His pale blue eyes darted around, but once again, nothing.

He knew he was way too early to expect an answer, but he was cold and bored and lonely, and it didn't hurt to try.

"I guess... Not yet. Okay." Zevon turned and trudged back up the sloped hill to the house. It was time to cook lunch.

CHAPTER ELEVEN
PRESENT DAY

JUST OVER FIFTEEN years had passed since he'd graduated from Hamilton High, and Tom Kepper had aged twenty-five years. Passed out on a tiny, single-sized bed in a cluttered guest room, the morning sun streaming through the slits in the blinds, he appeared to be closer to forty-five than thirty. He had put on a good fifty pounds in all the wrong places, his hair was a bedraggled mess and his worn-out clothes were stained and deserving of a quick trip to the garbage can.

A puddle of spittle had dried around the edges of his chapped lips and his five-day growth of beard. Nondescript tattoos had faded on his forearms, his wrists and fingers accented with bracelets and rings that he felt were stylish.

Tom lay contorted on the bed and his closed eyes began to wince at the direct sunlight shining on them. His body shifted and he let out a groan as the painful process of awakening began. Before any conscious thoughts came to him, the first sensations were the usual throbbing in his head from a late night out, a persistent pain in his lower back, a stiffness in his legs and a hot swelling in his bladder.

His right arm and leg were hanging off the side of the bed while his left side was pressed against the wall with a crumpled mass of blankets and sheets. *This is much smaller than my own bed*, he thought. He couldn't be at home. Slowly prying his eyelids open with the care and precision of an Egyptologist cracking an ancient sarcophagus, he proceeded to look around the room.

"Ohhhh... What the fuck...?"

Tom groaned, clutching his head as his eyes struggled to focus. It was a small room, with an old dresser across from the bed and a collection of old suitcases. Boxes overflowed with CD's and DVD's, and bags of softball supplies filled the corners.

A guest room that never had guests and had long been repurposed into a storage vault. His vision shifting in and out of focus, he zeroed in on a collection of framed family photos on the walls. His aunt Rita, his uncle Jim, his father. Old photos that Tom remembered growing up with.

He was in his father's house.

"Ohhh, shit..." Tom croaked, clearing his throat as what felt like small splinters shot through his brain. *What happened last night?*

"Sounds like somebody's up," came a familiar voice from down the hall, accompanied by approaching footsteps. Tom's eyes squeezed shut and he wished he could flip a switch and go right back to his stupor.

Striding into the room in his standard-issue police boots, and nearly fully dressed in his uniform for the day, was the monolith that was his father. Chief Paul Kepper of the White Feather, PD. Though not tall, he was a straight and sturdy man in his early sixties, able to whip the butts of most men half his age.

As usual, he was freshly showered, clean shaved,

wearing crisp and pressed clothes, with his stomach properly fueled for the day. In his left hand was a travel mug filled with coffee, and he put it down on the counter beside his son.

"Uhhh... hi Pop," The words creaked out of his throat. The Chief finished buttoning his shirt and got started on the tie as he looked down at his son with his best poker face.

"Have a good time last night?"

It was a very familiar tone that Tom had heard from his father many times, and the disappointment in his voice was palpable. Tom sat up with a grumble, lifting the coffee and popping open the cap to drink.

"What am I doing at your house?" Tom didn't look him in the eye as he spoke, just drinking coffee and letting the aftershocks in his head settle down.

"If you were anyone else," The Chief said, "You'd be waking up in the drunk tank right now."

"Mmmmmm, thanks Pop." Another sip of hot bitterness.

"Drink up, now," His father said through pursed lips. "Time for you to go home, bud. Watch some hockey, drink some... Water. Do whatever it is you do these days."

Tom shook his head, drinking the coffee, remembering this pattern that recurred every time he and his father saw each other. The disappointment, the shame, the judgmental and condescending tone. The self-righteous attitude that made his father think he was so perfect and made Tom feel like he could never possibly measure up.

"Good to see you too, Pop."

"I have to go to work now, Tom. People depend on me. You wouldn't get it." The disdain was well measured, his father felt. Tough love was the way to go in this case.

"You always know how to make me feel right at home," Tom snickered, shaking his head.

"You know what? I spent half the night pulling your comatose ass off the street, out of a puddle of your own vomit, and I am *done*, Thomas! I helped you get onto the force, you fucked me. I got you into rehab twice, let you come back home twice, and you fucked me! I clean up your messes again and again... I am done!" Steam nearly came from Chief Kepper's nostrils as his face turned red with anger.

"Sorry, Dad..." Tom had nothing else to say. He knew his father was right and the honest words cut him deep.

"Come on, now. Time to go," his father said. "Can't have you alone in here." Tom struggled to his feet, his bones creaking like an old oak staircase.

"Okay. Can I just go to the bathroom first?" Tom stole a quick glance up to his father's eyes in shame. Letting out a sigh, the older Kepper nodded and led him out into the hall.

AFTER TOM HAD EMPTIED his bladder and his father had set the house's alarm, they walked out into the brisk morning air. Tom pulled the collar of his corduroy jacket tighter and took another swig of coffee as his father climbed into his black patrol SUV.

He started up the healthy engine and let it rumble as he closed the driver's door. Rolling down the window, he searched his memory for the right words, not wanting to come off too harsh.

A long moment passed and all either could feel was a bitter emptiness and tension that stretched between them like a tattered net.

"Take care, Thomas," was the best the Chief could do. He rolled up his window and pulled off down the road as Tom watched, eyes fighting back the growing, burning sensation within.

"Yeah, I love you too, Pop," he whispered to himself.

CHAPTER TWELVE
PRESENT DAY

IT WAS AN UNUSUALLY warm day in White Feather for mid-March, and Claire took advantage of the sunshine. Still a bit chilly, she'd draped her favorite avocado-green sweater over her shoulders and her multi-colored scarf around her neck, striding out onto the streets of her old home town while conflicting emotions flooded her brain. A very uneasy and anxious Puffy Pants was struggling to get along with her parents' pets, but she'd found the litter box and food, so Claire figured the little fuzzball would be just fine soon enough.

Sipping from a to-go cup of "frothy caramel latte" as they called it at the corner cafe, Claire walked through the familiar streets and avenues, taking note of what had changed and what hadn't. It was Thursday, so the weekly farmer's market was set up on Main Street, and the thought of whether or not to go never even crossed her mind. She was going.

Walking around the roadblock signs, people buzzed all around her, some with dogs, some with young children. A flurry of noises waned in and out, random snippets of conversations, different sources of music with conflicting tempos, laughter and musical ringtones.

She navigated around through the crowd, slowly taking in the sights. Booths and vendors lined the stretch of road, selling everything from raw, local honey, to fresh produce, wood fired pizza, Mediterranean food, jewelry, and arts & crafts. The aroma of roasted peanuts was in the air, followed by that of a decadent funnel cake. Claire's mouth watered, wanting to try everything.

She smiled to herself as she saw young children at one booth getting their faces painted, their parents taking photos for Instagram, and another artist at the next booth drawing caricatures. One booth sold women's garments, including spring dresses and colorful scarves. Claire could never pass a display of scarves and not buy one, so she picked one printed with lavender and yellow and purchased it with her credit card from a very warm older lady. Carrying it in a bag, she moved on down the street.

Another booth featured drawings, paintings and other fare by a local artist, another smiling older lady who was very inviting of any form of attention. Claire nodded pleasantly and beamed a big smile at the lady as she walked in, looking at the paintings.

"Hello," she said, looking at the various paintings, in no particular hurry to get anywhere. Within a minute, she had zeroed in on an acrylic painting on an 11 by 14 inch canvas, featuring what she thought might be the cutest kitten she'd ever seen. She let out a little gasp, marveling at the tiny black and white fluffer, frozen in the moment of chasing a ball of yarn. If there was one thing Claire liked even more than scarves, it was cute pictures of kittens and puppies or any kind of baby animals.

But especially kittens.

"Now, this would be just perfect for my office," she gushed. "How much is it?"

TOM AND EDDIE sat in a window seat at a bar near the farmer's market. Eddie had finally found a contest he could beat Tom in: Drinking himself into oblivion and packing on empty weight. While Tom had gained fifty pounds since high school, Eddie had ballooned up to over 300. His skin was red, the hair on the top of his skull was thinning and the smell of alcohol seeped from every pore.

Eddie's eyes were fastened to the TV screen above, watching sports news as he drank from a bottle of Coors. Tom was content to people watch, massaging his temple and enjoying a cold Bud. His hangover had never left, but his usual pattern was to simply chase away the dragon with another dragon.

"Looks like Harris is getting traded in the fall," Eddie grumbled. "Fuckin' Atlanta."

"Lame," Tom managed. His thoughts still swirled around the morning's events at his father's house.

"This guy is such a douche," Eddie said, gesturing to the sports commentator on the screen with his hipster hairstyle and fancy suit. "Look at that stupid haircut. Want to like, smack it off his face..." Eddie finished the beer, his fourth so far. Tom wasn't far behind.

He had to be at work in a few hours, so he knew he'd better take it easy on the suds, if he wanted to stay employed and keep seeing that tiny paycheck every two weeks. Eddie looked over at Tom, who seemed to be off in his own little dream world. He was obviously troubled by something.

"Your dad again?" Eddie asked.

"Mm."

"Why don't you just try opening up to him about your feelings?"

"Suck a dick, Edward."

Eddie laughed with full resonance, the sound reverberating through his barrel chest in typical fashion as he gestured to the waitress for another beer.

"Seriously though, bro. You should talk to him. Your dad's a good guy. He won't stay mad at you forever. I don't like seeing you guys like this, man..."

Tom wasn't listening. His bleary eyes stared out the window at the passersby, when all of a sudden, one of them caught his attention. She was slender and fit, wearing a green sweater and a colorful scarf. Curly bronze hair and skin, and hazel green eyes. She carried a cup of coffee and two shopping bags in one hand and a painting of a cat in the other. Tom sat forward on his barstool.

"No way..." Tom said to himself. "I'll be back."

CLAIRE STRUGGLED to balance her various recent purchases in her hands as she continued to shop. Her frothy caramel latte almost done, she decided to trash it in order to regain the use of her right hand. She had almost reached the end of the street, where this little wonderland ended and normal traffic resumed. Only one of the remaining booths called out to her, which looked like a charming collection of art and local wares, so she drifted over that way to take a look.

Three fold-out tables featured hand-made toys, knick-knacks, wind chimes and dream catchers. There was also handmade jewelry, wood-carved statues, signs and ornaments. Buzzy, a friendly older man with a white beard and an all-denim style, grinned pleasantly as she began looking through the merchandise.

She ran her fingers across the features of some of the small, wood carved animals. Beside those were a few custom pieces of artisan furniture, light stands, a coffee table and a few hand-made wooden plaques and signs that hung from a post. One read "Welcome to the Miller's" and another, "McTighe's Apiary."

Claire was drawn in by the craftsmanship, attention to detail and rustic nature of the signs. They were beautiful and classy, stained wood that invited the eye and would make anyone feel welcome.

"These are great!" Claire said to the shopkeeper. "Do you make them yourself?"

"Naw naw naw, local boy," Buzzy said. "We get all our goods from local artists and craftsmen."

"I would love a sign like this to put outside my new office! It's so cool and unique and... Rustic!" Enamored, Claire's fingers ran across the smooth, lacquered surface of the signs.

"Yeah, he does really nice work. I can get you his card if you want?"

"Sure, that'd be great!" Claire beamed at the warm, friendly old man as he shuffled off to get the card. Claire began to continue browsing in Buzzy's little shop when another voice, strangely familiar, cut into the moment.

"Claire Carpenter."

Tom stood behind her, holding his shoulders back and keeping his gut sucked in. Turning around to face him, it took her a moment, but she finally recognized his face as her eyes filtered through fifteen years of hard life.

"Tommy? Wow, look at you! I... Hi!"

"Hi," Tom smiled and stepped in for a hug. It was an awkward embrace and she could instantly smell the alcohol on him. The last time he'd held her, he was lean and firm and smelled delicious to her teenage sensibilities.

She remembered how he would hold her so snug and tight, how he would kiss her, how they made love for the first time in his room when his parents were out on their weekly, Friday night date. She'd thought it would last forever.

Now standing here before her was a completely different person; disheveled, unclean, broken down and depressed. Buzzy returned with a business card in his hand, breaking the tension.

"Here you are, little lady!" He said, handing it to her.

"Thank you!"

Tom and Buzzy shared a respectful nod as the older man turned to help another potential customer.

"So how long you in town?" Tom asked.

"I'm *back*," Claire winced playfully.

"What? What happened to Brooklyn?"

"Just didn't work out."

"Yeah? Shit... Wow, well uh..." Tom was pleasantly surprised to hear this news and his inebriated head desperately searched for the next thing to say. "Well, you look great! I haven't seen you since what? Senior year? Since you moved."

"Yep, yep... Been a while."

"You, uh... Married?"

"Not anymore." Claire shifted her weight, growing uncomfortable.

"He just couldn't compete with me, huh?" Tom laughed.

"No, I..." Claire searched for the right words. "It just wasn't working out. I'm a veterinarian now. Starting up my own practice, so... Just wanted to wipe the slate clean. Fresh start, y'know?"

"Yeah, I hear you." Tom knew all too well. What he'd give for a fresh start. "Very cool! So you're a vet now! That's awesome! I remember you saying that was your dream!"

"Yeah, yeah! So what have you been up to these days?"

"Well, uh..." Tom's mind sprinted. "Y'know, I'm over at Powerhouse gym right now. Manager over there. Trying to do my music thing on the side." He was only a front desk associate at the gym and his "music thing" consisted of skimming through his old, unfinished Drum & Bass tracks and never finishing any of them.

"Oh, cool. I thought you became a cop after school? Working for your dad?"

"Yyyyyeah," Tom wavered. "That just really wasn't for me, y'know. Didn't really work out. You know how it goes." Better keep things work-related as vague as possible, he thought.

"Yeah, yeah..." Claire was no dummy; she could read between the lines. And the empty bottles.

"Hey, do you want to go get a drink? We could just, right over here...?" Tom turned and gestured to the bar across the street. Claire tried to not look visibly uncomfortable.

"Sorry, I can't. I just... Yeah."

"Yeah, okay. Another time, maybe." Tom had run out of material and the air between them was as thick as cold clam chowder. "So! I guess I'm gonna have to go get myself a dog, so I'll have an excuse to come see you!"

"Sure, okay." Claire chuckled, looking down. "Well, I

actually gotta go now. But it was nice seeing you again, Tommy."

"Tom. Just Tom. At your service!"

"Right. Gotcha."

The thought of going in for another hug occurred to him, but the awkwardness was tangible and they both started taking slow steps backwards. Tom pleasantly smiled and waved to her as he backed off.

"Welcome back, Claire. It's good to see you."

"Thanks," she smiled politely. "You too."

They both turned and continued on their own paths. Neither sure what to make of their little surprise reunion.

CHAPTER THIRTEEN
2005

DEEP NIGHT HAD SETTLED over Lake Yakonkwe.

The side door of the Lang's house creaked open and Zevon emerged, gingerly closing it behind him and tip-toeing down towards the water. Nearly two weeks had passed since nearly being beaten to death by Cyrus, and with a combination of stitches and prescription pain meds thanks to the local ER, he was on the mend.

When his father had finally seen him the next morning, he'd nearly given the boy a beating of his own for trying to hide it and not coming to him right away. He'd wanted to go to the police, to press charges, to hold those responsible accountable for their cruel actions. But Zevon didn't want to appear any weaker than he was. And he knew that Tom Kepper's father was a police Lieutenant in town, and that wouldn't help much either.

Now the swelling had gone down and the stitches would be removed soon. His ribs still hurt like a sonofabitch when he twisted the wrong way, though. Walking through the freshly-cut grass, he approached the water's edge. He looked all around, scanning the still, black body of water, looking for signs of movement.

"You there?" He whispered. Many silent moments passed, until he saw a hand emerge from the water nearly a hundred yards out, waving to him.

"Here," came that silky voice he remembered, as the hand went back down beneath the surface. Zevon smiled, jogging out onto the dock and hopping onto the small floating platform tied there. Untying the knot, he pushed off the dock and let the structure float out to the center of the lake. He lay on his stomach and paddled with his hands, stopping as he reached the area where he'd seen her.

After a few moments, she rose up from the black depths in slow, flowing motions. Her eyes beckoned and her lips smiled at him from below. She stopped mere inches before breaking the surface of the water, floating perfectly in place and looking at Zevon as if through two-way glass.

"Zevon," She spoke with a sensual smile, her voice clearly ringing in his ears as if she were right there beside him, with no distortion from being under water. He smiled back, seeing her image move with the ripples of the water as if looking through hand blown glass.

"Hi," he marveled at her unapologetically. He put his hand flat on the surface of the water, and hers came up to meet it. "Don't you need to come up to breathe?"

"I'm fine," she said bashfully.

"Are you like, a ghost or something?"

"No."

"Then what are you," he pushed. "Some kind of mermaid?"

"Don't be silly," she giggled.

"I must be going crazy. You can't be real..."

"How are you feeling?" She ignored his last statement.

"Eh, a little better I guess," he shrugged. "Dad's still mad at me. But what else is new?"

"I can't stand to see you in pain, darling." Her big, blue eyes never left his, genuine care and concern in their gaze. Her flowing blonde hair moved with the water, as did her gown, translucent at best. Her fingertips met his at the edge of the water, tracing the lines on the palm of his hand. He was hopelessly smitten.

"You're so beautiful," he said, unafraid of saying that to a beautiful woman for the first time in his life. She blushed at him from beneath the water.

"Thank you," she said as if she wasn't used to taking compliments.

"Do you really not have a name?"

The mysterious female shook her head left and right, her sumptuous gaze never fading. "Would you like to give me a name?"

"*Me?*" Zevon laughed, shaking his head in disbelief. "Oh come on, you gotta be kidding!" Her fingers interlocked with his, giving him an encouraging shake.

"You can do it! Think of something pretty!"

Zevon once again shook his head, laughing at the unimaginable situation he was in. There he sat on the surface of a lake, in the middle of the night, talking to a beautiful, etherial goddess who wanted him to give her a name. His mind searched through its memory banks.

"Okay, uhhh... How about Elizabeth?"

"No."

"Ummm... Melissa?"

"No. Not good. No."

"Aqua-Girl?"

"Very funny!"

She let go of his hand and splashed at him from beneath

the surface. They both laughed together as Zevon wiped the water from his face with his shirt sleeve. This was harder than it looked. How could a skinny, unpopular little outcast like him choose a fitting name for this exquisite, feminine force of nature?

"Think of something pretty!" She encouraged. "Something that has a special meaning to you." She watched him as the gears turned in his eyes.

"I don't know. I mean... I never really knew a woman who meant a lot to me."

"No? What about your mother?"

"My mother? I mean, I didn't even know her. I was just a baby when she died."

Zevon looked off into the distance, his mind reaching back to a dim and forgotten place. He had seen photos and a handful of early-80's VHS clips, plus stories from his father and grandparents, before they also died. She too was an artist and his father would muse that Zevon's creative side had come from her, along with his big, blue eyes.

"She was real pretty," he recounted. "Seemed like a great lady. But just... Y'know." A sadness had resided in him all his life and he figured that perhaps, it was the void left by her.

"You miss her, and you didn't even know her." The lady stared up at him, understanding of his pain.

"Pretty stupid, huh?" He tried to laugh it off.

"Not at all," the lady said, once again interlocking her fingers with his and gripping affectionately.

"What was her name?"

CHAPTER FOURTEEN
PRESENT DAY

"LILA!"

Zevon called out to the lake. It was night and the effects of winter had almost worn off. Most of the ice had melted back into the lake, the snow had almost completely dissolved and he could go outside again without a heavy coat. Maybe, just maybe, she would be awake by now.

"Lila, it's me... You there?" There was no answer. Only a quiet, still lake sitting in the black of night. Zevon let out a sigh, knowing he would have to wait a bit longer. "I guess not yet. Okay." He spoke almost to himself, shuffling back to his empty house.

THE DAYS PASSED and Zevon went on with his usual routine, doing his chores, working on carvings for clients, keeping the house clean and keeping his body in shape. Every day he would run around the lake, watching the ice dissipate. Every night he would walk onto the shore, watching for her to emerge and call to him. The sun was shining on a consistent basis now, birds were singing and all around were the signs of spring.

Zevon tended to Roland, Lemmy and all of his little pets, giving them food and water. He skillfully cooked for himself, serving up meals of grilled trout with steamed vegetables, chicken and brown rice, steak and potatoes. He sat by the television, eating by himself, watching the news and vapid reality shows when he simply wanted to turn off his brain.

He was not much of a drinker, but boredom had steered him towards having a couple of brews with dinner every night. Stretching out on the couch, satiated from a meal of fish, vegetables and beer, Zevon drifted off into a peaceful slumber, melting into the old couch like his old man used to do.

Late in the night he was still in his cozy cocoon, only sunken deeper down as his body displaced the seat cushions forward, as if the couch was eating him alive. The TV was still on and an infomercial was preaching the positive effects of their natural soap rather than the name-brand sludge most people bought at the store. Something began to fade into his head, a soothing voice coming to him from another place altogether. Slowly, he began to awaken as he heard it.

"Zevon... Zevon..." Lila spoke.

Zevon's eyes slowly fluttered open, focusing in on the TV screen. The image of the salesman in the infomercial faded out as her stunning face began to fade in. There she was, staring right at him through the screen, blonde hair flowing, skin radiant and delicate, eyes and lips beckoning to him.

"Zevon, my darling..." she said. "It's time." Zevon sat up, knowing what he had to do.

A COUPLE of hours north of White Feather on interstate 87 was the comparatively metropolitan city of Albany, New York. It boasted larger industries, larger streets and larger populations. Whereas White Feather had high schools, Albany had colleges. White Feather had one-lane dirt roads on certain side streets, and Albany had two-lane streets and those fancy traffic cameras on their red lights. A light rain had fallen and everything was fresh and wet in Albany, lights from the buildings above reflecting on the pavement below.

It was getting late, nearly 1 am, and some of the bars were closing. The young crowd slowly made their way onto the streets, relying on taxis, Ubers and designated drivers to get them home. But it was still not a grand, bustling city like Manhattan, and there were still plenty of quiet backstreets and unlit, dingy alleys away from the Saturday night action.

An old homeless man sat in one of these back streets, leaning against a dirty brick wall, content with the nearly empty bottle of bourbon in his weathered hand. He had burrowed himself into an unused and unseen corner, built a nest of cardboard, shipping crates and scavenged blankets, and he was hunkered in for the night.

He could hear the sounds of the young and affluent in the distance; the entitled and spoiled, spilling out onto the streets after a night of drinking, laughing and enjoying their privileged lives. The homeless man grumbled something incoherent in their general direction as he took another sloppy swig of bourbon, wiping his tangled grey beard afterward.

He turned his head to the sound of footsteps at the far end of his alley.

89

The silhouette of a young man casually strolled down the center of the slick backstreet. He was short and slender, but his proportions and the way he moved betrayed a man who was strong, healthy and athletic. Worn work boots were on his feet, a hood over his head.

The old man remained still, hoping this interloper would pass so he could return to his drunken fantasies of Lynda Carter in her classic Wonder-Woman costume. Instead, the young man slowed to a halt as he approached the old vagabond, looking down at him curled up in the shadows.

"Spare some change?" His voice was like a wind instrument that had several open leaks and a splintered reed.

"Do you have somewhere to go?" Zevon asked in his best concerned voice. "I could give you a ride."

"Naaaahhh…"

"There's a shelter pretty close. You must be freezing. Why don't you come with me? I'll drive you there."

This youngster was saying all the right things, but the old man didn't trust anyone of his generation any farther than he could throw them. Besides, this was his alley, his nook, his life and he didn't need no damn charity.

"Naaaahhh, I'm good." He waved a crusty hand, a dim smile on his face to be polite and get rid of this shadowy young figure. Zevon was persistent.

"You're sure you don't want to come with me? I'm parked just right down there. Get you some hot food?"

The old man could make out a dishonest smile on the darkened face of the young man in the hood, and alarms began to go off in his chest. He was no fool and no stranger to crime or violence, so when his heart beat faster and the little hairs on his arms and neck began to stand up, he knew something wasn't right.

"Nah man, thank you though..." the old man wheezed, his right hand creeping towards a baseball bat, hidden beneath his pile of dirty blankets. "You got a cigarette?"

"Oh, yeah. Sure," Zevon said, reaching into his jacket. "Here you go..."

"Ahhh, thank you brother!"

Zevon's hand came out from his jacket, brass knuckles now clenched in his fist and ready to strike. But the old man was already swinging, and the baseball bat clipped Zevon across the left temple with desperate ferocity.

"*Nnng!*" Zevon staggered and dropped to his knees, his equilibrium spinning out of control as the terrified old tramp took off running on atrophied legs towards the populated main streets.

"Help!" The old man bellowed with weak lungs. "Somebody heeeeelp!" He tripped and stumbled on the rain-slicked pavement, picking himself up and continuing to flee. Looking ahead, he could see a street corner only two blocks up ahead, where the cool crowd was smoking cigarettes outside of the Old Dog Tavern.

Zevon's head spun and throbbed, but his discipline and perfectionist nature could not let him lose grip. He had to pull it together and complete the mission, no matter what. He controlled his breathing, focused his energy and forced his spinning skull to level out and his eyes to focus.

The old man had a massive head start on him, and Zevon could see him getting closer to the mingling crowd up ahead. With a trickle of hot blood running down his face from the fresh wound over his left eyebrow, he felt the urgency of the situation and forced himself up onto rubbery legs, taking off running.

"*Help!*" The old man screamed again, looking behind to see the much younger man gaining on him like a jungle cat.

He'd dropped the baseball bat as soon as he hit the attacker and now he regretted it. All he could do was run, hoping that someone ahead would be able to help him and that the multicolored lights on the main street would scare off this predator who operated in the dark.

The old man waved his hands, wheezing and out of breath. Zevon knew that any second his prey would be close enough to be seen and heard by the others. He would either have to abort his mission or risk witnesses to his attack.

Either way, the old man could potentially identify him to police, describe his face to a composite artist and ruin everything. He would be thrown in jail forever, and then who would take care of Lila? Zevon shifted his engine into high-gear, his strong legs pumping like pistons and rocketing him forward, and just when he was within striking distance, he lunged forward through the air.

With practiced, cold precision, Zevon collided into his prey's back with a hard thud, arms wrapping around his throat and legs around his torso in one fluid motion. The impact knocked the elderly tramp off his feet and the two of them fell to the side of the alley, in the darkness where none of the hipsters ahead of them could see.

The old man's eyes bugged from his head in confusion and terror as Zevon's arms cinched around his throat like an iron vice and his legs locked around his waist.

Mere yards away from civilization and salvation, he struggled, more doomed than a mouse in a boa constrictor's grasp. Zevon was quietly happy with himself; he'd never heard of, let alone pulled off a flying-rear naked choke before, and it was a thing of beauty.

Cinching his arms tighter, he closed off the carotid arteries feeding blood to the old man's brain, which would result in unconsciousness in mere seconds. The panicked vagrant struggled in vain, one hand outstretched toward salvation as his head began to throb and the lights began to fade.

"It's okay... It's okay..." Zevon whispered as the old man's body went limp. Allowing himself to relax within their private, little dark pocket of the alley, Zevon breathed a sigh of relief. That was way too close, he thought. Now he would have to carry his prey out of there without being seen, which required another set of skills altogether.

THE TRIP back down Interstate 95 South took just under two hours, as Zevon was eager to get home and finish before morning light. He passed through four counties by the light of the moon, keeping an eye on the unconscious man tied up in the rear. By the time he crossed back into White Feather, it was 3:30 a.m. and he still had work to do.

He carried the old man into his work shed and locked the door. His quarry still breathing, still grumbling in his deep stupor, Zevon took his heavy duty scissors and cut off the filthy rags the man called clothes. He placed the old vagrant on the gnarled, wooden chair draped with plastic sheeting, his large, plastic jug beneath the grate in the floor below him.

With the emotional detachment of a deer hunter to a freshly downed buck, Zevon began what others would consider to be ghastly and unspeakable business. He pulled on his yellow rain coat to cover his clothes, sealing himself up.

He chose a large gouge from his tool kit, gripped his mallet in the other hand and steadied the old man's head, which was still lolling about loosely. With the head still, he aimed the gouge at the very top of the cranium and brought the mallet down with one forceful stroke.

The man's body jolted as the gouge cracked his skull and ripped deep into his brain, ending his life instantly. Zevon let the spasming body fall to the floor where the blood began to run into the drain, dripping down into the jug below.

He pulled the gouge from the old bum's skull with a hard yank and placed it aside, now picking up the next tool needed for this procedure, his hacksaw.

CHAPTER FIFTEEN
PRESENT DAY

4:33 a.m.

A mist lay across the land and a curtain of clouds covered the stars. The ground still wet from the rain earlier in the day, Zevon pushed his wheelbarrow down the back-yard hill to the lake. In it was a bloodied canvas bag loaded with the disarticulated body of the homeless man, and the two-gallon drum in which his blood sloshed.

The cargo jostled gently on the uneven, muddy ground. Zevon's body was tired and his grip strained, but he still eagerly hurried to the shore, halting at the edge of the dock and scanning the periphery of the still, black water.

"I'm back!"

He called out like a husband returning from a long day at work, "I got something for you! It's been a long winter! You must be starving!" He lifted the handles again and pushed the wheels over the lip at the edge of the pier, care-fully pushing it to the end of the long dock.

With an iron grip, he lifted the bloody bag from the wheelbarrow, carried it out onto the tethered raft, and placed it gently down. He came back for the container of blood, hefting it up and placing it too onto the raft, a macabre dinner on a floating table. Zevon expectantly called out, careful to keep his voice down, a big, proud smile on his face.

"Come on out!"

Nothing but the sounds of crickets, frogs and the exhale of light wind answered his call. The lake remained still, the surface gently rippling. *Where is she,* Zevon thought, anxiously looking in all of her favorite spots. "Lila, come on out! It's me!" He called again, but still nothing. He stepped onto the raft and began to untie the tether so he could float out into the lake with his offering. But finally, a voice called out to stop him.

"Leave it and go away."

The voice was rough and raspy, not the smooth and sultry tone he'd fallen in love with. The childlike playfulness was gone, leaving only a pained hunger. Zevon knew she got like this after not eating for a while. But he still desperately wanted to see her, so he kept looking.

Finally, he made out a movement in the brush on the edge of the water, a growth of bushes and reeds. There, he could see the head and shoulders of a woman, peering out from behind the wet shrubbery in the shadows.

"Come on, Lila..." Zevon called out to the silhouette in earnest. But this was not the darkened form of the glowing, full and plump figure of an earthy goddess, but rather a shriveled old woman.

Even though he could barely see her through the shadows and reeds, he could still make out small glimpses of a hunched posture, wrinkled white skin, cracked fingernails and once-lustrous hair now falling out. She hid from him like a wild, dirty animal, ashamed to show herself.

"I said leave it and go!"

The voice was cracked, strained and dry. Zevon clenched his teeth, hurt. She still kept him at arms length, even after all these years. *"I don't want you to see me right now, okay?"*

"Okay," Zevon sighed, his head hanging low. He stepped back onto the pier, untying the tether to the raft and letting it slowly drift deeper into the lake. Turning around, he gripped the handles of the wheelbarrow again, pushing it back to the shore as sunken, gray eyes watched him through the reeds.

He left the wheelbarrow on the side of the house and headed for the door, in dire need of a hot shower and some sleep. As he did so, the raft reached the end of its tether, and a dark figure plunged under the water to inspect its cargo.

AFTER A QUICK, hot shower, and cleaning the small cut over his left eyebrow caused by an old man's defensive strike, Zevon had collapsed onto his living room couch, wearing nothing but pajama pants. He fell instantly into a deep sleep, his entire body exhausted right down to his fingernails. His chest heaved and his abdominals flexed slightly with each breath, not a shred of fat covering them.

He dreamed of being a passenger on an old ship, a sailing vessel from another life. He was surrounded by people, all travelers from the old world, all staring at him as he walked the decks. Long coats and top hats, corsets and elegant bonnets, he stood out from them all and could not escape. No matter where he went on the ship, the crowd followed him and his heart rate began to speed up with a sense of urgency.

Through this hazy illusion, a voice cut through the fog.

Silky, warm, sultry and feminine. A voice calling to him in familiar, loving tones, childlike and playful, yet at the same time, nurturing and maternal.

"Zevon... Zevon..."

Lila's voice drifted through his dream, bringing him into the in-between realm of neither sleep nor waking. She continued to call for him, her urge growing stronger. The old sailboat faded away, and he found himself aware that he was on his couch, in his living room, having a dream.

He held onto that voice, letting it pull him until he found his eyes fluttering open, and he was fully back in his home again. The lights were all out and the digital clock on the microwave oven read 5:45 a.m. He lay still for a minute, eyes adjusting to the dark, but then there she was again, calling.

"Zevon... Zevon..."

He sat up like a bolt and quickly jumped over to the large window overlooking the lake. And there she was. Standing right at the edge of the shore, water lapping around her feet, Lila smiled at him. Glowing and beautiful. Lush and voluptuous, hair flowing in the breeze, she was the vision of perfection he'd fallen in love with long ago. Not even bothering with shoes or a shirt, Zevon hurried outside to meet her.

When he reached the shoreline, Lila was nowhere to be seen. Water lapped up against his feet as he scanned the undulating, black, mirrored surface. Then, several yards out, she rose from the depths like a ghost to greet him. Zevon waded into the cool water chest-deep, and she moved toward him as well, her smile warm and sincere.

"Hi," Zevon whispered.

"Oh, baby boy." She embraced him, her affectionate

arms wrapping around his back. He held her tight, his head resting against her ample bosom.

"I missed you so much," He said.

"I missed you too, my darling."

She ran her porcelain fingers through his thinning hair, stroking his head carefully. They remained in a close embrace, drifting deeper into the lake as if slow dancing into the night.

"I'm sorry I snapped at you," she whispered. Zevon lifted his gaze to look at her, peering into her gemstone-eyes and running his fingers through her hair, which remained dry and perfectly styled, despite having just come up from under the water.

"You get grouchy when you're hungry," he said. "It's okay... How was it?" Lila wrinkled up her cute little nose, shrugging.

"Old. Dirty... But good enough for now. Thank you, baby." She placed a delicate kiss on his cheek, tracing his bare back with her fingernails.

"Cleaning the filth off the streets..." Zevon began.

"And making the wicked pay. Together," Lila finished.

Zevon looked up at the sky. Soon, the sun would be rising and their dream world of shadows would transform back into a picturesque lake lined with neighbors, all clueless to the magic it held.

"Gonna be light soon," he pointed out.

"I know, Z. I know. Just a little longer..."

"You and me, Lila. You and me."

"Ahhh, I missed this. My baby boy. You take such good care of me..." Their dance continued through the water, never sinking down but tracing the surface, Lila controlling their movements with ease.

"And you take care of me too," he said.

"Promise you'll never leave me, Z." Lila's voice strained with worry. "Don't ever leave me for one of these young girls, throwing themselves at you, offering you things I could never give." Zevon pulled away to look her in the eye, surprised by this last comment.

"What? No no no..."

"I just... I just hope you never get tired of me," she said, her eyes glazing over with a fine layer of tears. Zevon held her tighter, staring passionately into her eyes.

"Oh Lila, please!" He urged. "You're my whole life! You're the only thing that makes sense in this world! Come here." Zevon pulled her in tighter and they fit together like an artist's hand had sculpted and molded them to do so.

Holding each other tight, they drifted in circles, slowly sinking down until the cool water enveloped them completely. Their heads submerged and they spiraled down, lower and lower into the cold depths.

Their dance continued without the need of air, the extended embrace uninterrupted by the restraints of the real world. They were simply two souls helplessly in love and endlessly devoted to one another. Soon they would have to part and go their own ways as the new day shone down on their lake.

But at least for a little while, they could simply swirl around the bottom, locked in their supernatural waltz.

CHAPTER SIXTEEN
2005

FIFTEEN YEAR-OLD ZEVON LANG strode through the hallways of Hamilton High School with an underlying confidence he'd never before known. Some of his classmates may have even called it a strut. A wry smile sat on his face all day as he glided through his classes and the linoleum halls, carefree and buoyant. His stitches had come out and his face was starting to look normal again after his showdown with Cyrus the neanderthal.

His hair remained a tussled mop without the slightest signs of male pattern baldness. His frail frame stood upright, shoulders back, as it never did unless his father reminded him to do so. Curious sets of eyes watched him as he made his way around the school, wondering what was different about him that day. They would never know, he mused.

He had a secret.

He'd been up nearly all night, waiting until his father fell asleep, then going out to visit Lila at the lake. He had come in just before dawn, showered and gone back to his room before his father woke up. He could not fall asleep no matter how exhausted his body was; his mind buzzed and raced with emotions.

When his father called him down for breakfast, he'd suffered through the tense and awkward meal of Honey Bunches of Oats before running out to meet the bus. He had spent the rest of the day in a dreamlike state, physically drained, but his mind on fire.

Come lunch time, Zevon ate the cafeteria's best interpretation of spaghetti and meatballs and gazed off, letting his eyes drift and go out of focus. He sat alone as usual, thinking about his new friend. Or was she his girlfriend? He had no idea who or what she even was. All he knew for sure was that she was stunningly beautiful, lived in a lake and hungered for human flesh and blood.

So Metal!

But even so, could he really do what she asked of him? Could he bring himself to kill? He felt deep in his core that he would do anything for her, anything to make her happy, to stop her suffering, to see those eyes and that smile again. But although he was drifting in a dream-land at the moment, he still knew his ass was firmly planted in the real world.

He was still a little runt, barely one hundred and fifteen pounds soaking wet. He had no strength, no fighting ability and no courage to perform such a horrible act... as murder. *How could I possibly do it, and should I?* Young Zevon's mind raced. He knew murder was wrong, on at least a base level. But everything Lila said made such good sense.

So many people out there *did* deserve to die. So many have committed evil acts, or simply made the world an ugly place. So many wished they were dead. Would it be immoral to stop the suffering of someone who just wants it all to end? Was it unethical to take the life of someone who brought nothing but pain to others? And if he didn't do it, Lila would be the one to suffer, and die.

After several weeks since first meeting her on that enchanted night, she had told him that she was starting to feel hungry again. She needed to eat at least once every couple of months, or she would become weak, sinking to the bottom of the lake forever. If Zevon didn't bring her a real offering soon, she would disappear from his life. Looking around the cafeteria, Zevon pondered...

Who would I like to kill?

Who could this world do without? Jock assholes like Tom and Eddie, maybe deceitful bitches like Becky, or self-righteous teachers like Mr. Wyckoff or Mrs. Reynolds? And how would I do it? With a gun? With a knife? Where would I even get a gun? How could I even get a body down to the lake with nobody seeing me, and how could I do it all without getting caught?

Young Zevon's mind spun in circles.

———

His last period of the day was Physical Education. Having changed into his gym shorts, Zevon made his way through the gymnasium, the sounds of his classmates echoing through the cavernous, polished hall. If there was one thing he knew for sure, it was that he needed to become more formidable if he was to satisfy Lila.

He needed to become stronger, faster, and learn how to fight. He sought out the side room where the school's wrestling team met for their practices, his eyes focussing on a stout, fire hydrant of a man.

Mr. Roberts was only an inch taller than Zevon, but had nearly eighty pounds of solid muscle over the boy. His shorts were high on his muscular legs and a polo shirt stretched over his hairy, barrel chest. The wrestling coach for the past four years, Roberts was a stern task master, but he was known for getting the job done and many of his proteges had gone on to win national medals. Zevon approached with a hesitant step as the man quietly looked over his printed roster, clearing his throat to get the coach's attention.

"Hi there," Roberts said, his black mustache bristling, unimpressed by this skinny, goth-punk with chicken legs.

"Um, Mr. Roberts?" Zevon stammered a bit. He noted that this felt eerily similar to the sensation of asking out a pretty girl on a date. "Um, my name's Zevon Lang. I uh... I'd like to find out about joining the wrestling team?"

CHAPTER SEVENTEEN
PRESENT DAY

AFTER A SEEMINGLY ENDLESS period of cold and rain, the sun was shining and the temperature had jumped up to a balmy eighty degrees. In the following days, it would drop back down to sixty and cloudy again, but for this brief moment, there was a window of lush warmth around Zevon Lang's house. The sky was blue and the grass was green, and all the little creatures and critters scuttled around excitedly, running their errands and going to their appointments.

If a person closed their eyes and focused on the many layers of overlapping sounds and smells, they would detect the aroma of Mrs. Strauss' famous, perfect pecan pie from two houses down, along with the fresh-cut lawn at the Jackson family house. They could hear the trotting steps of joggers and their dogs getting a much-needed workout, hear the tweeting of various species of birds and the muffled tones of a football game coming from the Lockett house across the wide street.

Claire Carpenter arrived in her faded-green Toyota Tacoma, slowing to a halt in front of the carved, wooden mailbox that read, "Lang." She held up the business card that Buzzy had given her and confirmed the address. A slight smile pulled up into a set of dimples that had earned her much attention and praise throughout her life.

She killed the engine, stepping outside. She walked up the front pathway to the porch, which was adorned with a collection of sculpted, wooden figures, beautifully stained and expertly placed. She ascended the creaky steps and into the shadow of the porch, ringing the doorbell.

She waited a few moments, adjusting the purse strap on her shoulder and taking another look around to admire the woodwork. After a minute with no answer, she tried the bell again. Again she waited, and again, no answer.

"Hello?" She called out, peeking into the windows. The interior of the house was dark. It appeared there was no one home, but the van parked in the driveway told her otherwise. She rang the bell and waited for another minute before detecting a sound coming from out back.

It was a thudding *chunk chunk chunk* that repeated every few seconds.

Claire pulled back from the door and trotted down the front stairs, making her way around the side of the house. She followed a small creek, passed the side door, the garden hose and what appeared to be a boat house or a work shed nestled in the trees on the edge of the property. The narrow channel opened up into a large, sloping backyard, leading straight down into a grand, regal lake.

Not far from the shed was a tree stump, and beside that, a growing stack of chopped wood. Standing in front of the stump with his back to her was a young man wearing blue jeans and a wife-beater, swinging a large axe at the targets he placed on the stump.

One by one, the pieces of wood were bisected and placed off into the pile on the side. Claire cautiously approached, noting the strong, wiry physique that wielded the axe, sweating in the humid sun.

"Um, hello? Mr. Lang?" She called out, startling him.

Zevon turned around, chest heaving, sweat on his brow. He froze, staring at her, not knowing quite what to say at first. A radiant young woman stood before him, skin like bronze and hair like copper, glinting in the sun.

Her eyes were kind and intelligent, her face round, soft and inviting. She wore a light pastel scarf that fluttered in the breeze and her airy, cotton pants and shirt were simple and effortless, yet elegant and alluring.

She looked like a beauty from some long and forgotten period of human history, a race of golden amazons completely unknown to him. His mind searching for an appropriate answer to her question, he settled on one that he felt would do just fine.

"Yes?"

"Hi," Claire said, taking a step forward. "I got your card from a vendor down at the farmer's market." Her voice was as clear as a bell and smooth as satin.

"Oh."

"Yeah, I saw all the signs you made, the sculptures and whatnot... Really cool stuff! I was thinking about getting a custom sign like that made, so the nice old guy gave me your card."

"Buzzy."

"Yeah... Hey, sorry to barge in on you like this. I would've called first, but the address was so close and it's such a nice day, so I just figured..."

"Okay," Zevon said, wiping off his axe with a rag and placing it down on the stump. He wiped the sweat from his brow and took a long swig of water from his bottle.

Claire noted his perfectly toned body, his bold eyes and

his quiet simplicity. This was a real man, she decided, smiling at him. Zevon made note of her dimples and the thought crossed his mind that they looked good enough to eat.

"I'm Claire, by the way! Nice to meet you," She warmly extended her hand and he shook it gently. "I used to live around here when I was a kid. Everything seems so familiar," she laughed.

"Oh yeah? You go to Hamilton?"

"No, New Roads School."

"Ah, rich parents."

"Sort of. Not really," Claire chuckled as Zevon picked up two armfuls of wood and carried them over to the open door of the work shed. "So, what kind of name is Zevon, anyway?"

"Oh, my uh, my mother named me after her favorite singer," he said, placing the chopped wood down in a pile. "*Awoooo, Werewolves of London...* That's what my father told me, anyway."

They stepped over the floor grates, now cleaned out from the fresh blood of the old homeless man that poured through them the night before. Claire admired the collection of tools as she looked around.

Chisels, gouges, picks, wedges, power tools, sand papers, adhesives, stains, a few unfinished sculptures in the works... All were neatly laid out in order and in their proper place.

"Cool," she said. "Wow, look at this place! So much neat stuff!" Zevon shrugged, giving her a sheepish smile.

"Eh, thanks."

Noting that Zevon's conversation skills were slightly lacking, Claire jumped in before an uncomfortable pause could swell up between them.

"So, I'm a doggy doctor!"

"Oh. Okay, great."

"Yeeeeaah," Claire smiled, nodding proudly. "Setting up my new office over on Gower Avenue... And I need a new sign to put out front!"

"Aha, okay."

"So, do you think you could like, do something nice for me? Something that says 'Doctor Claire M. Carpenter - Veterinary Clinic.'"

"Uh, yeah. Sure."

"Yeah? How much do you charge?"

"Oh, um... I mean, it depends on the size of the sign, the type of wood you want, detailing... Can't really give you an exact price right now. But, I mean, I'll give you a good deal, I promise."

"Well, I tell you what," Claire smiled. "Why don't I get back to you when I have more of a specific idea of what I want?"

"Uh, yeah. Sure. I mean, yeah."

Claire turned and walked back out into the sunlight, spinning again to face him with that big, glowing smile. Her hands clasped together in excitement.

"So I'll give you a call in a couple days," she asked. "Is that cool?"

"Yeah. Cool."

"Okay! Well, have a great day, Zevon! It's nice to meet you!" Claire waved at him as she turned to walk away. Zevon returned the gesture.

"Thanks, you too."

He watched her disappear back around the side of the house, noting how her lithe body moved against the light cotton fibers of her shirt and pants. There was something different about her, he decided, a grace and elegance that the others lacked.

It occurred to him that he wanted to touch her, but he forced that thought away as he glanced back at the lake. The water gently rippled in the sun. He turned back again as he heard her car's engine start and rumble away.

"Doctor Claire Carpenter," Zevon mused.

CHAPTER EIGHTEEN
PRESENT DAY

THE LIGHT of the setting sun shone orange through the windows of Zevon's den as grilled chicken and steamed vegetables digested in his gut. He sat cross-legged on the couch, his large sketch pad in hand, assorted art materials strewn out on the coffee table and a half-full beer resting on a coaster. It was a pleasant evening and the soothing sounds of Pantera's first album, *Cowboys From Hell*, filled the air.

Zevon's right hand held a mechanical pencil, and its tip whipped and whirled lightly across the surface of the paper. His lines began light and sloppy, gradually refining themselves with each stroke to form the sharpened image he wanted. He leaned over to the coffee table, pushed aside his ruler and grabbed his kneadable eraser, using it to remove excess scribbly lines and further refine the illustration.

Little by little, the image of a rectangular sign formed on the white surface - scalloped edges, the profile of a dog and a cat in the corner, and in the center, lettering which read, "Dr. Claire M. Carpenter - Veterinary Clinic."

Zevon took a swig of beer, now room temperature, and appraised his finished rough sketch. He leaned over across the couch to where Roland the frog's aquarium sat, holding the pad up for the amphibian to see.

"What do you think, Roland?" The frog did not answer. "Oh yeah? Too cheesy maybe, huh?" Zevon turned the sketch pad outward, pointing it at the row of aquariums and terrariums that lined the wall.

"What about you, Lemmy?" The snake sat immobile in his habitat, disinterested in Zevon's artistic expression. What could possibly be floating through the consciousness in the little creature's head, he couldn't begin to fathom. Was he angry? Was he lonely? Did he secretly want to be a film director in Hollywood? Zevon chuckled, turning the page, taking another sip of brew and plopping back down.

"Yeah yeah, everyone's a critic. Well, that's just one option, okay? *Okay?*" Zevon laughed, clicking his mechanical pencil and pushing a short length of graphite through the tip, ready to draw again. He smiled, nodding his head as *Cemetery Gates* began to play, its haunting and woeful tones filling his head with a flowing current of contemplation.

His pencil began to move again, gently at first, always gently at first. The light lines barely kissed the page, leaving the faintest marks as his practiced hand whipped and whirled, another sign beginning to form. It had to be beautiful, classy, ornate, yet subtle. Just like the person it advertised, Zevon thought.

Stopping for a moment, he glanced over at the back window. The lake sat in the fading, dying light of the day, the lights of its surrounding houses still glowing. He waited, looking out just in case she decided to call out to him. Sometimes it would be only a faint whisper.

Sometimes she would appear like a phantom on the TV screen, her eyes looking into his like a seductive advertisement for a new, scented body moisturizer. Of course, she didn't call to him every night and he supposed this would be one of those times. Turning back to his sketch pad, he continued to draw, singing along with Phil Anselmo under his breath as the illustration came to life.

TOM KEPPER SAT ALONE in his studio apartment, unless he counted his bottle of Hankey Bannister as a guest. No, it was more like a roommate than a guest. He had too many roommates, and none of them helped out with the rent at all. They all lay scattered around the dim hovel in no particular order, most of them empty, some on their sides and some on the floor.

There was whiskey, vodka and gin mostly, and an array of empty beer cans as well. Laundry in various stages of filth lay scattered around along with thousands of other small, miscellaneous items that had not found their proper place.

Tom took a pull of Hankey straight from the bottle as he rummaged through a pile of memories from his past. He threw aside an old hockey jersey and some dirty underwear and pulled an old cardboard box up from the dig-site. His eyes bloodshot, his beard bristling and his breath a potent stink, he rummaged through the old box like a careless archeologist.

He tossed items aside, from old, unpaid bills, to food wrappers, a stapler, a few old DVD's and more clothes. A small collection of books were at the bottom, and after a little more rummaging, he found the one he was looking for.

Stumbling back over to the couch and planting himself firmly down, he held out his senior yearbook from New Roads School at a distance where his bloodshot eyes could focus on it. He opened up the book, hearing the slight creak let out by its aging spine.

There were scribblings in multiple colors of ink from his classmates, wishing him well in the future, adorning the first few pages. Everything from the trite, "Good luck! Have a great summer" wishes, to more sincere entries like, "I'm sorry we didn't get to know each other better this year, but hopefully we'll see each other again and stay in touch" lined the pages.

Tom read through the notes of yesteryear with blurry eyes, taking another drink from his bottle.

Flipping ahead, he glanced through the photos. There was a section for the teachers, a section showing-off the various school clubs and of course, the sports teams. Tom stopped on the page for the hockey team, focusing on himself in the front row of the group photo. There he was in full uniform: slim, young, smiling, a conqueror of worlds.

He and all his buddies, together.

Tom bitterly flipped through the pages, finding the section of all the students' school photos. He breezed through the sections for freshmen, sophomores and juniors, and slowed down when he hit the seniors. He reached the C's and zeroed in on a photo he hadn't looked at in years.

Claire Carpenter.

There she was in her posed, school picture, beaming generously, somehow not coming off as insincere or tacky as so many of the others did. Her hair, makeup and wardrobe choices were simple and timeless and her visage did not appear dated in the slightest.

Tom let out a sigh, slowly turning the pages again until he reached the K's. And there he was, a big cocky smile on his face, a cringe-inducing, spiky haircut and a shirt and tie that looked completely out of place on him. Tom Kepper, star athlete. Tom looked at the photo of the boy looking back at him and quickly turned the page again.

In the section of candid photos, he found many images of fun times around the campus, moments in sports frozen in time and romantic dances at the school prom. There he found two photos with him and Claire together.

One was at the prom: him in an uncomfortable and ill-fitting monkey suit, and her in a sparkling, yet simple dress, looking like an angel as always. They were dancing cheek to cheek and had stopped to smile for the camera.

Tom smiled again as he looked at the second image, which was him and Claire together on the school quad with a few other friends, joking around. He had picked her up off the ground and was twirling her around while she laughed and held on for dear life. Tom remembered that moment with painful clarity.

Good times.

There was one more thing he wanted to see again, to further twist the knife into his own back some more, so he flipped to the very back of the book. There were a few more handwritten notes from friends, plus one from his hockey coach. Another note sat scribbled on a page by itself.

Tom's eyes fought back tears as he read.

"Tommy, my darling. Meeting you this year and getting to know you has been the most wonderful experience of my life. I came here as the new girl, but you made me feel at home, let me in and made me feel loved. I've never met anyone who makes me feel the way that you do. Whatever college may bring, please don't worry. We may have to be apart for a while, but we'll always be together. I'll come back, and I'll always be your little dumpling!

I love you always, your Claire."

CHAPTER NINETEEN
2005

IT WAS NOVEMBER, too cold for the adolescent Zevon to walk barefoot out to the lake at night anymore. Wearing his shoes, sweatpants and a hoodie, the diminutive fifteen year-old descended the slope of his backyard and walked up onto the pier. He shivered with the night wind, peering around for the one who had summoned him.

She was nowhere to be seen, not rising up against gravity and standing on the surface like the female counterpart of Jesus. Not shimmering just below the surface like a watery mirage. He waited a minute or two, but still no sign.

"Lila?"

It was a shout and a whisper at the same time, but he knew he didn't need to alert her to his presence. She knew he was there. After a moment, there was a rustle in the reeds and overhang of trees over to his left and he could see a shadowy figure wading waist deep through the cover of foliage.

"Here," her voice was strained, raspy, like she needed a drink of hot echinacea tea with a generous dollop of raw honey. She was closer to the shore than the end of the pier, so Zevon trotted back to the dry land and got as close as he could. She was a good fifteen feet away and he couldn't get any closer without swimming out, but the water was too cold at this point.

"Come closer, Lila." Zevon bent to get a better look at her, but she remained shrouded in shadows, nestled in a womb of reeds and bushes. "What's wrong?" He could tell by the way she was standing, the drooping of her shoulders, the effort of her breathing, that something wasn't right.

"You know what's wrong," she said. "I'm hungry. It's almost winter. The lake will freeze... I have to eat soon."

Zevon gulped, knowing exactly the ramifications of that statement. She had told him about her required diet, and he had been thinking about it for the past month, batting it back and forth in his head like a ping-pong ball.

Contemplating the mechanics and moral consequences... of murder.

He had been training with the wrestling team, started lifting weights and putting the junk food aside. His scrawny body was constantly aching, always stiff. Every day something else hurt.

This was all natural, Mr. Roberts had told him, par for the course. That if he stuck with it, he'd be "a real killer" some day. *Well, that's the idea,* Zevon thought. But could he actually go through with it?

"So, y-you want me to... to...?"

"Are you too weak to do it?" Lila remained in shadow, the glints of her eyes still meeting his, challenging him.

"No! I'm strong. I can do it!"

"Or maybe you don't love me enough."

"Of course I do! Please Lila, just — "

"Shhhh," she stopped him as his voice grew too loud. Neither of them could risk waking his father, or a nosy neighbor. Zevon calmed himself, stepping as close as he could to her without getting his shoes wet.

"Of course I love you," Zevon said. "I'm just scared, that's all. I've never... *killed* anyone before."

"You know what will happen if you don't."

"I know, I just... Oh, please let me see you. Come on."

Lila sighed, hesitating before taking a step forward through the reeds and into the soft moonlight. Her usually supple breasts and hips had diminished, and her skin was pale and sickly. Even her hair hung limp, it's color desaturated. She was still an undeniable beauty, but she looked like someone who'd had the flu for two weeks.

Her eyes were still blue, but didn't sparkle. Her skin was still smooth, but it didn't radiate, and lips that usually looked more delicious than fresh, tropical fruit were now chapped. Her shoulders slumped in shame as she let herself be seen, and Zevon could feel it without asking.

"Is this what you want to see?" She could barely look him in the eye. Her pride and vanity had been compromised, and now her adoring admirer had to look on her with pity.

"Lila, you look beautiful. You —"

"Don't lie to me!" She snapped. "I'm hungry!"

Zevon was taken aback, fearful of her for the first time. He could see the void within her, intermingled with sadness and desperation. She was hopeless, completely dependent on him, like a baby. Her eyes burned and her teeth clenched.

"I... What do you want me to do? I don't know how—"

"Go out and find someone."

"Someone? Just someone, anyone...?"

"Someone who deserves it, Z. Someone who won't be missed. Someone the world doesn't need. Someone *wicked*."

Her eyes followed him as he nervously paced, wringing his hands and racking his brain.

"S-So, do you want a man, or a woman, or…"

"A man," she said. "I always prefer a man."

"Okay… And what should I do? I-I mean how should I…?"

"That's up to you, Zevon. But you have to be careful. You can't let anyone see you. And you can't leave anything behind that will lead them to you. No footprints in the mud. No fingerprints. No trail of blood leading them to me, no puddle of blood in the trunk of a car… You need to be a ghost, Z. You can't afford to get caught. I need you."

Zevon began to cry, feeling the urgency and hopelessness of this surreal situation. His fingers ran through his shaggy hair as he paced, this whole thing becoming more of a reality by the minute. They had talked about this before, but now the time had come and he would actually have to perform the deed.

"You can do this, Z. Find someone. Someone who deserves it. Stab him, shoot him, smash his head in… Then bring him to me. But try not to lose too much of the blood. I want as much of the blood as I can get."

"Oh, Jesus Christ…"

"You'll do this for me, won't you? For us?"

"Yes yes, I'll do it."

"Tonight?"

"*What?* No, not tonight!"

"Why not?"

"Because! Y-You need to give me some time to think," he said. "It's one in the morning, I don't know who to go after, where to find them, how to do this… I-I need to come up with a plan!"

"Then when?"

"Soon, okay? Soon."

"The water will freeze soon, Z. I'll need to sleep for the winter... Don't take too long."

"I won't."

"Great." She flashed a faint smile his way, an encouragement as well as a warning. "Have a good night, my darling. Get some rest. I look forward to seeing you soon." She turned and waded back into the reeds, sinking down deeper into the black water until she vanished.

CHAPTER TWENTY
PRESENT DAY

THE SUN SHONE down generously on the courtyard at the Lean Bean coffee shop in downtown White Feather. A sparse collection of people made themselves comfortable on the outdoor tables, some reading books, some checking social media accounts, some gossiping about their friends' love lives. One older woman in designer fitness attire had just finished a spin class at the gym and was now rewarding herself with a caramel latte and feeding bits of oatmeal cookie to her dachshund.

Two young college boys sat in the shade of a tree, quizzing each other with index cards for their upcoming Psych exam, each with a simple cup of black coffee in hand. A young man with a balding head of close cropped brown hair sat at a table wearing jeans and a hoodie. No drink in his hand, he watched as humanity buzzed around him.

Zevon liked to watch, to study them, to imagine what was really going on in their lives. How alien they seemed to him; he may as well have been watching a nature documentary. He sat in human skin, easily able to infiltrate their ecosystem and appear as if he belonged. On the table beside him was his backpack, and inside that, his sketch pad and art supplies.

He had met with many clients before, sometimes in a public spot like this, sometimes in their homes, sometimes in his home. He had been commissioned to make everything from welcome signs, to sculptures of animals, to abstract furniture... But never before did his heart flutter quite the way it did as he waited there for Claire Carpenter.

"Hey," a voice called out from inside the coffee shop. Zevon turned his gaze to find Claire approaching with two cups of coffee in one hand and a small, brown baggie in the other. "Oh, you found a good spot!" Claire smiled as she walked to the table, smiling with ease. Zevon did his best to play it cool as she sat down beside him, smiling back politely.

"Yeah, it's a nice day. The weather, it's... sunny. It's nice..." He smiled with closed lips as she handed one of the cups over to him.

"Here you go," she said. "One black coffee."

"Thanks." He realized he should have asked for tea. This was going to make his heart pound even faster.

"Okay okay, so let's see it! The suspense is killing me!"

Zevon chuckled and unzipped his bag, reaching in and producing his sketch pad and a pencil. Claire took a sip of her frothy, sweet coffee and removed a raspberry crumb cake from the paper bag, taking her first nibble. Her eyes rolled back in her head as the buttery sweetness made her moan in near ecstasy.

"So, yeah..." Zevon cleared his throat, trying to remain professional and not contemplate just how smooth her bronze cheeks must be to the touch. "I uh, I tried to incorporate a kind of 'country doctor' feeling to it, came up with a few designs..." He opened up the book to show her the first page of sketches. Five rough designs in all on the first page, two of them larger than the others. "Trying to keep rounded lettering, y'know? Like a flowy kind of design? Toying with framing it with branches or leaves, maybe..."

"Mmmmm, wow! These look great!" Claire's eyes ate up the artwork as she ate her crumb cake. One design had rough edges, another framed with sculpted tree branches, and another had leaves. Zevon turned the page where four more designs were drawn, slightly more refined than the last.

"And then these here I put like, a dog and a cat in the corner, but I don't know. That feels a little corny, maybe too on the nose?"

"Mm hm, mm hm! Wow, you are so talented!"

"Thanks."

Zevon smiled and took a sip of his coffee, flipping to the next page. Claire looked over the next set of sketches, taking another bite of her new favorite treat.

"Oh my god, you have *got* to try a piece of this crumb cake." She held it out to him and he could smell its sweetness.

"Ahhh, no. I don't really... Eat that kind of stuff."

"What, you're on a *diet*? Look at you!"

"No, I just... I'm very careful about what I put in my body. All these things have chemicals and additives, saturated fats... I just want to stay... pure."

Claire rolled her eyes at him and took another mouth-watering bite. "You're no fun," she said, then redirecting her attention back to the art. "I like these ones here! With this texture on the edges and the real branches coming out!"

"Yeah, that's a nice effect I like to do. Leave a strip of the original tree bark showing while the rest is sanded down smooth."

"But I like the lettering more on this one over here," Claire said, pointing out the differences between the two designs. Zevon nodded, making notes with his pencil beside each drawing.

"Okay, got it."

"*Mmmmmmmm!*" Claire moaned as she took another bite of the crumb cake, just to torment Zevon. She broke off a small piece of the dessert, waving it playfully in front of his face. "Eat me! Eat me!"

"Shut up," Zevon finally broke out laughing and took it, popping it into his mouth. Claire clenched her fist and celebrated her triumph over his will.

"*Yes!*" Claire and Zevon laughed together and continued looking through the art, planning out the perfect sign to put outside her new office.

THEIR MEETING CONCLUDED, Zevon and Claire continued to talk as they strolled along the bike trail in the park. Joggers breezed by, people walked their dogs, people wheeled babies in strollers; humanity in all shapes and sizes. Not one of them had noticed there was an alien imposter in their midst.

"So, you really think you can get the sign done in two weeks, huh?" Claire sipped on the nearly empty coffee.

"Not a problem. And you're okay with the price?"

"Are you kidding me? It's very reasonable, no problem. This is so cool," she beamed. "It's gonna be great!"

"I'll do my best."

Claire finished off her coffee and tossed the cup into a trash can as they approached her parked truck on the street.

"Are you okay? You seem kind of, I don't know. Uncomfortable?" Claire phrased it as gently as possible.

"Oh no, I uh... I don't know. I'm just kind of shy, I guess," Zevon struggled for the words. "Going to places like this, being around people. I keep more to myself. Always been kind of an outsider, I guess. Kind of hard to fit in..."

"I know how you feel. Growing up half black and half white, sometimes it was hard knowing just where I fit in. Not black enough, not white enough... I can't tell you how many times some ditzy girl would ask me, 'So like, what *are* you? Like, Egyptian or something?' Ugh. Sometimes it's hard knowing who you are."

Zevon nodded as they continued to stroll. Here was someone who seemed to understand him, he thought. Someone who would not judge or make demands. Someone so very alive and *real*.

"Yeah, I wondered that myself," He said. "Like, where your family is from. I thought maybe Hispanic."

"Yeah, I get that a lot too."

"Well, you seem to do much better around people than me! I'm pretty much like, a hermit!" He laughed at his own expense and she smiled at his boyish cuteness.

"You know, next weekend is Easter," Claire said. "Do you have any family, or someone to spend it with...?"

"Oh, no. I, uh... No. I don't really do anything..."

"Well, one of my old girlfriends from school is having a big barbecue. I guess she does a big thing every year."

"Uh huh."

"Well, you should come! It'll be fun! Good food, good beer, good people..."

Zevon stammered, rubbing the back of his neck, searching his memory banks for an excuse.

"Come on! Get out of your shell! I mean, unless you'd

rather stay home and play with your wood?" Claire laughed and lightly jabbed his shoulder. Zevon couldn't help but smile bashfully.

"Ahhhhh..." His memory bank of excuses was failing him.

"Come on, this Sunday! You're coming! I'll text you the address!"

"I don't... text..."

"Then I will *carve* the freakin' address onto a tree for you! Okay, mountain-man?" Claire grabbed him by the shoulder and playfully shook him, eliciting more laughter.

"Okay, okay!"

"Okay, then," Claire had gotten her way, crossing over to her driver's door as she pulled the keys from her purse. "I guess I'll see you Sunday. Meantime, you've got some work to do, young man!"

"Yes ma'am," Zevon laughed.

ACROSS THE STREET from Claire's pickup was Power-house, the gym where all the serious, local gym-rats went to avoid the hipsters over at Planet Fitness. Tom Kepper sat at the front desk in his staff shirt and name tag, folding towels and greeting guests as they came in. His head throbbed despite the two aspirins he had taken earlier, but he fought through it and did his best to smile politely.

Tom stopped folding towels and his jaw clenched as something caught his eye through the front window — Claire was driving away. And Zevon Lang was waving goodbye to her, a big smile on his face.

CHAPTER TWENTY-ONE
PRESENT DAY

TOM FLOATED on the current of a comfortable, fuzzy beer buzz, drifting around his apartment without a care. It was another late night, he had put in his eight hours at the gym and he didn't feel like going out and getting plastered when he could just stay home and do the same thing, but much cheaper. Plus, if he went out, he might find himself waking up at his father's house again.

Here, nobody would bother him.

Flipping through the channels on his TV, Tom poured himself a double from a bottle of Sauza tequila. It wasn't top-notch stuff, he thought, but it was affordable and got the job done. With an insistent pressure building inside of him, Tom pulled himself to his feet, gliding over to his cluttered bathroom. He stood in front of the toilet, swaying from side to side as he emptied his bladder. The toilet rim was filthy with a collection of fallen pubic hairs and dried urine. *Who cares*, he thought. He didn't have any guests he was trying to impress.

He squeezed out a final stream, shook himself off and contemplated flushing the toilet. *Fuck it. Who cares?* He crossed over to the mirror and ran some water over his hands, splashing some onto his face and running wet fingers through his hair.

He turned off the faucet, looking into the reflection at the stranger before him. His skin was red, his eyes puffy and distant. Getting fatter every day, he thought. Not wanting to dive down the rabbit hole of self pity, Tom switched off the light, heading back into the living room.

A commercial for a local used-car lot was playing for the fiftieth time that hour, and Tom switched the channel with an annoyed grunt. Plopping back down onto the couch, he picked up his glass and took in some more of that purifying liquid fire. He lifted the remote again, changing the channel. *Everybody Loves Raymond*. No thanks. *Say Yes To The Dress*. Vomit. He came across a basketball game, but it wasn't really his sport and he had no emotional investment in either team.

He growled to himself and kept flipping, stopping on a local news channel. On the screen, a police investigation was in progress. Detectives interviewed a sobbing, middle-aged woman as a calm and steady news anchor described the unfolding events.

Tom left this on, taking another swig.

"There is still no word from county police on the whereabouts of fifty-three year-old Charles Frankfurt - " the stone faced anchor said. " - Who disappeared three months ago without a trace." A photo faded onto the screen of the man in question, a portly, middle aged businessman with thinning brown hair and a broad smile across his face.

"Frankfurt's car was discovered parked in the lot of the Barley Bar, where he was last seen. Neither his bank account nor his credit cards have been used, and local authorities suspect he may have met with foul play."

"Charlie wouldn't have just run off like that," the distraught woman on the screen sobbed. "He never would've abandoned his children... Somebody took him!"

Tom's inner cop-brain had begun to tick, mentally taking notes as if he were still on the force. The screen cut to the detective in charge, an uptight and unglamorous man who didn't like being on-camera.

"Currently we are pursuing all leads and would encourage the public to call us if you have any information that may assist in this case." The screen cut back to footage of the family and stills of Charlie Frankfurt in an emotional montage as the news anchor continued his report.

"Otsego County has a long history of missing persons cases, going back well over a decade, and many neighboring counties including Albany, Schenectady and Columbia all have similar reports. The apparent patterns in all cases lead many authorities to speculate that this is the work of a prolific and highly intelligent serial killer."

Tom's mind raced as he finished his glass of Sauza. He wanted to throw on his uniform and go right out and get to the bottom of this mystery. He'd load his gun, shine his shoes, walk out on the streets and be respected again...

But he knew those days were long gone. You can't burn a bridge, then hit it with a rocket launcher, then piss on the ashes, and ever think you can come back, he thought. Still, he sat back and contemplated a serial killer operating so close to where he lived. *Otsego is less than two hours away*, he mused. He and his dad used to go fishing up there when he was little. Now somebody else was fishing up there and they weren't looking for trout.

Tom shrugged and poured himself another double. What did he care? *Somebody else's problem*, he thought as he sank deeper into that comfortable, warm fuzzy feeling.

CHAPTER TWENTY-TWO
2005

BEING A "GOTH" and a Metal-Head had its advantages when it came time to running a clandestine, ninja mission. Zevon had plenty of black clothes and he had put together the best ninja outfit he could muster. Black jeans, black boots, a black hoodie and black gloves. His father's big, rumbling van, however, not very ninja.

But Zevon needed a vehicle, the old man had passed out after too many beers, as usual, and he'd never know it had been taken. Only fifteen, Zevon still didn't even have a learner's permit, but getting in trouble with the DMV was the least of his concerns.

He followed Cyrus around all night, watching as the hulking thug drove around with his once-crush, Stephanie Mayben. The couple got burgers and fries at a local cafe, then headed over to a quiet dead end where they climbed into the back seat of Cyrus's car for some pot smoking and other activities that Zevon didn't care to watch.

Stephanie carried herself with an air of obedience and subservience, doing what she could not to arouse the ire of the beast. Zevon wondered if Cyrus beat her and came to the conclusion that he must. Was it Battered Wife Syndrome? Stockholm Syndrome? She knew what he was, yet remained with him anyway. He sympathized for her, but she was enabling a monster. *Much like myself*, Zevon thought.

He had kept his distance, following from afar, waiting for the perfect moment to make his move. His instructions were simple: To find a man who didn't deserve to live. Watching this sleazy, slimy, dull, hairy, cruel mountain of human slime having his way with that poor, delicate, young girl, and remembering the pain inflicted by him, Zevon could think of no one better.

Vengeance was due.

Cyrus had dropped Stephanie off at home in the upscale part of town just after midnight, then driven off to his own home in a seedier area. It was a one-story, run-down little house on a sparsely populated street. Yards were big and each house was a good distance from the next.

The lawn was overgrown and Cyrus's 1999 Blazer was parked in the driveway. Zevon had parked on the corner, three houses down. He turned off the engine and slowly crept out into the night, a baseball bat in hand. Like a good ninja, he slithered forward through the shadows, finding a tree on the edge of the property that he could hide behind and peak at the residence. A light was on inside and he could hear running water.

All of the other houses were dark except for a handful of lights scattered along the street. There were no sounds of TV's inside, or music, and nobody walking their dogs. Zevon couldn't ask for a better set up. Still, he was standing right on the edge of the street, and if anyone was to walk by, his best ninja skills wouldn't save him. He knew he had to step over the threshold and get closer.

His skinny arms trembled and his knees all but knocked together. The fear was settling down on him like a fine mist. He was really about to do this. He had thought about it, fantasized about it, planned it, but now he was there, doing it. He was going after big game, hunting a man who had already beat him nearly to death, a man twice his size and strength.

Maybe this isn't such a great idea, he thought.

Zevon moved around the tree. He stepped forward with his right foot. He stepped forward with his left... He was officially trespassing. He could feel the cold dew from the long grass through the stitching in his boots. He trembled, grasping the baseball bat with both hands. But realizing he was now out in the open and completely exposed, he either had to move forward or pull back.

Cyrus had beaten him, humiliated him, emasculated him... There was no going back. Zevon slowly continued forward, heading around to the side of the house where he saw the bathroom light.

In full stealth-mode, Zevon glided under the window and could hear Cyrus brushing his teeth. Two thoughts crossed his mind: amazement that Cyrus actually brushed his teeth, and bafflement as to how he was going to pull this off. Hitting the lummox over the head with a club was the obvious plan, but how would he get him outside? Or should Zevon go inside to commit the act?

No, he thought, *better to lure him outside somehow*. The light clicked off in the bathroom, and Zevon followed the creaking of the floorboards inside as Cyrus crossed into his bedroom. Another light clicked on and Zevon could hear the big man taking off his clothes.

Zevon looked to his left and saw the side door of the house, up off the ground at the end of three concrete stairs.

A plan came into his teenage mind, a plan so simple and childish, it couldn't fail...

He began to whistle.

His lips pursed together and he did his best to imitate a bird directly beneath the bedroom window. Cyrus didn't notice at first, so Zevon upped the volume. Inside, Cyrus stopped moving. He heard. Zevon ceased whistling, giving it a few moments. The light in the bedroom turned off, Cyrus clearly getting ready to sleep. Zevon whistled again.

"What the fuck?" Came from inside the room. The sound of heavy footsteps hit the floorboards and walked to the window. Zevon hugged tight to the house, sensing Cyrus directly above him, peering out of the window into the night. After a few seconds, the floorboards creaked as he walked back to bed. Zevon's whistling resumed, this time including a very light rapping of the baseball bat against the side of the house.

"Motherfucker!" This time, Cyrus jumped to his feet and stormed to the window. Zevon continued to whistle, gently clicking the bat against the side of the house as he drew himself over to the side door. *"Who the fuck is out there?"* More sounds of stomping footsteps came, followed by the opening and closing of a drawer, then his bedroom door swinging open.

Zevon knew he was coming. Shaking with anticipation, knowing this was actually about to happen, he huddled down against the side of the concrete stairs leading to the side door. He was hidden in shadows, a little black shape curled into a ball. He heard the footsteps.

Cyrus reached the door.

The outside flood-light switched on and a moment later, the side door swung open. Zevon remained crouched, still in a shadowy nook despite this new harsh light. Cyrus stormed onto the small, concrete porch, nostrils flaring like a bull. Zevon noted a six-inch hunting knife in his right hand, and his blood ran cold. Cyrus looked left and right, not seeing anything.

"Who's out there?"

Zevon knew he had to make his move. If he didn't, this time he would be given far worse than just a beating. His gloved hands gripped around the bat. He drew deep air into his lungs. He dug his boots into the ground, preparing to strike.

His heart pounded.

"Hey..." Cyrus caught sight of the figure in black hunched over against the side of the stairs. "Who the fuck are *you?*" Zevon answered with one springing motion, leaping to his feet and whipping the baseball bat through the air with all of his might.

The blunt tool hit Cyrus square in the crotch with a dull thud, sending a signal of unmanageable pain through his body and a fluttering of stars into his eyes. Cyrus gasped and lurched forward, doubling over and falling over the three concrete steps with a bone-crunching crash.

His head hit the ground and he dropped the knife as both of his hands went defensively to grab his aching manhood. Signals of pain lit up all over his body, his brain overloaded trying to compute them all. He gasped and tried to scream but he was too busy getting his lungs to even breathe.

The trees above, the moon, the stars, all were spinning as Cyrus lay there in shock. Stepping into this swirling, impressionist painting was a figure in black, standing over him. Not a snarling monster or wilderness beast, but a lanky youth in a black hoodie, a trembling baseball bat in hand. A moment of confusion passed as he tried to focus on the face of this boy, until his eyes went wide in a recognition of rage.

"You... The little *freak!*"

Cyrus snatched his knife back off the ground and lashed it out, embedding the blade into Zevon's thigh. The youthful ninja took the scream in his throat and turned it inward, not allowing himself to make a noise as hot fire radiated through his leg. Without thinking, he raised the bat up high and lashed down.

The bludgeoning tool hit Cyrus on the crown of his head, knocking him out and causing him to drop the knife. Zevon raised the bat again, delivering a second blow, then a third. He stopped, looking down at his immobile prey.

His head was swollen, bleeding. Cyrus was out cold, but his chest still heaved. *He's not dead yet*, Zevon thought, *but maybe this was good enough. Maybe I can give him to Lila just like this, and she can do the rest.*

He looked down at his leg, blood oozing from the wound in his left thigh. His blood. He saw the knife laying on the ground beside Cyrus, the first two inches of it stained with red. His blood. He knew he had to be careful. Couldn't leave evidence like this to incriminate himself. It was time to move.

Keeping pressure on the wound, the young man turned and hobbled back the way he came, as fast as a crippled ninja could. He limped back through the front yard, back up the street and finally reached his van. He heard no movement from any of the neighboring houses and hoped he'd miraculously pulled this off without alerting anyone.

He opened the back doors of the van, where a large roll of plastic sheeting and a roll of duct tape were waiting. Zevon pulled off his hoodie, then his t-shirt, using the under shirt to tie a tourniquet around the wound. He then ripped off a length of tape and wrapped it around the leg tightly, sealing everything in. He put the hoodie back on, limped over to the driver's door and hopped in.

Zevon started the engine, kept the headlights off and carefully backed up the van. He passed two houses before he reached the edge of the lawn where Cyrus lay unconscious. Keeping the engine running, he lurched around again and opened the back doors, unraveling the plastic sheeting. He carefully laid it out on the floor of the van, making sure the plastic covered everything. Leaving the back doors open, Zevon headed back across the front lawn, his left leg throbbing with every step.

He reached the side once again, where Cyrus had not moved. Zevon crouched down with a wince, producing the tape and ripping off a short length. He taped his victim's hands together, then did the same to his feet. He picked up the bloody knife, wiping the blade off on his already ruined pants and tucked it into the back of his belt. Taking a few deep breaths, he knew this would be the hard part...

Moving Cyrus.

He had been lifting weights and training with the wrestling team for two months and his strength had most definitely increased, but Zevon Lang was still a skinny fifteen year-old boy. But, fueled with adrenaline and his ego bolstered by already coming this far, he knew he could do it.

He carefully positioned himself behind Cyrus, bent down with great pain and put his hands under the bloodied man's armpits. Snaking his arms through, Zevon got the best grip he could find across his chest and stood up, lifting Cyrus half off the ground. His leg screamed at him in agony, but he pushed through it.

One excruciating step at a time, Zevon dragged Cyrus backwards through the front lawn. His leg was on fire, and pretty soon, his arms, shoulders and back were also screaming at him in defiance. Sweat rolled down his face as he struggled to breathe quietly, dragging this tree trunk across the grass.

Halfway across the lawn, he stopped, dropping Cyrus down and catching his breath. *This is so stupid*, he thought. *Someone could come out at any moment.* But he couldn't turn back now. After a few more deep breaths, he scooped Cyrus back up from under his arms and dragged him to the rear bumper of the idling van.

The back tailgate doors were opening and welcoming, the plastic sheeting all ready to do its job. Now all he had to do was get this beast inside. Zevon stood there, thinking, contemplating the leverage. After a minute, he realized there was only one way.

He'd have to sit Cyrus up and put his back against the rear bumper, then stand over him, lace his arms under Cyrus's arms from the front, and squat him up. Cyrus would plop down on the tailgate, and from there, he could be easily pushed in. All Zevon had to do... Was squat.

Propping Cyrus against the bumper, Zevon stood over him, took a few deep breaths and squatted down. Taking his grip, hugging himself in tight to Cyrus, he made his first attempt. The dead weight came two inches off the ground before Zevon's pain spiked and he had to let go. This would never work, he thought.

But it had to. Lila would die.

"I'll give you strength," he remembered Lila saying.

"Come on! Come on!" He cursed under his breath.

Letting himself get angry, knowing the pain would come, but not caring, he went in for his second try. His body strained and tightened as he began to lift. His leg bellowed in pain, but he ignored it, his face going red, sweat pouring down.

With a herculean effort, he used every muscle in his little body, concentrated all of his power and completed the lift, dropping Cyrus's butt down on the tailgate of the van.

The vehicle's shocks squealed and bounced in protest.

CHAPTER TWENTY-THREE
2005

THE VAN RUMBLED back onto the gravely driveway of the Lang house around 2 a.m. Zevon tenderly backed in and parked. He killed the headlights, killed the engine and hopped out, putting all of his weight on his right leg. Gingerly, he closed the driver's door, limping around to the tailgate.

His left leg was numb at this point and the bleeding had stopped. But this would require some significant self-surgery later on, involving the sewing kit he usually used to stitch patches onto his Heavy Metal denim vest, and he was not looking forward to that.

Before opening the back of the van, he took a few hobbling steps towards the side window. There, his father sat in the same position as when he'd left, slumped over on the couch in front of the TV, which at this point was playing a long-form infomercial about an electric nose hair trimmer.

Zevon smiled, knowing the old man would sleep through anything, and returned to the van. He opened the back doors and peeked in. Cyrus lay inside, grumbling in an unconscious stupor, wrapped loosely in the plastic sheeting.

Zevon shuffled back over to the side of the house where he had his father's wheelbarrow waiting. He lifted up the handles and rolled the levered craft over to the edge of the tailgate, where he expected getting his cargo out would be a lot easier than it was getting him in. This theory turned out to be correct, as with a few good tugs and pulls, Cyrus slid out of the van and plopped down into the wheelbarrow.

A distinct *dong* resonated with the impact, echoing across the lawn, and Zevon seized up. Any moment, his father could come outside, angrily demanding to know what the hell was going on out there. He waited a few seconds, looking around for any signs of disturbance, then continued in his task.

Zevon closed the tailgate of the van as delicately as he could and turned back to the wheelbarrow, lifting the handles and pushing the substantial load down and around the side of the house. He winced, the pain coming back in his leg with an angry throb. His grip weakened and his lungs labored.

The boy pushed forward along the dark side of the house with a *clump clump clump* as the single wheel went over the uneven ground. The figure within the plastic sheeting stirred, moving slightly, slowly coming to his senses. Zevon knew he had to hurry. He came around to the backyard, finally seeing the lake and gasped with relief.

"Lila!" Zevon whisper-yelled. "Hey, Lila! I'm back!" He stopped at the shoreline, dropping the wheelbarrow down and gasping for air. He loosened up his fingers, stretching out the ache, then checked his leg. He was a wreck, but he'd completed his mission... Almost. A ripple ran through the cool, black water and a voice called out to him.

"Hi," she said. Lila emerged about twenty feet out, wading in closer to meet him. He smiled back at her, noting that she was even thinner than last time, her luminance even more faded. She stopped, waist-deep in the water, a pleased smile on her hungry lips.

"Let me see," she said.

Zevon grabbed the handles again, lifting up with great strain and finally dumping the plastic wrapped load onto the sandy shore. A pained voice moaned from within as Zevon proudly unwrapped Cyrus like a Christmas present, pulling on the plastic and letting him roll out into the exposed night air.

"I got you a big one! Here you go!"

"He's still alive."

The fact had not escaped Zevon. In fact, Cyrus was coming more to life by the minute, beginning to lift his hand and trying to sit up. Dried blood had formed in his hair, turning it into a bizarre modern art sculpture, and his eyes were both nearly sealed shut with a deep, bloody crust like dried tomato paste.

"Yyyeah, well..." Zevon struggled. "I mean, he's *almost* dead. Here, I'll just push him into the water and you can—"

"Finish it off for me, darling. Please."

"Well, b-but... I thought... I..."

"Where did you find him?"

"Oh, he's a real asshole, Lila. A bully. He and his friends were the ones who beat me up that first night we met. If anyone deserves to die..."

"You took someone you know? From *town?*" Lila's countenance shifted into worry as she looked down at the would-be victim. Zevon froze, unsure how to answer her.

"Well, yeah... I-I mean, yeah. I just thought..."

"People have seen you together, Z. People know you

don't like him. If he goes missing, they might trace it back to you."

"I... I..."

"And what happened to your leg?"

"Oh, this?" Zevon looked down and touched his bloodied bandage, shrugging. "I got cut, it's no big deal. I'll be fine."

"Did you leave your blood behind? Did you leave footprints?" Lila's anger was percolating.

"No, I was very careful. I tied it off, didn't bleed on anything... I promise. Look, I even took his knife." Zevon pulled the still-bloody hunting knife from the back of his belt.

"You need to be more careful, Z. If you leave blood, they can find you. If you kill someone you know, someone from around here, they can find you."

Cyrus was slowly coming to, getting himself up onto one elbow and rubbing the dried blood out of his eyes. Zevon looked down at him, feeling the urgency in Lila's gaze.

"Uhhhh... What the fuck, man..." Cyrus groaned, his battered skull aching as he spoke.

"It'll be okay, I promise," Zevon said.

"He's waking up, Z. You have to finish this now."

Zevon knew the moment had come. He could wait no longer. Cyrus was coming to his senses and Lila was becoming impatient. He looked down at his right hand. Cyrus's knife clenched in his grip. His heart sped up, his mind raced, but it was too late to turn back now.

"Do it, Zevon."

"Hey..." Cyrus uttered, looking angrily around through the bloody gauze of his half-sealed eyes. Slowly, he began to realize what had happened, and what was happening. "Is that you, *freak?* Where are you? Come here, you little fucker..."

Zevon swallowed hard, stepping behind Cyrus while the dazed brute began to reach out for him, grasping at thin air. He looked up to meet Lila's gaze. She nodded in approval. Zevon raised the knife up with two hands, ever so slowly above his head. He trembled and shook, his grip growing ever tighter on the knife's hilt.

"Come on, loser! I'm gonna fucking *kill you!*"

Zevon lashed down.

The blade arched straight into Cyrus's chest with a *chuft*, breaking through his ribs, severing arteries and his right lung. Cyrus gasped, choked and stammered. His reaching hand fell to the ground as his body convulsed and deep, thick blood coughed out of his lips.

Zevon yanked the knife out of his chest, and that's when the blood flowed; a gushing, arterial spurt that showered onto both the shore and the plastic sheeting crumpled around the victim. Cyrus grabbed at his chest, struggling for life. Shocked and petrified. The realization suddenly hit him that this was the end of his life.

Zevon raised the knife and brought it down again. Quicker this time. He wrenched the blade out, back up over his head, then delivered a third blow with even more force than the first two.

Chuft!

Zevon was sure that he had hit the heart, as Cyrus finally went limp and his body collapsed to the shore, his head splashing into the water. Lila smiled, feeling nourishment from the blood already seeping in to her water. Zevon looked up, his breathing heavy, his hands covered with blood. Lila looked back at him with a reassuring smile.

"Good," she said. "Now give him here."

Zevon crouched down, his leg cursing at him once again, and pushed Cyrus's body further into the water. Once Lila could reach her meal, she pulled him in closer, assessing the morsel as if a waiter had just placed a juicy steak in front of her.

"Next time, don't waste so much blood."

"O-Okay."

"And I prefer it in smaller pieces, please. And no clothes." She smiled as she slowly pulled back, deeper into the waters. Zevon panted, nodding his head.

"Okay."

"Thank you, Z. Now, clean yourself up. And take care of that leg." Zevon nodded as Lila pulled her meal under the water with her, disappearing into the chilled blackness.

CHAPTER TWENTY-FOUR
PRESENT DAY

LITTLE BY LITTLE, the small, square handful of cedar formed into the shape of an egg, with the help of an electric grinder and sandpaper in decreasing levels of grit. Zevon rotated the wood in his hands, moving it along the surface of the grinder and shaped it by hand. Sawdust kicked up inside the work shed, falling to rest on his sweaty, muscled frame.

He squinted slightly even though he wore protective glasses, an extra precaution that couldn't hurt. He switched the machine off when the piece of wood was roughly the same size and shape as a jumbo egg, then turned to his collection of sandpaper. He began with a coarse 40 grain, removing any excess material and finessing any uneven portions of the egg's surface.

He held it up close to his eyes, rotating the sculpture in every direction and inspecting it for any defects. He repeated this process three times, catching flaws and sanding them out by hand. He then moved to a fine 150 grain, smoothing the whole thing over. The sawdust was now just a fine mist in the air.

Zevon wiped the egg off with a rag, then rolled it around in his hand to ensure it was perfectly smooth. One level of even finer sanding would still come, but first he moved on to the all-important detailing. Using his trusty-old Dremel tool and his VonHaus kit of small-sized wood carving tools, he went about the process of personalizing and beautifying.

As Dave Mustaine screamed through the old speakers in Zevon's little boom box, he used a pencil to write in script on the wood surface, then drew a design of swirling vines and leaves. Once he was happy with the image he had drawn, he took up his tools and began to carve into it.

With a surgeon's precision, he carved along the lines, embedding them in the egg forever. Creating texture and relief, the vines and leaves came to decorative life.

He blew away the dust and wood shavings, finishing with the lettering. Flowing script was embedded into the egg; practiced calligraphy on a curved surface, a feat that would come out sloppy and amateurish if attempted by most. But Zevon Lang was not happy until it was perfect.

He wiped the egg clean, smiling and nodding his head in approval. Next would come a very fine sanding with a 220 grain paper just to smooth out all edges, followed by a very light and subtle stain.

He turned the egg around in his hand, reading out loud the name he had carved into it.

"Claire."

THE SUN HAD JUST FINISHED SETTING and the bathroom was sealed tight. The door was locked and so was the window. A towel had been draped over the window to protect from prying eyes, even though it was a second floor bathroom. Another towel had been draped over the mirror to protect from prying eyes, even though this was not a one way mirror used in any FBI interrogations.

The light was turned off. The sink had been turned on, the water running in an ongoing stream to muffle and disguise any other sounds that may come from within.

Zevon lay in the bathtub, soaking in the hot water, masturbating as quietly as he could manage. His eyes closed as fantasies danced across the insides of his eyelids. It was always a risky process, but it was the closest thing to intimacy that he knew. He stroked himself slowly with a gentle grip, trying his best to imagine and approximate sensuality.

He stopped for a moment to look at the door. Still locked. The mirror and window, still covered. He returned to the business at hand, the running tap covering the sounds of gentle splashing that his hands made.

He couldn't be too careful. He didn't want *her* to hear. She could come to him at any time, whispering in his mind, watching him through mirrors and television screens.

Lila would certainly not approve.

She would see this as low, base, shameful, sinful. But as lustful as she had once made him feel, she could not satisfy his carnal cravings. All she did was take. And judge.

So he carried on in secrecy, hoping like a timid teenager not to get caught by his parents. But his parents were dead. His beard bristled, his muscles bulged, and he was his own man. If Lila could not fulfill his needs, he would have to do it on his own.

He continued, drifting off into his delicious trance, where a beautiful woman with caramel skin and a succulent dimpled smile was there in the tub with him, doing the dirty work for him, bringing him to the point of ecstasy.

His eyes squeezed shut and his mouth opened with a faint whisper.

"Oh, yes... Claire..."

No AMOUNT of toying with his hair was going to hide the fact that the top of Zevon's head looked like a big, open landing pad for a helicopter. He stood before the mirror, a nice blue, button-up shirt tucked into his jeans, and decided to just let his hair be. He had shaved off the week-old growth of beard and moisturized his face and hands. He had brushed his teeth, flossed and used mouth wash.

He looked himself up and down in the mirror, pulse picking up, wishing he could sand down his rough edges just a little more with some extra fine grain paper. But this was him, he thought, take it or leave it.

He turned off the bathroom light, and headed into the bedroom, where he scooped up his keys and wallet. He slipped into his gray windbreaker and found the freshly-sanded and polished wooden Easter egg lying on the bed. He put the egg into his pocket, turned out the lights and headed out the door.

"LILA?"

Zevon stood on the shore. It was a half moon that night and the lake was coated in a pleasant bluish-gray glow. He waited a minute but saw nothing but the peaceful ripples of the water. He stepped right up to the shoreline, looked around again, waiting with fidgeting hands in his jacket pockets.

"Lila, are you there?"

"Hi, baby."

Zevon tracked the direction of her voice and found her under the pier, emerging head and shoulders from the water. He smiled and trotted over to the pier, walking out a few feet onto the wooden planks until he reached her.

"Hey you," he said. "How you doing?"

"I'm fine," she said, but he could tell she looked tired. Still beautiful and vibrant, but older, slight bags under her eyes. Her hair was damp and wet with water, whereas when she was at peak energy, she would emerge looking like her hair had just been professionally curled and dried.

The glow was gone. Her hands were clasped together, holding something close to her bosom. She looked Zevon up and down, noting his unusually polished appearance. "Going out?"

"Yeah," he said, trying to sound as nonchalant as possible. "I got invited to a barbecue."

"Oh, that's nice. Who invited you?"

"Just a friend. Well, client. Not really a friend, just someone I'm doing work for. Client." Zevon held the wooden egg in his hand, keeping it lodged inside his jacket pocket. Lila floated out a few feet from the pier, raising up slightly in the water to get a better look at him.

"Is this friend a man or a woman?"

"It's a... W-well, she's a woman. But she's not really a friend, like I said."

"Mmm," she mused with a close-lipped smile. "Okay. Well that sounds like fun. And you look very nice."

"Thanks... How are you doing? You okay? Getting hungry?"

"No, I'm fine."

"Yeah?" Zevon took notice of her hands gently clutched together. "What are you holding?"

"Oh, it's nothing," Lila said with a sheepish shrug. She opened up her hands, revealing a baby turtle the size of a small bar of soap, squirming innocently in her palm. "Just another little dear I found. Thought you might like him."

"Ohhh, how sweet! Thank you, I love him!" Zevon smiled at the adorable little guy, knowing he'd fit right in with the collection of critters he had up in the house. "But I don't really have time to take him inside right now. I gotta... Y'know—"

"It's okay, go ahead." Lila smiled politely and waved her hand in acceptance. "I'll let little Buster here swim off. Maybe I'll catch him again another time... Go to the party. Have fun."

"Okay," he could see her eyes turn downward as she drifted away. "I won't be back too late. Promise."

"Whatever. Have a good time, Z. Good night."

Lila drifted further into the lake, sinking down into her vast, murky home once again. Zevon let out a sigh and released his grip on the egg, realizing that his hands had begun to sweat and that he would have to wipe it off before giving it to Claire.

He walked back up the pier, took out his keys and headed off into the night.

CHAPTER TWENTY-FIVE
PRESENT DAY

A SICKENINGLY UPBEAT new song by Bruno Mars saturated the night air, along with the sizzling scents of lemon-chicken and beef patties on the grill in the suburban back yard. Cutout Easter Bunnies and eggs were taped along the railing of the deck, and plastic eggs were sprinkled around the property.

A mixed crowd danced and socialized, laughed and smoked, ate and drank. Young couples in their 20's and 30's mingled with senior citizens, and a few visibly stressed parents had brought their young children along. All were welcome here at the home of Claire's old friend and White Feather's biggest social butterfly, Sarah Houston.

Sarah, a full figured woman with sandy blonde hair and a line of gossip on everyone in town, stood with Claire. They sipped their beers and shook their heads at the woman standing in front of them. Mandy had short, curly-black hair, glasses, and was five-foot-two in heels. She took a sip of red wine, squinting her eyes suspiciously at her two friends as they silently judged her.

"*What?*" Mandy demanded. "I don't understand what's wrong with you two! We had a great time!"

"Mandy! That's just wrong," Claire said. "Four hours? Your blind date with this guy lasted *four hours?*"

"We got along so well! We just talked and talked..."

"Jesus, lord," Sarah said and took another sip of beer.

"Mandy," Claire explained. "A blind date is supposed to be like: You meet up for coffee, or lunch, you talk for a half an hour or maybe an hour, you test the waters..."

"You leave him wanting more," Sarah interjected. "You don't talk and talk and talk and talk for four hours straight, making it clear that neither of you has anything else to do and are just totally desperate!"

"Well, I'm sorry, Sarah," Mandy said. "Not all of us are married and have kids and have a beautiful house and a perfect life like you, okay? Some of us still have to go out there and find a man! Know what I'm saying, sister?" Mandy nudged Claire, expecting a *hoorah* but getting only a puzzled look in response.

"Claire!"

"Ummm, not really, Mandy."

"You bitches are really something! Jesus..."

"Ahhh, nothing's changed," Sarah mused.

"No, I mean..." Claire searched for the right words. "I was married for three years, you guys, and we all know how well that went. So, now... I'm in no rush to find a new man to hit me or control me or mess my life up any more. I'm starting my new practice, back in my home town! I got my girls, I got my favorite pie shop... I'm good! *I don't need no man!*" Claire affected her voice with a comedic accent and the three old friends laughed together and each took another sip.

Two strapping young men walked by the three ladies,

beaming with charming smiles and fashionable facial hair as they flexed their way across the lawn. Claire, Sarah and Mandy couldn't help but turn their heads, cracking each other up once again.

"Which is not to say that I can't have a little *fun* now and then! A little roll in the hay..." Claire amended. "I just don't feel the need to get into some serious relationship, y'know? *Ya hear me?*"

"*We hear ya!*" Sarah and Mandy answered in unison as two of Sarah's young children blew past them and cleared a path through the guests as if they didn't exist.

"Sterling!" Sarah shouted and chased after them. "You leave your sister alone!"

OUT ON THE STREET, a faded-old Chevy van rumbled to a halt a block away from the festivities. Zevon got out with a bottle of wine in his hand and closed the door, looking over at the house, which seemed to be throbbing with sound and movement. He checked his reflection in the driver's side window - Hair still fine. He checked his jacket pocket - The wooden egg was still there.

He stood for a moment, feet glued to the pavement, trying to pump himself up. People, he thought. Lots of people, all getting along and having a good time. Murder was easier than this. Taking a few deep breaths, he compelled himself into motion.

"Okay," Zevon said to himself as he crossed the street and moved around to the side gate of the house. He made his way around to the back yard, where the majority of the action was. Smiling people criss-crossed in every direction, drinking, talking, eating, laughing.

His body reflexively tightened as he penetrated deeper, taking note of all the familiar strangers. Some he knew from school, some he had seen around town over the years and most faces didn't have a corresponding name. A few people smiled and nodded at him as he found his way to the center of the yard.

The affluent house stood behind him, with people lining the deck that led outside. The large lawn sprawled out, enclosed by a high fence, with trees and bushes lining the edges. Picnic chairs, tables and lawn furniture were in full use as friends gathered around, making full use of the setting.

Off to the side was the DJ station, which was just a stereo connected to large speakers, and beside that was the grill and three large coolers. Zevon could smell the tantalizing meat sizzling and hear the juices popping; the collective sounds of laughter drowned out whatever top-20 Pop music hit was playing at the moment. Zevon stood immobile, taking all in.

Tom and Eddie had found themselves two seats near the coolers. Eddie had downed nearly half a bottle of Hennessy before arriving and was now working on his sixth Heineken. Tom had his third cold Bud of the night in hand, and nearly had to prop up his friend as the big slob kept leaning against him to whisper in his ear.

"Hey bro," Eddie said. "Claire's looking good tonight..."

"Shut up."

"She's right over there. You should go talk to her, Tommy. She still digs you, man."

"Damn, Ed! Quit breathing on me!"

Tom couldn't help but glance over at Claire, and she looked back. He smiled and raised his beer in an informal, distant toast and she returned the gesture. Tom took a swig of beer, contemplating what he would say and which of his smooth moves he should try. Eddie nudged him with a snort and gestured to a lone figure across the lawn.

"Better make your move before Xerox does! I heard they've been getting real friendly, bro!"

Tom's eyes found Zevon, standing like a lost puppy, wearing what might be his only nice set of clothes, clutching a bottle of wine. Tom had seen him around town once in a while through the years after high school, and he had changed dramatically.

Tom used to be the jock, and Zevon, a pile of chicken bones. Now, it was the outcast from Mars who filled out his clothes with lean muscle mass, while Tom filled his shirt with a belly full of suds.

Zevon's eyes scanned the crowd for familiar faces, finding Tom's and making eye contact. The two men shared a moment together from either side of the lawn. Years ago, this may have triggered a fight or an onslaught of insults, but now they simply acknowledged each other.

Zevon nodded his head and Tom followed suit. The look in old Xerox's eyes had changed, Tom thought.

They no longer had the look of easy prey.

CLAIRE and her two girlfriends walked down onto the lawn from their high ground on the deck. Claire enjoyed her drink, and relished in the warm, social atmosphere. Sarah waved and smiled at everyone, ever the good host. Mandy continued to rattle on about her woes concerning men and dating etiquette as she eyeballed every male in the crowd.

"Whatever," Mandy said. "I guess it's just as well. All men are the same. God forbid I ever find one that's just honest and good and actually likes me for *me*, doesn't treat me like shit..."

Claire shook her head, searching the party for familiar faces, her focus landing on the strangely handsome young artist she had invited. Zevon stood off to the side, bobbing his head to the music in a nervous attempt to fit in. Claire smiled, and it occurred to her that he looked like a puppy who'd lost its mother.

"I don't know," Claire said to Mandy. "Once in a while you meet a man who's... Different. See you heifers later."

Claire stepped through the crowd, trying not to bump into anyone, but the effects of three beers made that difficult. She cut a path toward the lonely puppy standing by himself, sneaking up on him. She approached from behind, coming in and delivering a playful jab to his shoulder. He turned, startled, and Claire beamed like a child who'd just pulled off the world's greatest prank.

"Hey, you!"

"Hi, Claire."

She threw her arms around his neck and gave him a strong, tipsy hug. Zevon did not resist, hugging her back. He'd seen people hugging before, so he approximated the motion. Claire noted just how firm and solid his body felt against hers, and what an effortless, yet irresistibly masculine scent he had. She let go before it started to feel too awkward.

"I'm so glad you came," she said. "And you brought wine!"

"Yeah, well... I didn't know, uh, if I should bring anything, so... Yeah. I figured, like... I'd bring wine?"

"Sweet! Let's pop it open and have some!"

"Ah, I'm more of a beer guy, myself."

"Well, I think we can manage that."

Claire took Zevon by the hand, leading him off toward the coolers. Her hand was so soft and smooth, her natural beauty and glow intensified by her alcohol consumption. Her smile was honest and glowing; her enthusiasm to spend time with him was itself intoxicating. Zevon followed her lead, his tense body slowly beginning to relax.

Tom watched in silence as Claire and Zevon made their way across the lawn, hand in hand, smiling. There she was, his beautiful girl, back after so many years, holding hands with Zevon Lang.

Zevon fucking Lang.

Tom finished off his beer and went to throw it in a recycling bin, doing his best not to pay attention. But in the corner of his eye, he saw her opening the bottle Lang had bought and pouring herself a glass. He saw her passing Lang a cold beer. And he saw them heading off together to talk. Tom cracked a new beer for himself and took a hard swig.

Zevon and Claire had found a spot on the patio stairs to sit and talk. He had nearly finished his beer and her empty wine glass sat on the step beside her. She was leaning in, hanging on his words as she gently led him through the telling of a painful story.

"That's so terrible, Z. I'm so sorry. I don't know what I'd do without my parents."

"It's okay," he said. "I never really knew my mom."

"And your father? Was it a car accident, or...?"

"No," Zevon said, thinking quick. He wanted to tell her

the truth, but wouldn't dare divulge the whole story. "No, he was drunk, but it wasn't drunk driving. He, uh... He was fishing, out on the lake behind our house. He had started the day off with a bottle of scotch... Went to get in the boat... Slipped, hit his head on the dock, fell in the water..."

"He drowned?"

Zevon nodded his head. "Found him floating out there. We never got along so great, but... I never wanted something like that to happen. By the time I got to him, it was too late."

"Oh my god," she said. "And you've been living in that house all alone ever since?"

"Since I was nineteen." Zevon put his beer down and picked up a paper plate that he'd loaded with chicken wings, going back to work on the tender meat. "So, I try not to drink much. Just a little beer. Try to keep my body pure, y'know?"

"Mmm, I see that!"

"Well, I try."

Claire could see him struggling with his own shyness as he nibbled at his chicken wings, and decided a good non-sequitur was in order.

"So," she started. "How's my sign coming?"

"Good! Got the main frame done, another day to finish roughing out the main shapes, then another few days for detailing. Actually, here! I uh, I brought you a little something..." Zevon figured while they were on the subject, this would be a good time to present her with the carved egg. He pulled it from his pocket and offered it over to her. "Happy Easter."

"What's this?"

"Just a present, a little something. No biggie."

Claire turned the egg over in her hands, marveling at its smooth surface and the flowing lines carved into it. She read her own name, framed by vines and leaves, polished and lightly stained to perfection, and gasped.

"Ohhh, Zevon! That's so sweet! Thank you so much!" She hugged him tight and he accepted the warm sensation.

"You're welcome."

She pulled away, just far enough to look into his sapphire eyes. He gazed back at her, enchanted. A smooth player would have turned the moment into a kiss, but Zevon Lang just sat there, bedazzled. She smiled, grabbing his hand.

"You want to dance?"

"Ahhhh, no. I don't think so. No no no no no..."

"Oh come on," she urged, standing and pulling at his arm. "Have some fun, Zevon! Live a little!"

"I don't know how to dance," he laughed. "Claire, no! Stop!"

"Just think of it as exercise," Claire teased. "You just ate a bunch of chicken with the skin still on it! Oh, nooo! Time to work off those calories! Come on, feel the burn!"

Zevon's resolve would only go so far, and he found himself being pulled to his feet by the irresistible creature.

CHAPTER TWENTY-SIX
PRESENT DAY

THE FUNKY and soulful fusion of Blues and Hip-Hop created a fun vibe as G. Love And Special Sauce pumped through the speaker system. Party guests misled out on the lawn, dancing and drinking. Sarah Houston danced with her husband while their youngest child clung to their knees, refusing to give them a single moment of intimacy. Tom and Eddie sat off to the side, getting sufficiently juiced to maintain their reputations. Mandy stood off in a corner, texting a man who wasn't there rather than dancing with a man who was.

Claire guided Zevon to the center of the crowd with a gentle hand and a warm grin. She moved her shoulders and hips, encouraging Zevon to do the same while G. Love spat his unique brand of Bluesy rhymes.

"Just move your body to the beat," she said. "See? Like this." Her curvy figure surged and flowed beneath her form-fitting, summer dress. Zevon swallowed hard, trying to follow.

"I don't know any moves!" He said. "What do I do?"

"Just let your body go free! Have fun!"

Claire took his hands, leaning back and spinning around him. She pulled back, popping her hips with attitude, moving her feet to the pulse of the beat. She was not a polished, professional dancer by any stretch, but she knew how to move and have fun.

She gyrated her body, striking out with her hands in no formalized, practiced gestures, but punctuating each movement to the bang of the bass drum. Zevon bobbed his head, working his knees up and down. He began to lose himself, enjoying the moment and feeling the music.

"There you go," Claire said. "Woo! You got it!" She stuck her tongue out at him and made a silly face, and he couldn't help but laugh. Zevon's robotic motions became more relaxed. Instead of trying to execute perfect, choreographed moves, he let the rhythm flow through his body, moving to the beat and allowing himself to be silly.

He flashed a comical look back at her and she erupted with laughter. Zevon Lang was approximating dancing, and a wide smile stretched uncontrollably across his face. Perhaps getting a bit overzealous, his wide movements were quite sloppy, and he bumped into another party goer behind him with a thud. Zevon turned to see the man look at him with an annoyed glare.

"Oh, sorry man! I'm sorry!" The man nodded in acceptance and they all went back to dancing with their partners.

Tom tried to stop himself from watching Zevon and Claire dancing as he finished another beer. The sense of bravado that fueled him in his youth was nowhere in sight, and he was done trying to think of a way to get to Claire alone. *Much better to sit in a corner and stew*, he thought.

Meanwhile, his trusty companion, Eddie, swayed with weighted eyelids to a beat all his own, sweat beading up on his red face.

"*Nnnnnng*," Eddie groaned. "I don't feel so good, Kepp..."

"You don't say. Is it all just spinning around? Just spinning and spinning and spinning?"

"Shut up..." Eddie had clearly passed the threshold, and as much as Tom enjoyed toying with him, he also didn't want to spend the rest of the night covered in his friend's vomit. Tom laughed and rose to his feet, putting his hand on Eddie's shoulder and started to help him up.

"Come on, dumb-ass," Tom said. "I think we need to get you to a bathroom, stat."

ZEVON AND CLAIRE DANCED, surging with the crowd, soaking up the smiles and happy energy around them. Zevon spun around, striking a pose and making Claire bust out with laughter. Her partner making fun of his own inability was far sexier than any skilled dancer could be.

Feeling his confidence build, Zevon took her by the hand and pulled her close. Their bodies pressed together and each could feel the other's warmth. Their faces were inches apart, their eyes locked together, his hand on the small of her back. Her lips parted, but Zevon did not even register the invitation.

He pulled back again, trying to impress her with some funky dance moves. She laughed once again, clapping her hands and egging him on.

"Yeeeeaaah, Zevon! *Woooooo!*"

Zevon thrust his body to and fro, snapping out his

arms, spinning, popping his hips. It was a combination of reckless goofing and trying to execute moves far too advanced for him. Unaware of his surroundings, riding on a cloud of alcohol, adrenaline and endorphins, he was in a zone.

No one else existed; only he and Claire.

Losing himself as he moved across the slick lawn, Zevon's feet conspired against him. He slipped, losing his balance and knocked into a young couple before falling to the ground.

"Hey! Watch it!" The young couple protested, gawking at him as Zevon looked up at them from the lawn. Claire gasped and went to help him up.

"Oh my god! Are you okay?"

Zevon ignored her question as he pulled himself up, noting all the people who were now looking at him, laughing. He took Claire's hand, allowing her to help him stand. He turned to the young couple he'd knocked into, exasperated.

"I'm sorry, you guys," Zevon said. "I just... I'm sorry..."

The young couple went on with their dancing, as did everyone else. No one considered his little spill to be a big deal, except him. Zevon appraised himself, feeling the throb in his back from connecting with the ground.

He reached his hand to the back of his jacket and found that he was covered in dirt. A brown streak ran from his left shoulder all the way down to the back of his legs. He wiped the dirt on his hands onto his pants, shaking his head at his own clumsiness.

"Great," he said.

"You okay?" Claire asked.

"Yeah," Zevon shrugged. "Think I need to clean myself up a little. You know where I can...?"

"Yeah, yeah. Just right through that door. Bathroom's right there."

"Okay, thanks. I'll just... Yeah."

Zevon skulked off to find the bathroom as Claire watched. Not far from her was another party guest, a large figure with a shaved head, wearing baggy shorts and a Quentin Tarantino t-shirt. His bulging stomach filled with burgers and beer, Jordan Keenan laughed at Zevon's misfortune, seizing this moment and strutting over to where Claire stood.

Zevon entered the house through the sliding door, making his way to the bathroom as the outside music faded to a dim hum. He rounded the corner and found the bathroom, discovering Tom Kepper leaning on the wall beside it.

Through the closed door, Zevon heard the unmistakable sound of Eddie heaving his guts out into the toilet bowl. Tom and Zevon shared a look, no one else inside but the two of them.

"Oh, hey. Hi," Zevon said.

"Hey. Lang. How you doing?"

"Uh, good. Hi."

"Having a good time?"

Zevon nodded, not interested in small talk.

"Eddie may be a while," Tom laughed. "There's another bathroom upstairs." Tom pointed in the direction of the stairs and Zevon nodded politely as he turned in that direction.

"Okay, thanks," Zevon said. "Uh, hope he feels better."

Tom noticed Zevon's stained clothes as he turned, a slight smile cracking across his face, and he couldn't resist —

"Took a little spill, huh Lang?"

Zevon stopped for a second, but didn't turn and didn't answer. He continued on back down the hall, heading upstairs as Tom chuckled to himself.

Reaching the second floor, Zevon found the guest bathroom and headed inside, locking the door. He turned so he could see his backside in the mirror, noting his ruined clothes with a frustrated hiss.

He pounded down on the sink, clenching his jaw as he looked into his own eyes in the mirror. Letting out a sigh, he turned on the hot water, took his jacket off and began the task of cleaning himself up.

———

"Hey, Claire! Welcome back! Remember me!"

Jordan Keenan held his arms out as if expecting a big hug. Claire forced a smile and nodded her head.

"Hi, Jordan. Yeah, of course I remember you." *Unfortunately*, she thought. The towering ox dropped his arms and took another step closer, taking another gulp of beer as he looked her up and down. He would never become the next great white rapper, but no one dared to tell him that.

"You lookin' fine as hell!" Jordan said, trying to be charming. "How you been?"

Claire smiled politely and shrugged, taking a sip of wine as her eyes were already scanning around for Zevon.

"Haven't seen you since senior year," Jordan continued. "Yeah, you lookin' real good..." He may as well have been drooling over a steaming plate of fried chicken, biscuits and gravy.

"Thank you," she said, rolling her eyes and walking away.

"What's the matter, Claire?" Jordan said as he followed her through the crowd, unfazed. "C'mon, let's have a drink and catch up!"

"I'm here with someone."

"What, that little weirdo? Boy, you sure know how to pick 'em, Carpenter!"

"He's a nice guy, Jordan. And I don't think it's any of your business. You don't even know me, so I'd appreciate it if you'd just..."

Jordan easily passed her with two long strides and stepped in her way, blocking her like a mountain of trailer trash. "Oh come on," he said. "Don't be like that!"

"Please just leave me alone." She turned again and tried to walk away, but this time felt a large, meaty hand wrapping around her arm, easily stopping her escape.

"Where you goin', huh? What's with this attitude? I'm just tryin' to be nice and you're actin' like you're miss fuckin' thing! Come on, Claire, let's have a drink!"

***

ZEVON CAME BACK out into the back yard, his windbreaker now draped from his arm and his dirt-stained clothes sufficiently cleaned up. He cringed at the loud, obnoxious Rap song being played at the moment and hoped the Metal Gods were not watching him.

He slowly walked through the crowd, nodding his head and smiling politely as he headed back to meet Claire. She was not where he'd left her, and his eyes glanced around until he noticed a scene developing. There she was, standing helpless as some troglodyte gripped her arm, not letting her go.

Without missing a beat, Zevon began his walk over to

them, his face falling slack and his eyes going blank. A button had been pushed in his head, and Zevon had to remind himself that he was surrounded by normal, civilized people, all of whom could easily identify him in a police lineup. Controlling his breath, he focused his energy on staying cool and calm as he approached.

"Jordan, look! I'm not interested, okay? Please just…"

"Oh come on, Claire. Don't play fuckin' games like that!"

Jordan's grip did not let up, but an expression of relief fell over Claire's face as Zevon stepped up to them, casually inserting himself into the conversation.

"Hey, Claire," Zevon said. "I'm back."

"Zevon! Hi!" Claire stepped towards him, but Jordan's grip remained strong. The six-foot four-inch beast looked down at the little space alien like an oddity at a local carnival.

"Ze-*what?*" Jordan said with a laugh. "Unbelievable."

"This is Jordan," Claire said, trying to remain civil and calm, despite the tremor spiking in her pulse. "We went to New Roads together."

"Hey, how you doing?" Zevon nodded to Jordan, remaining calm and casual as he reached out for her. "Claire, you want to get something to eat?" Claire crossed towards him like a bullet, but Jordan's grip tightened, cutting off her circulation.

"I'm talkin' to the lady right now, homeboy," Jordan glowered down at him. "Private conversation, okay?"

"Let go!" Claire was done pretending to be cordial and patient. So was Zevon. His jaw clenched, his muscles tightened. He did not want these people to see his ugly side, but the partygoers were beginning to notice the conflict developing and a circle slowly formed around them.

Zevon looked up at Jordan with his cold, blue eyes. Steady and confident.

"Do you really want to do this?" Zevon said.

Jordan let go of Claire's arm and stepped up into Zevon's face, hefting his chest out and putting on his most intimidating face. His eyes stared back into Zevon's, not a spec of fear within. He was the big dog and always had his way.

"Oh yeah?" The big dog barked. "You got somethin' to say, *pussy*?" With a sharp *whack*, Jordan thrust his right hand into Zevon's left shoulder, pushing him back with impressive strength. "Go ahead, say somethin'!"

"Just stop, buddy," Zevon said. "You don't want to do this." Another shove and Zevon staggered back again, Jordan stepping right back in front of him. Claire had frozen in place, as did the rest of the crowd, none brave enough to step in. Another man's blood might boil, but Zevon's began to freeze.

His heart rate became calm as he could feel the situation unraveling in slow-motion before him. The size and strength of this stranger, the alcohol on his breath, the sloppiness and inefficiency of his movements; all aspects of his opponent's demeanor fell into place. He had no fight training and despite his natural size and strength, was utterly out of shape and had no stamina. And worst of all, he was underestimating his smaller opponent.

"What's the matter," Jordan goaded. "Huh, little man? You scared? Huh, *bitch*? You scared?" Jordan reached out with his right hand again, making contact with Zevon's left shoulder. But this time, the smaller man trapped the hand while stepping back, pulling Jordan forward and off balance in a blur of motion.

The crowd collectively gasped as Zevon expertly

twisted the hand away, stepping off to the side and securing a tight wrist lock. With a face devoid of emotion, Zevon wrenched the wrist off to the side, using leverage to break the larger man's wrist, snapping ligaments and tendons away from the bone with one simple twist.

"*YIIIIAAAAAAHHHHH!!!*" Jordan bellowed in shock and pain as fire shot up his arm and he fell to his knees, finding himself completely at the mercy of this man he'd so vastly misjudged. But there was no mercy or sympathy in Zevon's eyes as he methodically jumped onto the back of the wild boar. His legs cinched around Jordan's waist and his arms snaked around his neck as the crowd gawked in utter disbelief.

"Oh my God!" Claire could do nothing but stand and watch the event unfolding, both horrified by the violence and secretly pleased that her sensitive artist was also a knight in shining armor, willing and able to fight a dragon for her.

Tom emerged from the house after making sure Eddie had voided an entire week's worth of beer and fried food, finding the crowd outside circled around one central point. He made his way out onto the lawn, unable to see the action happening on the ground past the wall of onlookers. But he'd been in enough fights to know that a scrap was unfolding, and he ran forward, edging his way through the crowd until he could see the struggle playing out on the freshly-cut suburban lawn.

Zevon Lang had attached himself to Jordan Keenan like a backpack, his arms cinching tighter around his neck as the big man flailed helplessly. Tom watched in disbelief and the crowd hooted and hollered as Zevon's arms coiled tighter, locking in and setting into a rear naked choke.

Jordan tried to defend himself with his one good remaining arm, pulling at Zevon's arms to protect his own neck. But Zevon had the choke sunk in, deep and tight, and within seconds, he could feel the blood supply to his brain cutting off and his head becoming swollen and hazy. Reluctantly accepting defeat, Jordan slapped at Zevon's arm, the universal sign of surrender...

Zevon Lang would not let go.

"Zevon?" Claire implored, looking down at him and seeing the total empty expression on his face, like a snake with its prey. His eyes did not blink and his grip did not loosen. A random stranger called out from the crowd—

"Let him go, man! He tapped!"

Switched into kill-mode, Zevon did not hear the pleas and did not care as he felt Jordan's body finally go limp in his grasp. Zevon held the choke, holding tight well after his opponent was unconscious. Tom stood in shock, seconds away from jumping in and doing something. Claire shouted out, finally breaking him from this trance -

"*Zevon!*"

Like a bolt, Zevon came back to reality, looking up at the crowd circling him. His arms relaxed and he released Jordan's neck, pushing him down onto the ground and stood back up. One party goer held out a cell phone, filming the whole thing as he laughed and cheered.

"Daaaaamn, dude! That was *sick!*" The crowd began to dissipate, and Zevon found himself standing there, eyes locked with Claire's, knowing that she'd just had a glimpse of who he really was.

"I-I'm sorry..." Zevon said, the crowd parting for him as he took off across the yard. Claire didn't waste a minute and followed after him, both grateful and dumbfounded at what she just witnessed.

Tom looked back down at Jordan, lying in the grass, out like a wet sack of rice. Beside him was Zevon's wallet, which had fallen from the breast pocket of his windbreaker. Tom stepped in, checking first to see that Jordan was alive. The drunken brute murmured and began his slow ascent back to consciousness. Tom reached out and picked up the wallet, opening it up. Zevon's driver's license stared up at him.

***

ZEVON STORMED DOWN THE STREET, cursing himself as Claire chased after not far behind. He reached his van, punching into its side and trying to catch his breath. He had been cold as a reptile during the actual act, but now his adrenaline was kicking in.

"God damn it!" He fumed, pulling his key out.

"Zevon! Z, wait!"

Claire caught up to him and he struggled to meet her eyes. They both tried to catch their breath, neither knowing what to say. The air was thick between them, and with words failing them both, Claire reached out and pulled him in by the collar.

She pressed her lips into his, kissing him softly. He didn't stop her, slowly allowing himself to kiss her back. He held onto her shoulders as her hands rested on his chest. The kiss lingered, tongues lightly flicking together, each intoxicated with the other's warm essence.

Zevon finally pulled away, hesitating to continue along this unknown road. This was a new feeling to try to process, or maybe a very old one. Either way, something about it felt wrong, despite everything about it feeling so right. He looked her in the eye, not sure what to say.

"I... I shouldn't... I gotta go."

"Really?"

"Good night, Claire."

"...Good night." She sighed.

He stepped away, smiling as he unlocked his driver's door, slowly opening it as she watched. He climbed inside and started the engine. Releasing an exasperated sigh, Zevon Lang drove back off down the road, and Claire Carpenter returned to her friend's party on the quiet suburban street.

CHAPTER TWENTY-SEVEN
2005

LIEUTENANT PAUL KEPPER STRODE through the halls of Hamilton High, his sharp-soled shoes providing a steady tempo. He was ten years away from earning the monicker of "chief," twenty pounds lighter, and his hair had not yet gone gray from the crushing frustration and stress of being a cog in a faulty machine. Tom followed two feet behind, slouching as he felt the eyes of his classmates tracking with them.

It had been a week since Cyrus Kushan had vanished off the face of the map, and as yet, no evidence had turned up. Kepper had interviewed everyone in the Kushan family, interviewed the roommate, Aaron Bell, and interviewed the girlfriend, Stephanie Mayben, but still nothing.

Cyrus had taken Stephanie out to their favorite diner, come home, and just disappeared. His car remained parked in the driveway, and all his personal affects, including his wallet and keys, still lay on his dresser where he'd left them.

The only item missing from Kushan's home was his hunting knife, which raised suspicion. Aaron Bell hadn't seen or heard anything, and neither had any of the neighbors, but despite the lack of evidence, lieutenant Kepper had that all-too-familiar, sinking sensation in his stomach that something had happened to young Cyrus.

He had graduated from Hamilton High two years prior, and Kepper had arrested the troublesome youth three times since he was thirteen years-old. The first time was for driving without a license at thirteen. The second arrest was for assault, and the third was for driving under the influence. He was the type of kid who'd made plenty of enemies, any one of which would be eager to help him perform a vanishing act.

"This way, Pop," Tom said and angled down another hall, leading them to a conference room. Walking inside, they were greeted by Mr. Matthews, the school principal. A slouching-slug of a man, he sat on the edge of a desk, facing a collection of seats occupied by a handful of students. Eddie was there, vigorously chewing gum, along with Nate, Becky, Jared and Stephanie. Lieutenant Kepper nodded to the group, and Mr. Matthews rose to shake his hand.

"Thanks for coming, Paul," Matthews said.

"Sure thing," Kepper said. "Hey everybody."

The group murmured greetings as the officer and his son walked in, Tom sitting down with his friends. The room was dim and all postures were slouched. Nate swirled a box of Tic-Tacs on his desk. Becky had the look up a puppy who'd been caught knocking over a jar of cookies, and Stephanie sat with clasped hands and a furrowed brow.

"Still nothing?" Stephanie asked.

"We're still following leads, but no. We haven't found him yet. I'm hoping maybe one of you can help." The lieutenant glanced around the room at the disinterested lot.

"Come on, you guys," Matthews gently urged.

"I mean, I already told you everything I know,"

Stephanie said, hands wringing together. "Cyrus wouldn't have just run off like that..."

"Can you think of anyone who might have wanted to hurt him?" Kepper's question elicited a chuckle from Eddie.

"They'd have to take a number, Mr. K," Eddie joked, but quickly realized no one else was laughing. "I mean, Cyrus has beef with plenty of people."

"Such as?"

"I don't know," Eddie continued. "Cyrus sells weed. Calls himself 'Evergreen.' Maybe someone he sells to?"

"Do you know the names of anyone he sells to?" Silence. The lieutenant looked down at his son with raised eyebrows. "Tommy?"

"Uh, no. No, Pop..." Tom squirmed in his chair.

"Lieutenant," Stephanie's voice cracked. "Do you... Do you think somebody ki- Do you think Cyrus is..." Kepper stepped forward reassuringly, looking into the young girl's strained eyes.

"I don't know, Stephanie. But he didn't vanish into thin air. And I'm going to do my best to get to the bottom of this."

"Come on guys," Matthews continued. "Think. Who did Cyrus have beef with?" The group sat for a moment, thinking hard.

"He and Jack Lawson hated each other," Nate said. "They been getting in fights since junior high." The group nodded and murmured their agreement as the lieutenant wrote the name down in his pad.

"He stole fifty bucks from Dylan Filco over the summer. He's a senior," Eddie added.

"He beat up Xenon a couple months ago too," Becky timidly added. Kepper continued to write, puzzled.

"Xenon?" The lieutenant asked.

"Zevon Lang," Matthews clarified. "Sophomore."

"Yeah," Jared added. "Zevon was trying to hit on Stephanie, so Cyrus and his boys jumped him."

"Mm hm."

"And last year," Stephanie continued. "He beat up another guy who was talking to me at the movie theater. I don't know his name... Cyrus was... He gets very jealous..." Stephanie couldn't hold back the tears any longer, and Becky rubbed her shoulder.

The list would go on and on if they thought long enough. Cyrus had done plenty of damage in his day and trying to track down everyone he'd wronged was going to be a challenge to say the least. So Paul Kepper decided to start with those close by.

ZEVON SAT out in the quad, soaking up sunshine and leaning against a tree as he sketched a portrait of a beautiful woman rising up from under water. He had just finished a Tupperware full of grilled chicken, brown rice and steamed broccoli, then topped it off with a strawberry protein shake for dessert.

The hard work and rigid diet were no fun, but they were paying off. Zevon was beginning to feel stronger, faster, healthier. His father didn't understand and would shake his head whenever he saw him cooking "that health food crap," but Zevon didn't want to be a weakling forever.

A long shadow cast across his sketch pad, accompanied by purposeful footsteps. Zevon looked up to see a police officer standing over him in silhouette, a brown and tan uniform on his strong frame, a mustache on his lip and the name Kepper on his chest. Zevon swallowed hard and kept his cool.

"Zevon Lang?"

"Uh, yeah?"

"I'm lieutenant Paul Kepper, White Feather PD. Can I speak to you for a minute?" His voice was dry and sober, not an ounce of humor in his demeanor. Zevon recognized that last name, and his heart and stomach traded places. Tom's father. He put the sketch pad down and struggled to his feet.

"Uh, yeah. Sure," Zevon said, trying to hide the pain in his left leg. He had performed self-surgery after his first kill the other night, utilizing the same sewing kit that he usually tasked for stitching Iron Maiden and Judas Priest patches onto denim jackets.

There were now seven sloppy stitches and some bandaging holding his thigh together beneath his jeans, and though Kepper knew nothing of this, he did note how wobbly the boy was on his legs, as well as his overall slight and frail physique.

"I'm asking around about Cyrus Kushan. I understand you had some trouble with him a few months ago?"

"Uh..." Zevon's eyes focused past the lieutenant, noting that Tom stood in the distance with his friends, watching them. "Uh, y-yeah. He uh, kind of beat me up, him and his friends. W-why?"

"Did you know that Cyrus has gone missing?"

"Um, no," Zevon fidgeted.

"Hasn't been seen in a week. Just disappeared."

"Oh," Zevon tried to think quick and say something smart, but decided less was more. Kepper looked him up and down as the boy rubbed his hands on his jeans, his arms as skinny as broomsticks. He couldn't be more than five-foot-three, not even a hundred pounds. Kepper sighed, asking the obligatory questions before moving on to more serious suspects.

"Where were you last Monday night?"

"Um, at home. Just had dinner, watched a movie..."

"Anybody else there with you?"

"J-Just my dad."

Paul Kepper nodded his head, looking back at his son watching them from the edge of the quad. He tried to imagine this awkward runt somehow besting a violent brute like Cyrus and almost laughed. Still, he had to ask:

"You don't know anything about what happened to Cyrus, do you, Zevon? You have anything to do with him going missing?"

"Sir?" Zevon put on his best dumb, confused face, looking like an innocent doe with a shaggy head of hair. Kepper released a small sigh which turned into a laugh, smiling back at the youth.

He imagined his own son must give this poor kid hell; he knew he would have back when *he* was in high school. And with a name like *Zevon*, Jesus! Poor kid.

"No, I 'spose not. You have a good day, young man. Stay out of trouble now." Paul Kepper nodded at him and turned away, heading back across the quad.

Zevon held back a smile and restrained himself from doing a full-blown victory dance right there in the middle of the quad.

CHAPTER TWENTY-EIGHT
PRESENT DAY

ZEVON'S POWERFUL, muscled legs propelled him around Lake Yakonkwe on a fine, warm morning. He wrapped up his routine as the sun beat down on him, slowing to a jog and letting his high-performance engine rev down. He passed Murray Siedelman as the old-timer stood on his back porch, enjoying his morning coffee.

"Hey, Murray!" Zevon called out and waved.

"Beautiful day," Murray smiled and took a sip from his oversized cup of brew.

Zevon changed clothes and got to work, opting to move his chair out from the work shed and sit in the sun, facing the lake. He carried a small collection of chisels and gouges outside, placing them on the large tree stump and brought Claire's new sign as well.

Working through the embarrassment from his behavior at the barbecue last night, he held the sign on his lap, carving away at its surface. Slowly, the details began to form into three dimensions.

A RUSTY, old Honda Civic slowed to a halt on the curb in front of the Lang house. At one time, it had been a red, cute little number, but now it had faded into a muddled marbling of tones including yellows and browns, and a collection of small dents and scratches told of its rocky past. Behind the wheel, its driver was in much the same condition.

Tom Kepper turned off the engine.

He had showered, shaved and even combed his hair. He was relatively sober and had chosen a shirt that didn't show off his gut too badly. On the passenger seat beside him was a wallet, crusted on one edge with dried mud. He picked up the wallet and flipped it open once more to regard the state driver's license — Zevon Lang.

"God damn it," Tom flipped the wallet closed and got out of the car, sucking in his gut and adjusting his belt as he made his way over to the house, wincing in the bright sun.

ZEVON GENTLY HAMMERED the 20-gauge chisel along a guide line on the wood sign, creating an etched groove that would soon form into a winding vine on the surface. He wiped away several small curves of cedar that looked like little Fritos, running his hand over the still-rough surface with a smile.

He heard a rapping at the front door and habitually ignored it. Whatever they were selling, he didn't want it. He continued his work and after a minute, the knocking went silent. But then, he heard a familiar voice from around the front of the house.

"Lang? Hey, Lang?"

Zevon turned around as he heard the voice coming

closer. In a moment, Tom Kepper appeared around the corner, standing in between the house and the shed. Zevon sat motionless, chisel in hand, covered in wood shavings.

"Hey, it's me. Tom."

"Hi."

As if I could ever forget, Zevon thought. His old antagonizer, the leader of the high school jock-asshole-squad, as he once called them. *What the hell is he doing here now?*

"Real nice place you got," Tom said as he glanced around, admiring the lake's scenic beauty. "Right on the water."

"Can I help you with something, Tom?"

"Oh, I uh, I found this..." Tom stepped forward, holding out the sullied wallet in his hand. "You dropped it last night." Tom placed the wallet down on the tree stump by the new sign. In the drama and struggle the night before, Zevon hadn't even realized he'd lost it. He might just have to be a little grateful to the old jock-douchebag, he thought with a wince.

"Thanks."

Tom saw a dark maroon stain on the tree stump, and the ex-cop in him noted that it looked just like blood. But he pretended not to notice; a man working with sharp tools every day was bound to slice his hand once in a while.

Right?

Still, Zevon Lang had always creeped him out, and he could never put his finger on why. He looked around at the setup, impressed with all the product old Xerox was able to crank out of the little workstation.

"Wow, so you got your own little business here! Nice, man!"

"Thanks."

Tom smiled, trying to be friendly. It was a wise decision,

as Zevon wasn't a little shrimp anymore, and he held a hammer and chisel in his hands. Tom tried in vain to suck in his gut, but he could no longer pretend that he was the more athletic of the two. He nodded his head, noting that Zevon was not giving him much to work with in the way of small talk.

"So, uh," Tom began. "I saw the number you did on Jordan Keenan last night. Wow."

"Are you here to arrest me?" Zevon asked. "Oh, that's right. You're not a cop anymore."

"Nope, I'm not." Tom tried to ignore the dig, casually strolling around Zevon and kicking a small rock. "And you're lucky. I don't think he's pressing charges."

"Whatever," Zevon continued to chisel at his sign. Tom stepped in closer and leaned over to get a better look at the sign in progress. Shaking his head, he couldn't pretend he wasn't impressed with the craftsmanship.

"Wow, that's cool..."

Zevon stood up, putting the sign down. He could not concentrate or enjoy his work while his now-flabby, has-been nemesis paced around him. He produced a bandana from his back pocket and wiped the sweat from his brow.

"Where did you learn to do that?" Tom asked. "I mean, you broke Jordan's wrist, choked him out cold..."

"Oh, just watching movies and UFC. Y'know," Zevon lied as he took a long gulp from his water bottle.

"Ah-hah." Tom smiled politely, knowing he was not getting anywhere with this line of questioning. "Well, you freaked a lot of people out with that shit. Some said you took it too far."

"He had it coming," Zevon said.

"I guess he did," Tom nodded. "So, you and Claire are getting pretty friendly, I see?"

"Yeah, so?" Zevon suddenly felt defensive. "I'm making a sign for her. She's a client. Why, you know Claire?"

"God," Tom laughed, still walking around casually, hands in his pockets. "We were going steady for almost two years! We almost got married!" Zevon gripped his chisel tighter.

"Oh yeah? Mm."

"We met senior year," Tom continued. "After I left Hamilton and went to New Roads. I was playing hockey, she was a straight-A student. We tried to make it work, but... Life just pulled us apart, y'know?"

"Mm hm. Yeah. I never knew her back then. Just met her recently."

"Yeah, she's a really great girl," Tom said. "Really nice person, y'know?"

"Yeah, she is."

"She really... Deserves nothing but the best."

Zevon just nodded his head and maintained eye contact. He knew what old Kepper was trying to imply. The two men stood there in the sun, a swollen, unspoken silence between them.

Whatever the deal was with Zevon Lang, Tom would have to wait for another day. For now, he had gotten his message across, so he decided to cut the growing tension -

"Anyway, shit! One of these days, I'll have to hire you to carve something for me!" Tom laughed. "Maybe like, a trophy rack or something? You do really great work!" Tom playfully slapped Zevon on his sweaty shoulder.

"Thanks."

"Anyway, sorry to bother you. Just wanted to drop that off." Tom extended his hand for a shake. Zevon looked down at the open palm, wanting to break it more than shake it.

But he switched the chisel from his right hand to his left, and conceded to a shake.

"Thanks again."

"Okay, cool." Tom let go and backed away, returning back around the side of the house. "Have a good one. See you around."

Zevon nodded with a grunt and returned to work.

CHAPTER TWENTY-NINE
PRESENT DAY

FLEETWOOD MAC WAS ADJUSTING to her new surroundings as well as any spoiled, long-haired cat could be expected to. She inspected every box that was opened up, noting the familiar scents of the items as her mother and grandmother, Claire and Brenda, unpacked. Fleetwood did not recognize this new word, "condo," nor did she know or care what the meaning was, but this new place seemed big and blank and empty.

Her litter box as well as her food and water had already been set up, along with her favorite toys, so that was a bit comforting. There were a few good nooks and crannies for her to hide in, and the view from the front window was spacious and pretty, but completely different. With a twitch of her whiskers, she watched Claire and Brenda walk all around this new space, wondering if this was to be her new home, or if she'd ever go back to the apartment she knew and loved.

Claire carried a large box into the living room, placing it down on the floor beside the feline with a dancing step. The cat rubbed against her hand and followed her as she continued bringing things in and moving them around. Rubbing Fleetwood's neck, she smiled and sang along as Natalie Merchant played through the color-changing iPod dock plugged into the wall.

Her voice was a bit sharp, but neither she nor Fleetwood Mac cared. Brenda came in with a smaller box, putting it down on the new sofa the moving crew had brought in for them.

"Hoo! I'm gettin' tired! Baby, is this okay here?" Brenda gestured to the box and Claire nodded her head.

"Yeah, that's fine, Ma. You just take it easy. I'll put everything away later." Or maybe she'd let it all sit in boxes for the next two months, whichever suited her better.

"Sure, but I want to help."

"Just do light stuff. Remember your back?" Claire pushed a dresser against a wall in the living room and decided that was a good place for it. A lamp would go on top, books below. "Watch out, Puffy."

She walked back across the room, where Fleetwood had intentionally sat blocking her path, only to be shooed away again. She grabbed a lamp and brought it back to its new home on top of the dresser. Brenda looked around, contemplating the decorating possibilities.

"You up for some tea?" Brenda asked.

"Of course! All the mugs are in the kitchen in boxes still. Just give me a minute…" Claire's whole life was splayed out before her; all of her clothes, books, movies, music, photos, decorative pillows and living essentials overflowed from boxes and plastic storage tubs. Nothing was in any kind of order yet and it was driving her mad. If Fleetwood Mac could talk, she'd echo the sentiment.

"Poor Puffy looks stressed," Brenda cooed.

"Eh, she'll be all right," Claire said. "Takes cats some time to get used to a new place."

"How about you? Are you... Adjusting okay to moving back? How are you feeling about everything?"

"Mom, I just got the key. Tonight's my first actual night in this place."

"I mean coming back to town after all this time. Seeing your old friends again. Meeting new guys..."

"It's uh..." Claire tried to focus, but her feelings were too scattered and complicated at the moment. "It's a lot. I mean, it's great to be back, great to see you guys, of course. Seeing the girls again is great... But, I — I don't know. It's a lot."

"What about this new guy you've been seeing?" Brenda pressed, hoping for some juicy gossip.

"Mom, I'm not *seeing* any new guy. Come on."

"That guy that you were telling me about." Brenda said. "What's his name? Mr. Hunk with the biceps."

Claire laughed out loud, shaking her head. She pondered, not knowing how to answer the question. The last time she'd seen Zevon, he had left her with so many mixed messages and uneven emotions. There was a hunger for more, a craving and a potent curiosity. A yearning to peer into his big eyes and see his soul... Yet, a strange fear that she may not like that soul once she saw it.

A warning light kept blinking deep down. There was the seeming innocence and noble quality of his character, and there was the base animal desire to caress those biceps and feel the rest of his firm body next to hers. But there was something else that she just couldn't quite place.

"I don't know, Ma," Claire said, continuing to unbox her life. "I'm just moving into a new house, moving into a new office and starting my new practice soon... I have a lot on my plate right now. Thinking about meeting a new man so soon is... Not my priority."

"But what about *Mr. Hunk with the big biceps?*" Brenda bounced up and down like a giddy schoolgirl, craving the latest dating gossip with a playful giggle. Claire laughed and shook her head.

"He's a nice guy, Ma. But, I don't know... I don't know if he's ready for any kind of relationship either. He's very... Guarded. Innocent? Naive? I don't think he's very experienced with women..."

"Ooh, good! That means you can *teach* him!"

Claire laughed, "No, I mean... It's almost like he's still a little boy? Still hasn't grown up yet. I don't know. Whatever, he's a nice guy, and very talented. He's making the sign for my office, but other than that... I don't think it's something that's gonna work out."

"Honey, your father is still a little boy. Heck, sometimes he's more like a dang infant..." Brenda pondered. "Come on, let's bust out those mugs, make us some tea."

Brenda headed toward the kitchen while Claire smiled, knowing that all her silliness and lust for life had come from that beautiful, strong woman. Claire began to follow when she heard the faint tones of her cell phone ringing from her pants pocket.

She dug out the phone and looked at the screen. She let it ring a moment as she contemplated answering. Mixed feelings. She let out a sigh and pressed talk-button, holding the device up to her ear and putting on a friendly voice.

"Hi, Zevon."

CHAPTER THIRTY
PRESENT DAY

TOM SAT motionless in his car. His eyes were glued to Zevon Lang's house. The street was wet and the sky was gray. Lang's van was parked in the driveway, but he would have to leave some time. *Wouldn't he?* Regardless, Tom could not get the image of the bloodstain on the tree stump out of his mind. *Did Lang cut himself while working, or was it animal's blood? Or could it be something else?* Either way, this was his day off and he had nothing better to do than to find out.

He had been sitting there for two hours already, slouching behind the wheel, parked in front of Murray Siedelmann's house where Zevon wouldn't see him. He drummed on the steering wheel with his fingers, keeping tempo with an old LTJ Bukem song, when he finally saw what he had come for. Zevon was leaving. He carried something large and heavy wrapped in a blanket, unlocked the back of his van and placed it delicately inside. He got in the van and started it up, backing out of the driveway.

"Here we go..." Tom said, sitting up as he watched Zevon pull away. After the van disappeared around the corner, Tom sprang into action, grabbing a backpack from the passenger seat and getting out of the car. He checked around — The coast was clear. He trotted over to the Lang property, onto the driveway and headed around the side.

Tom's shoes squished in the wet grass as he made his way around to the back yard. There before him was the lake, gray and still, a light mist hanging above. It almost seemed to be watching him. Moving with a purpose, he headed straight for the old tree stump where he saw Zevon working before.

And there it was, the spot of blood.

Tom removed his backpack and unzipped it, pulling out a plastic baggie, a Q-Tip and a spray bottle full of saline solution. He spritzed the bloody spot on the stump, then quickly rubbed the Q-Tip all around on it. The cotton soaked up the substance, turning it pink. Tom smiled and placed the Q-Tip inside the plastic bag, sealing it back up.

"Alrighty then," Tom said. He put the items back in his bag, looking around. He'd give that evidence to his contact on the force, have it tested for DNA, see if it added up to anything. If Lang was up to no good, he'd get to the bottom of it. He strolled over to the work shed, glancing in the windows. The door had been left unlocked, and Tom slipped inside.

The air was dank and dim. The tools and supplies were kept in pristine condition. There were rolls of plastic sheeting in stacks, which raised his eyebrows. His eyes moved to the floor beneath his feet. Not wood panels, but a raised-metal grate. A curious feature for a simple work shed, but still... Proof of nothing. Oh, what he'd give to have a search warrant and a full CSI team at his disposal.

On the work table sat a nearly-empty bottle of water. He knew Zevon had drank from it, that his DNA would be on the mouth. His fingerprints would be all over it. He pulled out another baggie, opening it up and folding it inside out. With his hand inside the bag, he picked up the water bottle, then pulled the bag inside out again. He sealed the bag and tucked it away. The blood would hopefully provide some answers, or at least be a small puzzle piece to help him put this picture together.

It had rained the night before and the streets were still glistening. A blanket of clouds still hung overhead, threatening to open up again at any time. Claire steered her pickup through White Feather, slowing down on Gower Avenue as she reached the small plaza where her new office was. The lot was nestled between a coffee shop and a laundromat, with a 7-11 at one corner and Rancho's Tacos at the other.

She parked in her newly-appointed spot and almost at once noticed the faded-blue van on the other side of the lot. Sitting on the tailgate with a small bouquet of flowers in his hands was Zevon Lang. He wore the nicest blue jeans he owned and a rust-colored jacket, clearly trying to make himself as presentable as possible. Taking a deep breath, she stepped out of the truck and headed over to him.

Zevon stood up as he saw her approach, fidgeting to find the best way to stand. He smiled brightly and held up the flowers, struck by how amazing she looked in her casual cargo pants and tight-fitting green shirt that matched her eyes. His heart pounded; it took his best effort not to stare at her perfectly-pink lips or her bouncing curls of bronze hair. She smiled at him, shaking her head as she regarded the flowers.

"Hi, Claire."

"Hey," she said. "How's it going? Are these for me?"

"Yeah, they're for you," he said, opening his arms to give her a hug. She came in close and casually embraced him, being mindful not to cross the invisible line she'd drawn for herself. The last time they met, she was drunk and had kissed him under the moonlight. Now, it was a cool, gray day, and she saw him in a different light. Still, she gave him a good, firm hug, and noted that he seemed to hang on just a bit too long.

"You look so pretty!" Zevon said, handing her the bouquet. She took it with a smile, and he subconsciously leaned forward, almost expecting another kiss. But she just smelled the flowers.

"Thank you. How are you?"

"Good, good!" He said. "Are you ready to see it?"

"Yes," she said in a playful tone. "Show me my sign! Don't keep me waiting!"

"Okay, okay!" Zevon turned to open the back of the van, shaking with anticipation. "I hope you like it. I-I think you will. I hope. I worked real hard on it..." The door opened up and inside, a heavy work blanket was wrapped around something large and rectangular. Zevon rubbed his hands together, pulling up the edge of the blanket and tossing it aside.

Claire gasped as she saw her finished sign.

It was beautiful, sanded and stained, detailed and polished. "Claire M. Carpenter, Doctor of Veterinary Medicine" scrolled across the face in whimsical script, etched deep into the cedar block. On the top and bottom were real branches, bark still intact, framing the whole piece with a rustic style, with carved branches and leaves continuing onto the smooth surface in the middle.

The sculpture, the design, the craftsmanship... Everything was perfect. Claire's mouth hung open in amazement.

"Oh... My... God..." She whispered.

"You like it?"

"I love it! Oh my God, thank you so much!" Claire grabbed onto Zevon's shoulder with her free hand, steadying herself. He smiled, proud of himself.

"Wow," she said, at a loss for words.

"Want to hang it up?" Zevon's eyebrows bounced, his confidence soaring.

A large, wooden frame stood mounted at the entrance to the plaza, a slot for each business there to hang their signs. The other signs were made of a thick plastic, except the coffee shop, which had a wooden sign, though much less ornate and intricate than Zevon's handiwork.

Together, Claire and Zevon lifted the heavy placard into the empty slot in the frame, easing the hooks on either side into the metal eyes. Zevon's measurements were precise, and the sign fit perfectly in its place, hanging out-front now for all to see.

"All right!" Zevon hooted, hurrying a few steps back to take a better look. "Come on, come on!" He gestured for her to come to where he stood, and she joined him with an approving smile. They stood shoulder to shoulder, admiring its elegance and glossy, high-polished beauty. Claire's eyebrows perked up and she produced her cell phone from her purse, turning on the camera function.

"This," she said. "Is going on Instagram!" She took a picture with a giggle. "Here, you get in there now! Go, go!" Claire motioned for him to stand beside his handiwork with a wave of her hand. "Stand next to it! The *arteest* and his work!"

"Ahhh, I don't know..." Zevon hesitated with a blush as

she urged him forward, reluctantly complying. His shoulders slouched and he struggled not to look at his feet. Posing for pictures was not one of his strong suits. But he stood beside the sign for her, hands in his pockets with a closed-mouth smile. Claire aimed the camera and took a photo, noting to herself just how uncomfortable he looked.

"Got it," she said, putting her phone away.

Zevon wasted no time walking back up to her, hoping she would throw herself at him like in the movies, professing her love and praising his talent. Claire smiled at him as he stood before her, opening up her purse again and fishing down into it.

"Well, Mr. Lang," she said, producing her wallet. "You are amazing. You rock. I can't thank you enough." She unzipped the wallet and pulled out a check, holding it out for him to take. "Well earned."

Zevon shifted his weight, reaching out with both hands to rub her shoulders, trying his best to be smooth and suave. From what he'd seen in the movies, on TV and in the books he'd read, this was how it was done. He took a step closer to her, not taking the check, but caressing her shoulders gently as he lowered his voice.

"Nah, it's okay," he said. "It's on the house." Zevon leaned in for a kiss, slowly pulling himself forward, closing his eyes and readying his lips for another sweet taste. But Claire pulled back, not wanting to lead him on.

"Haha, no really, Zevon. Here." She handed the check over again, but he laughed it off, showing off his great generosity.

"Ah, forget about it! Some guys give women fancy dresses and diamonds. I give them big blocks of wood!" Zevon laughed, finding that particularly clever. But Claire pulled away from his hold, uneasily shaking her head.

"Listen, Zevon..." She tried to phrase it the best she could so as not to hurt his feelings. "I think you're a great guy. And... I-I just don't want you to get the wrong impression about the other night. I was pretty drunk..."

"Oh. Okay," Zevon's brain spun within his skull. "I thought you... You liked me..."

"I do! You're so cute and so sweet and talented... I just need to focus on me right now. And I don't want to move too fast, y'know?" Her eyes pleaded for understanding.

"...Okay."

"Okay? You sure?"

"Yeah. Uh, it's cool."

"Okay, great. Here, take it. You earned it!"

Her hand stretched out again, offering the check once more. Zevon noted that his body felt like it was a distant shadow from where he was, like he was watching someone else take the check from Claire's hand. Like he was in a surreal dream, drifting and floating in the clouds.

He looked down and saw his hand holding the slip of paper, his name printed on the front. Nodding his head and tucking the payment into his jacket pocket, Zevon did his best to save face.

"Okay," he said. "Okay, sure. Whatever you want. Thanks."

"Great. Thank you so much, again! You did such a great job!" Claire stepped forward and gave him a big, warm friend-hug. Not to be confused with a hug she might give a brother, and definitely not a hug she'd give to a man she loved. This was a hug that placed Zevon firmly in the no-fly zone.

The friend-zone. Purgatory.

"Oh. Okay," he said, watching her pull away and head

back over to her truck. "Well, maybe I can help you set up, move stuff around, get the office ready..."

"Oh, I already have people doing that," she said, fishing her keys from her purse. "I'm good, really. I have a bunch of errands I have to run right now, actually." She unlocked her driver side door and picked up the bouquet of flowers that rested on the hood to take with her.

"Oh. Well, maybe another time. Maybe we can have coffee again once things... Settle down."

"Totally," she said, tossing her purse into the passenger seat and laying the flowers down gently. "Thanks again for the flowers; they're beautiful!"

"Okay, well... Keep in touch, then. Let me know when you're free... We'll hang out..." Zevon watched her close the door behind her and start up the engine. She rolled the window down and smiled at him again as she began to back up.

"Absolutely! Thanks again, Zevon! Have a good one!"

With that, she was gone, pulling away from him and into the street. Zevon watched her drive away, standing immobile, processing the turn of events. Maybe he hadn't done a good enough job on the sign. Maybe she was just playing hard to get. Maybe she still loved Tom Kepper.

Maybe...

Theories and scenarios danced through his head in a barrage of imagery and echoing voices. He looked up to the sky. It looked like rain again.

CHAPTER THIRTY-ONE
2007

WIRY MUSCLES FLEXED in the seventeen year-old Zevon's arms as he pushed the empty wheelbarrow away from the lake and back up to its resting place on the left side of the house. It was a moonless night, approaching 3 a.m. and the August heat lingered through the early hours.

Zevon put the wheeled contraption back in its place, turning back to look at the ebony, glassy lake. Lila was happy with the meal he had brought her and he was happy to have done his job well.

He stood shirtless, new facial hair growing along with new muscles, and took a sip from his water bottle. He picked up a small towel draped over the right handle of the wheelbarrow, wiping himself down, starting with the neck and working it all over his body. New abdominals flexed, pectorals and deltoids shifting beneath taut skin as he wiped filth and sweat away.

His hair was cut shorter, not a formless mop anymore, and still no signs of balding. He was coming into his own, becoming a man. He was getting good at his secret job, using his budding strength, wrestling skills and intelligence to pluck men from the streets and deliver their bodies into Lila's clutches.

Still, the clandestine task of dismembering bodies and neatly draining them of blood in a wooded area by the lake felt a bit too hairy. He glanced at the empty space between the left corner of the house and the lake, thinking that might be a good place to build a work shed to take care of such grisly business.

Either way, she was his and he was hers, and he'd be damned if he'd let anyone or anything come between them. Someday they could be together alone, without having to sneak the van out at night and tiptoe around his father.

But for now, he didn't have any money of his own at seventeen years of age, and his father was adamant that if he wanted a vehicle, he would have to pay for it himself. He had held a part-time job at a local theater last summer, but was fired for poor attendance, and had done some free-lancing with McKay's Woodworks, fixing up antique furniture. But nothing steady, nothing that would buy him a car.

He still had a lot to figure out, but for now, things were running smoothly. Every couple of months, Lila would need to eat, and he would sneak out in the van once the old man had passed out drunk. Each kill became easier than the last, and striking only in neighboring counties ensured that the PD never came knocking.

He had this down to a science. Taking another sip of water, Zevon pulled his shirt back on and headed inside.

THE SIDE DOOR creaked open and Zevon slipped into the dark house. He passed the laundry room, crept across the living room where the TV still flickered with infomercials, and made his way for the stairs.

His father sat asleep on the couch in his favorite spot, immobile as the youth tiptoed across the room, as he had done so many times before. Zevon made it to the foot of the stairs when suddenly, the TV clicked off and his father's shadowy figure stood up behind him.

"You have a good time tonight, son?" Charles Lang said, wavering on legs made of beer foam. Zevon froze in place, every sinew tightening.

"Dad! I, uh... I..." This had never happened before. When the old man was out, he was out for the night. Zevon turned to face his father's silhouette, smelling the Coors Banquet on his breath from across the room.

"I said, did you have a good time tonight? Driving around in my van? *Do you know what time it is?*" Charles took an uneven step forward, his furrowed brow coming into the faint light from the window. Zevon stammered as he searched for an answer that would make some kind of sense.

"What? N-No Dad! I-I didn't... I just went for a walk..."

"It's three in the fucking morning, Z!"

"I-I'm sorry, Dad. I didn't mean to wake you, I-I... I just like taking walks at night, a-and..."

His father strode across the distance between them, getting right up in Zevon's face, spitting fury.

"Don't lie to me, boy! You think I'm *stupid*? You think I don't know what you're *doing*? You're sneaking out, taking the van, going God-only-knows where!"

"N-No Dad, I swear! I..."

"You think I don't check the odometer? Where do you go at night, huh?" Zevon stammered, unable to formulate an answer. His father looked him up and down, studying his sweaty, filthy clothes, shaking his head in disgust. "Just look at you! Where the hell do you go at night, *huh?*"

"Dad, I'm sorry! I-I..." Zevon backed against the wall as his father cornered him. When he couldn't answer, he received a sharp, antagonizing push.

"*Huh?*"

"Dad, I-I was just out with some friends! I'm sorry, I..."

"You don't have any friends! What the hell were you doing, Z? Where do you go at night?" Zevon almost got a buzz off of his father's hot breath alone, standing still and taking the abuse like a good soldier obeying his drill sergeant.

"Okay, where is it?" Charles demanded.

"W-Where's what, Dad?"

"Where is it? C'mon, empty your pockets!"

Zevon squirmed as his father grabbed at him, frisking him and trying to yank his pockets inside out. Zevon resisted, fighting off the aggressive, invasive hands.

"Dad, stop! What are you doing?"

"Where's the drugs, son?"

"*What?*"

"You're selling drugs," he fumed. "Where are they? Don't lie to me, son!" Zevon fought back tears, along with the urge to push back and show his father firsthand what he had been up to in the middle of the night.

"Dad, I'm not selling drugs! Please!"

Satisfied the boy had no contraband on him, Charles Lang turned and stormed up the stairs, leaving a perplexed Zevon in his wake.

"Oh, no? Well then, let's just check in your room!"

"Dad, stop!"

Zevon launched up the steps, chasing after his father as

the brute burst through his bedroom and flipped on the lights. His face swelling red with anger and alcohol, Charles wasted no time and tore into his son's possessions with abandon.

"Let's start in here, shall we?"

Zevon pulled at his father's shoulders, trying to stop him as he yanked out the top drawer of his dresser. Underwear and socks spilled out onto the floor and they were savagely inspected.

"Dad, *stop!*"

"No? How about this one?"

The next drawer was wrenched off its track, tumbling to the floor. Charles tossed through the t-shirts inside, fishing through everything and finding nothing but apparel. Zevon gripped his old man's shoulders, pulling him away, only to be pushed back against his bedroom door. His father snarled and paced around, looking for possible hiding places to uncover illegal contraband.

"Where is it, Z?" His father tore into his bedside night-stand, rummaging through the drawers. "What are you selling, son? Heroin? Meth?"

"Dad, please..." Zevon's eyes lost their fight with tears, and a hot stream began to flow. He gave up fighting and watched as his dad searched through the top bedside drawer, then the bottom. Pens, notebooks and antacids, rulers, protein bars and cherry lozenges; all were tossed to the floor.

He made his way to the bottom drawer and Zevon squeezed his eyes in shame as his father came out with his secret stash of DVD's. Perplexed, Charles flipped through each, reading their titles.

"'Big Wet Asses #3'? 'Butt-Woman?' 'Baker's Dozen #12...'?" Mr. Lang tossed the smut aside, shaking his head as he continued his search. "Classy, Zevon. Real classy." With no incriminating substances found in that drawer, he stomped over to the closet and threw it open, whipping the hangers aside in his growing fervor.

"God damn it, Z! *Where is it?*"

"Stop it, Dad! *Stop it!*"

Zevon launched forward, grabbing the old drunk by the shoulders and yanking him back with all his new-found strength. Mr. Lang garbled a protest as he fell backwards and crashed into the foot of the bed, knocking the mattress a foot off its frame with a crunching *thud*. Zevon stood over his father, chest heaving, fresh sweat glistening on the cannonballs he called his shoulders.

"Get out of my room!"

Charles Lang looked up at his son, and for the first time ever, realized he did not know this strange young man standing before him. He was powerless in his own house, at the mercy of a stranger he could neither help nor control. Zevon was all he had left, and now even he was gone.

"Z, please... I-I'm worried about you. I'm just trying to help... M-Maybe we should get you back in therapy. Find someone you feel comfortable talking to. It's been too long..." Tears welled-up in his eyes, and the two generations of Langs looked on each other through blurred lenses.

"*I said get out!*"

Charles sat up with a lurch, slowly pulling himself to his knees, then up onto wobbly feet. He dared to look his son in the eye again and saw a blazing fire. He sighed, shoulders slouching as he lumbered to the door. Zevon stepped out of his way, muscles tight and ready to strike.

"Zevon, I..." But it was no use. He knew there were no more words. He continued on, shuffling through the doorway with his head hung low.

As soon as he cleared the doorframe, Zevon slammed the door behind him. He creaked back down the stairs, sitting back into his molded spot on the couch, while Zevon put his bedroom back together.

Neither one of them got any sleep the rest of the night.

CHAPTER THIRTY-TWO
PRESENT DAY

ZEVON LEFT CLAIRE ANOTHER VOICEMAIL. This would be the second, just to make sure she'd gotten the first one two days ago. He put his phone down and stared out the back window at his lake.

The land was in full bloom, pollen in the warm breeze and the sun presiding over all life. People of all ages, shapes and sizes were out to enjoy the perfect weather. Zevon figured he may as well join them. He hadn't gone on his run yet that morning, and he was a creature of habit, after all.

He took off into the day, shaking out his thick legs briefly to get the blood flowing, then began his run around the lake. Periodically, he glanced over at the water, in case she wanted to signal to him. But he hadn't heard from her in over a week, nor had he heard back from Claire.

His mind wandered in many different directions as his feet kept him in a locked, physical route. Murray waved like he always did as Zevon passed by. He wondered what other errands he had to do, as he had no commissions at the moment. He had plenty of wood, plenty of groceries and his laundry was clean.

Back at the house, Megadeth blared through speakers and propelled him through his weight-training circuit. Arms and abs today, followed by twenty minutes of shadowboxing drills and stretching. He finished, dripping sweat on the floor, blood surging through his veins and air pumping in his chest. He had pushed himself hard, but still felt there was more left to do. Picking up his phone again, he checked for missed calls, but there were none.

Zevon went about the rest of his day. He showered, ate clean protein and watched a 90's Rom-Com with Kate Hudson by himself. He checked his phone again. Maybe Claire would call him back tonight. He looked out the window again as the sun began to sink, turning the sky into a swirl of oranges, purples and reds. Maybe Lila would call for him tonight.

TOM KEPPER AGONIZED over the decision, but finally decided to pour the steaming, black coffee into his mug instead of Hanky Bannister. Once poured, he contemplated tossing a shot of Hanky into the coffee as well, but fought the urge. Instead, a touch of milk and a generous dollop of honey were added to the hot beverage.

Honey is always better than sugar in coffee, Tom thought, and he didn't care if people made faces at him for it. He stirred up the drink, took a hot sip and sat down at his computer as a half-moon began to rise in the young night.

"Let's see," he said to himself, typing keywords into the omniscient search engine. Terms like "murder statistics in upstate New York" and "missing persons cases in New York" began to generate results. He scooped up a pad of paper and a pen and started writing down key information.

He was surprised to note that the town of White Feather averaged only 1.8 murders annually. Up in Albany, it was much higher. One's chance of becoming a victim of a violent crime there was one in twenty four, with an annual average of six murders a year. Other large cities like Schenectady and Troy were comparable, while smaller towns like Mahopac, Chappaqua and Lake George averaged between four and five.

As high as the murder rates were, the missing-persons rates were even higher. Some towns had well over a dozen missing persons a year; human beings who had one day vanished into the ether without a whisper, the vast majority being men. In White Feather, as he discovered, there were only two open missing persons cases, and one was from back in 1992.

The other was Cyrus Kushan in 2005.

Tom continued to drink his sweet, hot coffee, his head now buzzing with life and purpose again. The numbers intrigued and perplexed him. It seemed while all the surrounding towns and cities maintained a somewhat even average of violent crimes and missing persons, White Feather sat in the middle of all this criminal activity, virtually untouched.

Curiosity piqued, Tom continued searching, entering the keywords, "Charles Lang."

CLAIRE PARKED her Tacoma in the dim parking space at her condo, her stomach filled with her father's famous fried-chicken cutlets. Dinner with her parents always left her feeling warm and happy, frequently cracking her up at how cute they still were together after all these years.

Her mother had surprised her with a new scarf, this one light, green and earthy, and she wore it home with pleasure. They had also given her a bottle of wine, a bar of dark chocolate, a Tupperware of leftover chicken cutlets, and had loaned her their vacuum cleaner.

She hopped out of the truck, gripping a fabric shopping bag full of goodies in one hand and the vacuum in the other, and walked across the lot to her condo. She flipped through her keys with the hand holding the bag of goodies. She delicately tried to ace both tasks at once, finally succeeding to grip the key as she rounded the corner and headed across the courtyard to get to her front door.

Passing by the other condos, all small, modest and comfortable in their design, she saw her new home and prepared to open the door.

As she drew near, she stopped.

A large vase filled with flowers sat in front of the doorway, blooming with color and screaming of a romantic gesture. She slowly approached the gift, noticing a small card hanging by a ribbon on the front. Having a good idea who these were from already, Claire hesitated to flip open the card.

CHAPTER THIRTY-THREE
PRESENT DAY

IT WAS PISSING DOWN.

It wasn't raining, it wasn't pouring... It was pissing down. Tom waited under the old bridge on Tomahawk Landing to avoid the angry barrage from the skies. The heavens had opened up two hours earlier and Tom had gotten drenched getting to this destination. He had parked his car and gotten out, pacing with hands in his pockets, waiting as puddles swelled into ponds. The sky above lit up with an electric charge, and the following thunder bellowed at the lone figure.

This is stupid, he thought. *Dumb on so many levels*. But he was following his instincts, following the evidence. And if that meant heading out into a storm for a clandestine meeting like a character in some second-rate pulp detective novel, so be it. All he needed now was a trench coat, a fedora and a cigarette dangling from his lips. Tom shook his head as he continued to pace. *Stupid.*

He heard the purr of an engine approaching and the splash of tires through water, followed by headlights sweeping over him. A black Ford Focus slowed down as it approached the bridge, pulling around and parking in front of Tom's Civic. He recognized the face through the rain-speckled window and approached the vehicle, opening the passenger door and getting inside.

"Hey, Tom." Chuck Nash had joined the force at the same time as Tom. Clean shaven, a scheduled haircut every two weeks, he was a veritable Ken-doll. He didn't drink or smoke, and did everything by the book... Until now.

"Hey Chuck," Tom said. "Thanks for meeting me."

"Yeah, sure. No problem. Man, it's really coming down out here tonight, huh?"

"Yup."

"So how ya' doing, Tom? You're looking good."

"Doing fine, thanks. How are you and Holly? The kids good?"

"Yeah, they're fine. Shannon just lost one of her front teeth. Hannah's in high school now..."

"Cool. That's good."

The two men ran out of small talk. Silence fell in the car but for the sound of the pounding rain and thunder outside.

"So, uh... You got it, right?" Tom asked.

"Yeah, I got it," Nash said, pulling out a file folder from the side compartment of the driver's door. "But why...?"

"Don't ask."

"Come on, Tommy."

"Here, just take the money." Tom pulled a few folded bills from his coat pocket and passed them over to Nash. The driver hesitated, but sighed and took the money after a moment. He held up the file folder for Tom to see; he too had serious doubts about this little transaction.

"If you get caught with this..." Nash started.

"Yeah yeah, Nash. I didn't get it from you. I know."

"This could cost me my badge, Tom."

"I know, I know. Don't worry."

Tom held out his hand and Nash gave him the folder. Tom immediately flipped it open and started glancing through it. The papers were official police and medical examiner reports. The victim: Charles Lang. Nash watched him with concern.

"I don't understand why you want the files from some suicide back in 2009, that's all."

"Because I don't think it was a suicide," Tom said, skimming through the pages. "What about the blood-work from the tree stump?"

"Well, the lab boys told me it is human. It's not this guy Lang's blood, though."

"Is it his father's?"

"Nope. Not enough matching DNA markers. No relation."

"Interesting."

"Ran the fingerprints from the water bottle through AFIS too," Nash said. "No hits. Your boy Zevon Lang is clean, bro."

"Clean, huh? Then whose blood is that on the tree stump in his backyard?"

Nash sighed. "Good question. What're you planning to do, Tommy?"

Tom closed the folder, sitting back in his chair and letting the question sink in. He hadn't thought that far ahead.

"I don't know... Thanks, Chuck."

Tom slapped the folder against his friend's arm and hopped out of the car, closing the door behind him. Nash watched as Tom walked back to his own car and got in.

"Don't mention it."

LATER THAT NIGHT, Tom sat in his car as the rain continued to piss down. He had parked on a suburban street, a community of new condos flanking him. One block ahead was Claire Carpenter's new home. The lights were on and her truck was outside.

Tom's lap was occupied by the spread-open file he obtained from Nash, the passenger seat a treasure trove of fast food and gas station snacks. *This is stupid*, he thought again. This would definitely be considered stalking. *She is not his girl anymore*, he thought. And he was not a cop anymore.

Definitely stupid.

As he delved through the files on the suicide of Charles Lang, however, he became more confident that his protective services were needed. The medical examiner's report detailed the cause of death as a suicide via gunshot wound to the head. Everything, from the photos to the analysis of gunshot residue and blood-spatter on the victim's hands, corroborated the findings.

The lieutenant who'd handled the crime scene, Fuller, one of his dad's old friends, reported that the deceased's son, Zevon Lang, was there when the body was discovered. He was found on the pier behind their house, holding his father in his arms. Photos taken of Zevon at the scene showed the young man covered in his father's blood.

Everything pointed to suicide, yet the alarms in Tom's head would not stop ringing. Why would Charles Lang shoot himself on the dock behind his house, in the middle of the night, in front of his own son? And why would Zevon be covered in *so much* blood?

Some blood would make sense, of course. A person

cradling the body of someone who'd just shot themself in the head would naturally be sullied with blood. But looking at the photos of Zevon at the scene, he was covered in blood, nearly head to toe. Some of the blood was spattered on his face in small droplets, which Tom knew could only come from being up close to the victim at the moment of death.

Zevon was hiding something, Tom knew it. He couldn't put his finger on it and he couldn't prove it, but he also couldn't leave Claire all alone in there. Not with that psycho running around. He had been getting close to her, made a fancy, new sign for her...

The little weirdo was getting attached, Tom knew, maybe even falling for her. And why wouldn't he? Claire was wonderful, beautiful, intelligent... Of course he was falling for her. The thought of that slimy-little monster dreaming about his Claire, or putting his grubby hands on her, made his stomach churn. But once again he reminded himself, *she's not my girl anymore.*

"Stupid, stupid, stupid..."

Tom took a sip from his coffee thermos and settled deeper into his seat, bracing for a long night as the rains continued to pepper his car. His eyes moved from her house, to the left side of the street, then over to the right side.

He would continue to scan the street until daybreak, a silent guardian angel. A protector against the forces of darkness. Yes, he thought, that sounded better than *stalker*.

CHAPTER THIRTY-FOUR
PRESENT DAY

THREE DAYS HAD PASSED and Zevon had not received a jubilant phone call from Claire, thanking him profusely for his generous gift. The sun had set, dinner was eaten, the dishes were finished and Zevon could think of nothing else to do other than pace his living room and bite his nails. He tried to watch TV, but nothing could hold his attention. He could take a shower, but he was already clean.

He looked at the clock — 10:15 p.m. She was very busy, he knew, setting up her new office, decorating her new home. But still, she must have gotten those flowers. And there was a definite connection between them, he thought, and he knew she felt it too.

His eyes twitched over to his cell phone. Still on the coffee table where he had left it. He considered checking it again for missed calls, but he had turned the volume all the way up and had kept that little device with him day and night. He knew she hadn't called... She hadn't called. *Why hasn't she called?*

Maybe she's sick. Maybe her new house is being fumigated, and she's staying with her parents and forgot her cell

phone at her place... Maybe I should try calling her again.
He had called the previous day and it had been enough time
that another call right then wouldn't seem too pushy.
Would it?

Fuck it.

The phone was in his hands and dialing Claire's
number before he even knew what was happening. The
phone went up to his ear and the ringer purred in electronic
tones as he began to pace once again. Roland, Lemmy and
all his other woodland critters sat around him in their artifi-
cial habitats, disinterested in his actions.

Zevon bit his nails, humming under his breath and
praying that this time, she would pick up. But he once again
heard that hollow *click* on the other end of the line, and
Claire's voicemail picked up the call. Zevon's shoulders
dropped as he let out a sigh, listening to her almost musical
voice.

"Heeeey, you've reached Dr. Claire Carpenter," the
voice beamed. "Please leave a message and either me or
Puffy Pants will get back to you just as soon as possible!
Thanks!" The recording signaled its beep in his ear, leaving
Zevon racing to find the right words as he rubbed at the
back of his neck.

"Hey, Claire! Hey..." He swallowed hard, trying to
sound as casual and relaxed as possible. "Uh, it's Zevon
calling again. Just want to say hey. Don't know if you got my
other messages, or... I-I mean, you probably didn't. I know
you're busy with everything, umm..."

Zevon continued to pace, his feet digging through the
carpet, burying himself deeper into the floor with every
word. But he powered on, determined to dig himself out
rather than in.

"But uh, yeah... Haven't seen you in a while. Hope

everything's okay. Um, d-did you get the flowers I left for you? I-I don't know if they're the kind you like, so... And hey, even a vet needs to relax once in a while, right? You should like, come over sometime! I'm a good cook, and I'm told I give good massages, so... I'm just... I'm here for you. And I want you to know that. I... I don't really have any friends or anybody, but... I mean, you're so nice to me. A-And I feel like we have this connection, y'know?"

A lump had begun to grow in his throat, lonely fire glazed over his eyes and it took his greatest effort to restrain it. His voice cracked and halted as he rubbed his free hand from his neck up to his bald scalp, comforting himself and trying to control his breathing.

"Anyway, call me, okay? Let me know everything's all right? All right... Thanks... Uh, talk soon. Bye."

He pressed his finger down and ended the call, letting his arm drop limp to his side as he released an exasperated groan. He shook his head, painfully aware of how clumsy and un-Metal that was. He looked around at his friends in their aquariums and terrariums, a silent and harsh audience.

"Shut up," he said, turning away.

He looked at the mirror on the opposite wall, assessing his image in the glass. Red, puffy eyes. Hair almost completely gone from the top of his head. Pointed, angular features. *No wonder she wouldn't answer*, he thought...

But then, a figure stepped out from behind him in the mirror. A woman. Long wavy hair, eyes like the sea, beauty like none other; it was of course, Lila. She existed in the mirror but not in the room, a ghostly reflection with a melancholy gaze.

"Don't look at me like that," Zevon said, crossing into the kitchen. In the window above the sink, there was her reflection again, her eyes full of doubt and judgment. Zevon turned again, not wanting to meet that stern gaze, running up the stairs, down the hallway and into the master bathroom. He slammed and locked the door, but as he feared, when he looked up, there was her reflection once again in the bathroom mirror over the sink.

"Where exactly do you think you're going?" She said.

"Leave me alone!"

Zevon yanked a towel off the rack, tossing it over the mirror's frame, blocking off the reflection as his pulse pounded. He stepped into the empty bath tub, pulling the shower curtain closed behind him as he closed his eyes and squeezed his hands over his ears.

"You're not real!"

"Oh, please."

"Stop it!"

At once, the hot and cold nozzles in the tub began to turn on their own, squealing as they spun, opening the pipes up wide. But it wasn't clear water that gushed from the faucet, Zevon realized. It was blood. Thick, deep and red, it pumped like a syrupy merlot into the tub, splashing around his bare feet and rapidly filling up the tub.

"Oh, no... Jesus!" Zevon dropped his hands from his ears, panicking, feeling the warmth splashing up over his ankles like arterial bleeding from an open vein. He reached for the lever to open the drain, but it was stuck, leaving the drain sealed. He stood back up as the tub continued to fill.

He pulled at the shower curtain to open it up, but he could find no edge. What had once been a plastic sheet that could be opened and closed, had sealed shut, becoming more of a plastic sack, a chamber, a vessel that would hold the liquid inside.

"Stop it!!"

Zevon clawed at the plastic curtain, looking for a way

out, only to slip and fall back into the tub with a burgundy splash. Now nearly a foot deep, the blood covered him in speckles and blotches, the smell of iron tingling in his nose.

The faucet roared with a constant *fwoosh* of rich, salty blood as Zevon slipped and tried to regain his footing. He stood back up, drenched, looking like a suitable prom date for Carrie White. He pulled and stretched and pounded on the shower curtain, but it continued to swell like a balloon, soon knee deep, then waist deep.

"Lila, *please!*"

She had never done anything like this before. He wondered, *am I asleep?* Was this just a feverish nightmare fueled by guilt? It couldn't possibly be happening, but it was. The towel blocking the mirror fell to the floor, and there she was, glaring at him in the glass. Thick, hot blood surrounded him, now chest deep.

Zevon gasped for air, his pulse throbbing and panicked. The blood grew deeper and deeper still, and the last thing he saw before it flooded his eyes was the image of Lila looking at him from the mirror's lens, distorted through the blood-soaked shower curtain. Zevon thrashed and held his breath, completely submerged in this macabre womb as it swelled, as if to give birth.

The drain opened by itself in an instant, and Zevon felt an intense suction as the blood rushed through it around his feet. The pull from the drain sucked him down, pulling his feet into the impossibly small hole as he screamed.

He had once been to a water park as a child, and had slid down one of their long, waterslide tubes, loving every second of it. This was much the same, except he felt his whole body inexplicably flushed through a hole the size of a tangerine. His lungs cried out for air as he helplessly slid through a channel of hot blood.

From feeling like a red blood cell pumping fast through a hot vein, Zevon suddenly felt a cold rush around him as the warm liquid fed into a cold, large body of water. He swirled in the current of an underwater flush, feeling himself floating and searching for his bearings.

No longer hot, but cold. No longer thick, but light. He was underwater and he felt the air left in his lungs pulling him up, so he went with it, swimming upward toward a shimmering surface.

Zevon emerged from the lake, bursting up from below the surface and gasping for breath. The shore was only a few yards away, so he swam to it, his body exhausted. It was a warm Spring night and the moon was half full.

He checked around, finding no trace of blood on him, or in the clear water. His bare chest heaved as he slowly began to calm down, sitting partially on the sand with his legs still in the water. His eyes looked back over the lake, scanning over the misty surface.

Lila floated on her back, many yards out in the dim light, looking up at the stars. She lay on the surface as if it were a firm mattress, requiring no effort not to sink down below. She was the lake, and the lake was her. She did not turn her head to look at him, only stroking the water with her index finger as she gazed upwards.

"Do you love her?" She asked.

"What are you talking about?"

"That girl. Claire. She's very pretty, isn't she?"

Zevon waded out a bit deeper, holding his hands out as he drew nearer to her.

"Oh, no. No, Lila. I love *you!*"

"Do you fantasize about her? Do you touch yourself when you think about her...?"

"No! Of course not!"

"You're lying!"

Lila's voice cracked, her eyes glassing over with tears. "You're twisted and crooked! You're wicked and un-pure, just like the rest of them! You... You want to... You want to..." Her rage sizzled through clenched teeth until, in a flurry of motion, she went from several yards away to being right in his face in the blink of an eye.

Zevon staggered back as a wave splashed into him, knocking him to his back on the sandy shore. She stood at his feet, towering over him, looking tired and hungry and spited.

Zevon recoiled from her angry glare.

"Am I not enough?"

"Y-You are! You're all I need, Lila! I swear!"

"Tell me I'm beautiful."

She was visibly depleted.

Her hair hung limp, loose and wet. Her skin was pale, her lips dry and her eyes adorned with tired bags. Her body was thin, her curves diminished. Still a goddess, but an aging one, twenty years past her prime. She was clearly hungry, and in need of replenishing. Zevon told her what she wanted to hear.

"Y-You're beautiful. You're so beautiful..."

Lila could hear the lie and betrayal in his voice. Her eyes clenched and her fists balled as a burning fury brewed in her chest, resonating into a scream from hell. For just an instant, any life within her drained and Zevon saw her the way she never wanted to be seen:

Body drained of any muscle or tissue, pale skin stretched and shriveled across her bones. Sunken, black eyes and jagged, moldy teeth lodged into rotten gums. The raspy scream came to an end, and she shifted back to her usual, beautiful self. Her body filled back out, her eyes and face reforming to their normal, yet still depleted state.

Zevon cowered in shock.

"*I'm hungry!*" She demanded.

"Okay, okay..." Zevon staggered back to his feet, the water lapping at his toes. "Just let me put on some dry clothes. I'll drive over to Poughkeepsie, or maybe Millbrook, find somebody for you. Don't worry..."

"I don't want another drunk from Poughkeepsie or some bum from Millbrook!" She said. "I want something *fresh*. A special treat... How about your new girlfriend, Claire?"

Zevon's face dropped and his eyes went wide. "No. Absolutely not."

"Why? She means nothing to you, yes? You say I'm all you need?" She circled him slowly, lightly tracing her fingers across his chest.

"But, she-she's a friend!"

"You want to do wicked things with her! Impure things!"

"No!"

"Liar! Then bring me what I want!"

"But you only feed on men! You never —"

"I prefer men. But sometimes I do crave something a bit different. Now give me what I want!"

"I can't," Zevon protested. "She's a friend! And she lives in town! I don't take anyone from White Feather, nobody within the Putnam county jurisdiction! We talked about this!"

Lila growled like a lioness, scratching him as she circled.

"And she's not wicked," he said. "She's not filthy or

impure. She's nice. She's a good person. And you know how I feel about killing women, and..."

"*I want a woman's blood!*"

Lila's piercing scream once again drained any humanity from her visage, allowing Zevon to once again see the shriveled, decrepit hag for but a moment. She faded back to her normal self when the scream ended, but her eyes still held on his with a twisted, demanding rage.

Zevon staggered.

"Okay, fine... I'll go find a woman. Someone *wicked*. Okay?"

Lila smiled, satisfied her pawn was still under her control. She raised an index finger and playfully tapped the tip of his nose like a button.

"Boop!" She giggled. "Thanks! See you soon."

With that, Lila smiled and let herself fall backward, splashing down into the lake, her body instantly dispersing into the water as if she'd never been there at all. Zevon stood in silence, ankle deep in the water, head buzzing.

He knew what he had to do. He had to keep his word. Sloshing away from lake Yakonkwe, he headed back to his house to prepare for a busy night ahead.

CHAPTER THIRTY-FIVE
PRESENT DAY

TOM'S DAY had been tedious and dull, folding towels, scanning membership cards and watching men in much better shape than himself parade around at the gym in sleeveless shirts, guns locked and loaded. He'd thought that working at a gym would help keep him in shape, but the motivation had long ago withered away. Training before his shift started would be way too early for his liking, and training after he clocked out would mean remaining in this place that he was sick of.

All he wanted to do was grab a burger and some beers. As Tom drove his old Civic through the small-town streets that night, a burger and fries were definitely a must on the agenda. The beers could be avoided, but he'd have to see how his will power felt about that prospect.

He tapped the wheel as Rusty Randall and his sidekick, Dollar Bill, rambled on about sports news through the aging radio's speakers. Rusty's soothing Southern twang was a relaxing intoxicant of its own, and every day, Tom looked forward to his insights, philosophies and speculations about everything and anything sports. Tom chuckled at Rusty's histrionics and turned onto Wilcox Boulevard, stomach rumbling for some meat.

"Well, I don't know about that, Bill," Rusty Randall said in his famous drawl. "If Jennings tightens up on his D, they just might be able to pull out of this slump they've been in all season..."

"Yeah, that'll be the fuckin' day," Tom said, deliberating between Burger King and Cookout Burger.

He steered down the road, flowing with the sparse traffic on the dark, small-town street. A few blocks down, a surely majestic meal awaited him in a paper bag handed through a drive-thru window, but something caught his eye on the right shoulder of the road ahead. He slowed the car and took notice of a dog, a medium-sized terrier, limping down the side of the road with an apparently broken leg.

"Oh, no..."

Tom pulled over onto the shoulder, slowing to a halt as the pup continued to limp ahead. Getting out of the car, Tom jogged over to the injured, whimpering animal.

"Hey, buddy. Hey there."

Frightened and in pain, the dog turned to look up at Tom, tears in its eyes. Tom knelt down, putting his hand on its back and stopping the animal's halting gait. Its tail wagged in both excitement for help and trepidation. Tom gave the canine a quick looking-over, noting the left hind leg it kept raised off the ground as he gently stroked its back.

"It's okay, it's gonna be okay," Tom said, slowly wrapping his arms around the dog and lifting it up. "Come on, buddy. Gonna take you to see a friend of mine." Tom carried the dog back to his car. His drive-thru feast would have to wait.

"Yeah, looks like a hairline fracture," Claire said, examining the dog on the table in her new exam room.

Tom gently kept his hands on the little guy so he wouldn't move around too much. The office was nearly finished with all the furniture in place and most of the equipment set up. A few things still needed to be unboxed and there were decorations to hang, but the essentials were there. Claire had run over to meet Tom there, wearing only her casual house clothes. Tom admired her willingness to help, despite not even being open for business.

"Poor guy..." Tom said. "Hey, I told you I'd have to get a dog so I'd have an excuse to come see you, right?"

Claire laughed. "Yes, you did... Hold here."

Tom did as she asked, holding the dog steady as she tried to set its broken bone straight. The animal whimpered.

"Nice new sign you got out front. Zevon Lang, huh?"

"Thanks," she said. "Yeah, it's a little much. And he's a little... I don't know."

"Yeah, that guy's a weirdo, Claire. I'd steer clear if I were you."

"Mm."

"He was right there when his father shot himself. Some people even think Zevon might have..."

Claire turned, surprised. "He *shot* himself? Zevon told me his father hit his head and drowned."

Tom shook his head, his face dour. "He shot himself... Or at least, that's what the M.E. says... I don't trust that guy, Claire. Really. I'd stay away if I were you."

Claire nodded, soaking in this new information. She sighed, her own feelings affirmed. She went back to work.

"Toss this," she said, handing him the wrapper to a bottle of Ketofen as she filled up a syringe with the clear liquid. Tom threw the wrapper into the trash bin behind him as she gently injected the anti-inflammatory pain medicine into the dog's thigh. Tom smiled, petting the animal's head.

"You're a lucky boy. You're Dr. Carpenter's first patient in her new office!"

"Yup. And I don't even officially open my doors till Monday morning. God help me." They both shared a gentle chuckle as Claire continued to work.

"I'm proud of you, Claire," Tom said. "This... You did good. You're doing good."

"Thanks, Tom."

A wicked smile cracked across his lips as a memory snuck into his mind. "You still afraid of Cabbage Patch dolls?"

With that, Claire cracked up laughing, trying to contain herself as the unexpected recollection hit her like a surprise punch. "Shut up."

"Yeah, you are."

"It was just the one with the bright-blonde hair and the crazy eyes! And it just startled me that one time, so don't..." She glanced over at Tom and saw him cracking up, gleefully reveling in her embarrassment. "Oh, shut up!"

They both released their laughter, cheeks flushing red, shoulders heaving. The good old days... Tom looked at her smile, the open abandon of her laugh, her pure and innocent beauty. The laughing spell trailed off after a few moments, and the dog's agitation eased as the medicine began to work its magic.

"There you go," Claire said to the dog as she put its leg in a splint, wrapping it tight with gauze. "You're gonna be just fine."

They both stroked the animal tenderly, his hand on its

head, hers on its thigh. After an empty pause, Tom mustered up the courage to look her in the eye.

"I missed you," he said.

"Don't."

"You went off to the city for school, never came back... I never got a chance to... To say I'm sorry."

"It's okay, Tom. It's ancient history."

The dog had relaxed thanks to the medicine, and Claire gingerly lifted him off the table, carrying him over to a large carrier and easing him inside.

"Yeah, I know," he said, moving with her around the room. "Just wished I had a chance to put things right."

"We were all just kids. And besides, we never officially 'broke up.' We just kind of... Drifted apart." Her eyes offered forgiveness rather than struggling with heavy baggage. Tom however, still buckled under the weight of guilt.

"You deserved better," he said, struggling. "Better than a piece of shit like me. The drinking, the drugs... I'm sorry."

"It's okay, Tommy. It happens." Claire locked the cage and let the little guy sleep, standing up with a stretch. "And that should do it for you, buster! You're gonna sleep like a log, and I'll see you tomorrow morning!"

Tom struggled for the right words, but just saying *I'm sorry* over and over and over again could never summarize his feelings or assuage his liability for past acts.

"Is that it?" He asked.

"That's all I can do for now. Besides, I don't usually do calls after midnight! Gotta get back to sleep! Give little buster here an X-ray first thing tomorrow. See if he needs a cast. And hopefully we can find his owner!"

Claire picked up her light, knitted sweater and put it on, putting her tools away. She moved towards the door and

Tom followed with deflated posture. She clicked off the light and they moved into the front reception area.

"Do you want me to drive you home, or...?"

"I'll be fine, Tom. I got my truck outside, remember?"

"Right. Duh."

Tom nearly kicked himself, feeling like an imbecile for forgetting. "Well, uh... Maybe another time we could hang out, catch up some more...?"

"Sure, maybe coffee sometime," she said, keeping things vague and polite. Keeping Tom Kepper at arms length was good for her health, she had learned. She led them outside and locked the door behind them. "I'm going to be pretty busy, but I'm back now. I'm sure we'll have time to catch up."

Claire backed away towards her truck with a cordial smile. Tom stood beside his beat up old Honda Civic in the dark parking lot, watching her go.

"Okay," he said. "Sounds good." He fished his keys from his pocket, waving goodbye as she climbed into her driver's seat.

"'Night, Tom."

"Goodnight, Claire."

She closed her door, started her engine and drove away. Tom took a deep breath. Another night of guarding outside her home was ahead of him.

Right after picking up his burger and fries.

CHAPTER THIRTY-SIX
PRESENT DAY

KEISHA'S real name was Francis Luna Delgado, and she was twenty-two years-old, not eighteen, like she told her clients to arouse their perverted interests. She had skimmed through high school without a care, getting by on her good looks, dating popular boys and graduating with a degree in rolling blunts and drinking forty-ounce bottles of malt liquor. She'd gone straight to work at a string of fast food restaurants, and despite not going to college, she had earned a new degree in heroin and any other opioids she could get her hands on.

Her firm figure and healthy, fresh Latin features had faded and the boyfriends had become less studley, less popular and more abusive. Living with her mother and younger sister had become unbearable, and trying to scrape together a living serving tacos through a window had become an exercise in futility. Any money she made went straight into her veins, and that became the only pleasure she knew or strived for anymore.

Her name-tags and restaurant uniforms were left behind, replaced with tight mini-skirts, mesh tank-tops and pink pumps. Her hair became teased and dyed green at the tips, her makeup amped up into bold and saturated colors, and the girl once known as Francis became a streetwalker known as Keisha.

She and a few other girls would hang out near local bars in Poughkeepsie and surrounding towns, sometimes at gas stations or truck stops, enticing men for an invite to their back seat. She would angle out her hips, stick her breasts forward and pucker her lips together.

Men would stop, take her to a secluded spot and Keisha would let them make a filthy mess of her for a few crumpled-up bills. Being high helped, as the majority of her clientele were older men, crusty, stinking, ugly and vile. She didn't want to know what their wives' names were or what position of prominence these men might hold, and after shooting up, she didn't have to care.

On this night in particular, it was just after 1 am and Keisha was flying high. Her gaze drifted and her mind floated in a warm cloud of cotton candy as she sat in the front seat of a faded-blue van, heading south on the highway. Eyes struggling to stay open, Keisha gazed out the window as the road blurred past, every passing set of headlights leaving a phosphorescent trail that lingered behind.

The guy who had picked her up was younger than the usual fare. He was small but looked strong; probably had a great body under the black hoodie he wore, she thought. He didn't smell like alcohol or cigarettes, or like he had gone a week without showering. He was polite and classy, and Keisha wondered if she might actually have a little fun with this one. They neared a turn-off spot she was familiar with and Keisha raised a lazy finger to point it out to her new client.

"You wanna pull over in here, baby?" Keisha said. "It's nice and quiet... Nobody will bother us..."

Zevon said, "No, there's a real nice spot I want to show you. You'll like it. Not much farther now." He gripped the wheel tight, smiling in his best effort to be reassuring.

"It's your money, dude..."

Zevon smiled and continued driving, crossing over the Putnam County line and into the town of White Feather.

ZEVON ARRIVED AT HIS HOUSE, parking the van. All the lights were off, as were those in the surrounding houses. The dim light of the half-moon kissed the landscape. Zevon killed the engine and jumped out with practiced stealth, jogging around to the passenger side door. Keisha's head rested on the window, her mind shifting in and out of consciousness. Zevon lightly rapped on the window, then opened the door.

"Here we are, Keisha."

She struggled to raise her groggy head, looking around at the unfamiliar scene with confusion. The young man who had picked her up stood outside the door, arms held out to help her. She grumbled from within her dream world as he gently took her arm, coaxing her out.

"We're here," he said. "Come on, now."

"Ohhh, okay..."

Keisha stumbled out with Zevon's help, nearly falling when her feet hit the ground. Zevon kept his arm around her, his grip right at her elbow, keeping her steady. He glanced around in all directions, making sure no curious eyes were on them. Gently, he closed the passenger door with the faintest *rap*, guiding her forward to the house. She groaned, swaying in delirium as he guided her, steering her not to the front door, but to the left side of the two-story home.

"Here we go..." he encouraged.

"...Where are we going?"

"I want to show you my lake. It's beautiful in the moonlight." He walked her around to the darkened side, lifting her so her feet barely took any weight, guiding her across the nebulous, uneven ground. They emerged from the shadows and into the backyard, where the moonlight reached and the landscape opened up onto the scenic view of the lake.

All was quiet and still, the lake calm and glassy-black. Keisha's eyes focused on the water, glancing around at the back yard in bewilderment.

"You want to do it... Out *here*?" She asked.

"Yeah! Go ahead and take off your clothes. You look so beautiful." Zevon led her down to the shore, hiding his raw nerves with a smile.

Keisha held her hands to her chest, shivering despite the warm, Spring air. "Where are we?"

"This is my place. Don't worry, it's totally private. Just have to keep our voices down. Don't want to wake the neighbors."

"It's so coooooold..." Keisha's common sense tried to fight against the chemicals pumping in her veins. Zevon rubbed her shoulders and smiled, throwing in a playful chuckle.

"Oh, come on! I'll keep you warm!"

Zevon turned her to face him, aiming her back to the lake. He let go of her shoulders, letting the girl sway on legs made of gelatin. He took a step back, trying to make his feeling of pity translate into a leer of admiration.

"Go ahead," he said.

Keisha released a sigh. Men had asked her to do much dirtier and kinkier things than this. She began with her hot-pink, mesh shirt, pulling the garment off and tossing it aside while trying to maintain her balance. She decided her four-inch heels would have to go next if she didn't want to fall on her face, so she kicked those off to the side as well.

Zevon's forced smile strained, his heart pounding, every fiber of his body screaming at him to stop.

"Very nice," he said, swallowing hard.

Several feet behind Keisha, a series of bubbles rose to the surface of the lake. Zevon pretended not to notice as Lila arose from the water, head first, floating up to the surface, her feet standing atop the gentle waves like a dark messiah. She looked at Zevon with tired, angry eyes, piercing him with disappointment.

"What is this shit?" Lila snarled.

Keisha neither saw nor heard the entity behind her, and continued to slowly disrobe for her paying customer. Her bra came off, then her mini-skirt, both items tossed onto the shore.

"Keep going," Zevon said. "S-So sexy..."

Now wearing nothing but panties, the young woman who called herself Keisha wobbled forward, putting on her sexy-face as she reached up to put her hands on Zevon's chest and kiss him. He quickly grabbed ahold of her wrists, gently easing her back towards the water.

"What?" Keisha asked.

"I have an idea," Zevon feigned enthusiasm. "Let's go in the water!"

"Huh? It's gonna be freezing!"

"Nah nah, it'll be fine!"

Lila, hands on her hips, stood tapping her foot on the

surface of the water as Zevon eased Keisha backwards. This was not how they did things. Someone could see, someone could hear. They did things nice and clean; that's the way she wanted it. She was a lady, not a monster. She liked her meals prepared.

"Zevon..." Lila said, her tone growing more impatient.

Despite her intoxicated state, Keisha began to resist. Her arms pulled at his grip and her muscles tensed. She couldn't think clearly, but she could tell that something wasn't right.

"I don't know," Keisha said. "I don't like this..."

"Keisha, please. It'll be okay. J-Just go in the water."

Zevon pushed forward, driving Keisha back inch by inch. Her feet touched the water and an electric shiver shot up her leg. Keisha's body tensed, the cool water jolting her slightly out of the haze she still dwelled in. She squirmed and struggled as Zevon continued pushing, her feet soon ankle-deep.

"Please," Keisha whined. "I don't want to do this..."

Lila snapped through gritted teeth, "Zevon, stop it! Do it right! Kill the little whore and chop her up!"

Keisha heard no harsh voice behind her, nor was she aware of another woman's presence. All she knew was that the gentle grip on her shoulders had grown tighter, and this strange, strong man was pushing her deeper into the black water. Her heart thudded in her rib cage and her subconscious fought the drugs in her veins, forcing her out of her mind's dark tunnel.

"Please, please..." Zevon begged, his eyebrows in knots, nervous sweat beading on his face as he pushed her further, now knee-deep. Next door at Murray's house, a light turned on inside. Lila hissed with urgency.

"People are waking up, Zevon! You have to end this now!"

"I don't want to," Zevon said, tears brewing in his eyes. "You do it!"

"Who are you talking to?" An increasingly confused and frightened Keisha begged.

"Please! I don't want to!"

"That's not how this works!" Lila snapped. "You finish this little bitch *right now!*"

Keisha shrieked, fighting the strong grip, water splashing around them. "Please let me go! *Help! HELP!*"

"*Do it, Zevon!*"

His jaw clenched and a tear ran down his cheek, Zevon's eyes locked onto Lila's as he let go with one hand, silently pulling the folding knife from his pocket. In that moment, he didn't know who he was more disgusted with, Lila or himself. His thumb flipped open the folding blade with a *click*.

"God damn you..." he said, his eyes burning into Lila's.

"*HEEEELP! HEEE —*"

Slit!

Keisha's screams suddenly ended with a swift slash as the blade whipped before her eyes in a blur.

A sharp sting traced across her throat.

There was very little pain, but she could feel her body going cold from the inside, while a torrent of warmth spilled down her chest. She tried to scream but only found a hissing of air, like a deflating tire. She tried to breathe but could not fill her lungs.

Keisha staggered as Zevon held onto her left arm, her astonished eyes searching for answers. Her free hand reached to her throat but could not stop the hot gush of life draining from her body and into the cool water.

The world was fading, her body numbing, and a young woman who was once known as Francis Luna Delgado slumped to her knees, the lake swallowing her whole. Zevon controlled her descent like a gentlemanly dance partner, looking down into her confused eyes.

"I'm sorry," he said.

Zevon let go of her arm, dropping the body down face-first and letting her float toward Lila. Lila wasted no time, sinking down low and grabbing the dead girl with an angry glare at Zevon. She hurried to pull her meal out of view, dragging Keisha off to the side and into the reeds where they both sank down and out of sight.

Zevon's head hung low, standing knee-deep in a warm puddle of blood that was rapidly dispersing into the lake, feeding the monster that owned his soul. He turned and headed inland, shaking the water off as he stepped onto dry ground.

"That you, Zevon?"

Zevon turned to see Murray standing on his back porch, clad in his favorite bath robe, his gray hair a disheveled mess. Even with his glasses on, Zevon was no more than a shadow at this distance, but the commotion had been enough to bring him outside, curious and concerned.

"Hey, Murray." Zevon waved.

"You hear that? Sounded like people fighting!"

"Yeah, I did hear something..." Zevon thought quick. "So I came out here to check it out. I don't see anything, though."

"Maybe we should call the police?"

"Ah, what for? Probably just someone's TV turned up too loud, watching horror movies or something."

"But it-it sounded like..."

"I tell you what," Zevon smiled. "I'm gonna stay up a

while longer. If anything happens, I'll call the police. And you get back to bed! You need your beauty sleep!" Zevon shook a finger at the old man with a playful laugh.

"Ha!" Murray scoffed. "Okay then, Zevon. Goodnight. Be careful." Zevon watched as Murray trudged back into his house, the lights blinking off a few moments later.

"Yeah, you too..." Zevon whispered to himself. He shot a glance over at the shadowy area of reeds. There was Lila, still as a statue, submerged in the water up to her eyeballs like a crocodile. Those eyes looked deep into him, and he looked right back.

Neither of them moved. She was a serpent and he was nothing more than her slave. *Who is the real monster here,* Zevon wondered.

Slowly, the serpent's eyes sank below the water without a blink, leaving Zevon alone in the dark. He went back inside and collapsed on his bed.

He couldn't get to sleep for what seemed like hours, and when he finally did, he dreamed of blood on his hands and Keisha's pleading eyes looking up at him as she fell into darkness.

CHAPTER THIRTY-SEVEN
2008

IT WAS HALFWAY through his senior year of high school, and Zevon had become quite the physical specimen. In addition to his steady regimen of weights and wrestling, he had begun training at OSS Combatives in the downtown heart of White Feather. A mixed-martial arts training facility, they offered classes in Brazilian Jiu-Jitsu, Muay Thai and Kickboxing, and Zevon soaked it up like a chunk of fresh baguette dipped in broccoli-cheddar soup.

Three days a week, he worked at a local furniture wholesale store, Marris Brothers, where he built and repaired an assortment of wooden furniture. Any remaining slivers of free time went to the construction of his very own work shed outside his father's house, as well as his usual nocturnal activities.

He kept himself as busy as possible, avoiding his father at all costs. They were two ships in a misty harbor, sailing around each other and going about their own business. Now that Zevon had a job, Charles Lang had given up refusing the use of his van. The boy was going to do whatever he wanted to anyway, so as long as he put gas in the tank, they were square. He would see his son lifting weights, constructing his shed, coming and going at will. He was a grown man now, a physical force beyond control, and though his father would never admit it, he had come to fear the boy.

Zevon parked the van at his house after a grueling, two-hour session of Jiu-Jitsu. He was caked in dry sweat, his body exhausted as he hopped out of the van and snatched up his gym bag. There was a strange car parked out front, a black Lincoln Town Car with government plates. Zevon approached the front door with trepidation. He heard muffled voices inside and put on his game face, twisted the door knob and walked in.

Charles Lang sat at the dining room table, sipping a cup of coffee. Across from him was a handsome black man of fifty-five, wearing a perfectly-pressed Army officer's uniform, his black shoes gleaming. The two men stopped their conversation and turned to face the youth who stood in the entryway.

Zevon's eyes flicked between both men, but only the officer made eye contact. His father looked down into his coffee cup, shifting in his seat. The officer smiled pleasantly.

"You must be Zevon," he said in a Louisiana baritone.

"What the hell is this?" Zevon's whole body tightened, looking at his father for answers.

"Uh, Z... This is Lieutenant Willis. He's from the Army."

"I don't believe you," Zevon snarled. "We already talked about this. I'm not joining the damn Army!"

"You're eighteen years-old, Z. You're about to graduate high school, you have no college plans..."

"Yeah, so?"

"So, you can't just keep living here with me forever. Working three days a week at a furniture outlet."

"After I graduate, I'll be working full time!"

"Zevon," Lieutenant Willis interjected. "Your father is just thinkin' about your future. The Army would afford you a lot of opportunities, open many doors. If you were to come down to the recruitin' office, I can show you an assortment of jobs you could choose if you enlist. Not to mention education paid for by Uncle Sam..."

"I don't want to go to any recruiting office! Dad, we talked about this! Why did you bring him here?" His father did not reply, but merely released a weary sigh. "You just want me gone. That's it, isn't it?"

"I'm just looking out for your future, Z. Which you're not even thinking about..."

"Yes I am! I have a job! I have... Responsibilities! I have to stay here!"

"Zevon, please..."

"I can't believe you brought him here without even asking me!" Zevon paced, his arms waving, his finger pointing in accusation. They were ganging up on him, trying to drive him away. Trying to keep him away... From her.

"Listen, son," Willis stood, confident as he walked closer to where Zevon stood. "Your father wants what's best for you. He doesn't want to see you working at some furniture store forever. He wants you to make somethin' of your life. We can help you with that. We can teach you discipline, we can..."

"I have discipline!" Zevon said. "I've been working hard and staying busy! You don't know a damn thing about me!"

"Your father has told me quite a bit..."

"*He* doesn't know a damn thing about me!"

Charles Lang hung his head low as the stranger he called his son seethed. He knew the boy's words were the truth.

"What are we going to do then, Z?" His father asked. "This just isn't working. You refuse to see a psychiatrist or to talk to anybody. You won't let anyone help you..."

"I'm not crazy!"

"You can't just stay here forever, Z."

"*I'm not going anywhere!*"

The three figures stood frozen in position, eyeing each other like gunfighters in a Sergio Leone standoff. Lieutenant Willis decided to break the tension by speaking first.

"Well, I can see this is goin' nowhere. At least not today. Tell you what, Zevon? I've left my card with your father. Think it over. The Army has a lot to offer, and we can always use good, strong young men like you."

"Thank you so much for stopping by, Lieutenant," Zevon said through clenched teeth. "You have a wonderful day, now." He walked to the door and opened it, waiting for the Army man to take the hint.

"Well then," Willis sighed, nodding to each of them. "Mr. Lang. Zevon. Have a nice day." Straightening his collar, Willis made for the door, walking past Zevon with a forced, polite smile. Zevon didn't make eye-contact, waiting for the man to leave and then slamming the door behind him.

Charles Lang shook his head. "We gotta figure something out, Z... We can't keep doing this."

"Oh, I've got it all figured out, Dad. All I need from you is to just *leave me alone.*" Zevon stomped up the stairs and into the bathroom. He desperately needed a shower. Charles remained seated, staring into his coffee mug, choking back tears.

CHAPTER THIRTY-EIGHT
PRESENT DAY

CHIEF PAUL KEPPER picked through his to-go salad with a plastic fork like a scientist examining an alien life form. The doctor had told him to lose twenty pounds and that his cholesterol was up. But despite these warnings and the fact that his pants had become uncomfortably tight, he was still on the verge of running across the street to Sugar's for some ribs, baked beans and Mac & cheese. The desk in his office was clean and organized, the office itself sparse and utilitarian.

A calendar of scenic views marked the days; a few wanted posters and missing persons bulletins were the only decorations. The walls were white and the carpet was gray, and there was no red neon light giving the place any flair or style. It was just a room.

Papers on the desk, file cabinet in the corner, umbrella for when it rained and two chairs in front of the desk for guests. After determining there was no beef or pork to be found hidden at the bottom of his salad, he sighed and stabbed some spinach, crunching it into his mouth.

Through the open door, he heard two sets of footsteps

coming down the hallway towards him. One was the unmis-takable squeaky clod of a cop's standard-issue boots, the other one softer, perhaps a pair of sneakers. Chief Kepper leaned forward to see as Officer Nelson came into view through the door, and behind him, a nervous and charged-up Tom. The chief shook his head, letting out a sigh as they drew near.

"Great," Chief Kepper said under his breath.

"Hey, Chief?" Nelson poked his head in the door, giving a light rap with his knuckles. Tom wasted no time, pushing past Nelson and into the office.

"Need to talk to you, Pop."

Tom's eyes were sober and serious. He pulled a back-pack off his shoulder and dropped it on his father's desk. Paul Kepper glanced over at the officer, burning him with his laser-beam eyes.

"S-Sorry, Chief. I'll just... Yeah."

Nelson hurried out of the office, closing the door behind him and escaped. The Chief looked Tom up and down as he rifled through his bag, pulling out a notebook and a stack of papers, looking more focused and determined than he'd been in years.

"So, how you doing, son?" The Chief feigned hospital-ity. "Would you like a little plate of salad?"

"No, Pop..."

"There's spinach, kale, walnuts, apple slices..."

"No, Pop. Listen... We got a problem. I think... We have a serial killer in White Feather."

Tom's father looked up at him, his face an expression-less, immobile sculpture. His eyes blinked. He lifted a plastic fork loaded with greens into his mouth and began chewing.

Crunch. Crunch. Crunch.

His expression remained blank.

"Pop?"

"A serial killer," Chief Kepper chewed. "You do realize there hasn't been a homicide in White Feather in over two years? And that was an isolated incident, and we caught the guy, so...?"

"No, I mean he lives here in town, but he doesn't kill here! He's smart! Look..." Tom picked a state map off the top of his stack of papers, unfolding it and crossing around to give his father a better look. Putnam County, where White Feather sat, was outlined with a highlighter. Also scattered around the surface of the map were numerous red stickers, pinpointing locations.

"I started looking up all the homicides and missing persons cases in the area, going back twenty years," Tom continued. "Everywhere there's been a missing person, I put a red sticker..."

Chief Kepper nodded his head, following the story so far, entertained at the very least. Nearly all the red stickers lay outside the boundaries of Putnam County, with only two inside. On a map peppered with red stickers, their pattern resembling that of a shotgun blast, White Feather was a suspicious, vast, empty space. Tom continued in his zeal, pointing at the map with an accusatory finger.

"Here in White Feather, very little crime. Only a couple homicides, like you said, and one missing person in the last several years. But look at the surrounding counties! Dozens and dozens of missing persons reports, people never found... All conveniently just outside of your jurisdiction."

"Fascinating. So?"

"So," Tom fumed. "Most serial killers are lazy! They hunt where it's convenient, where it's easy! But I think we have one living right here, and *he's* smart enough to not shit where he eats! That's why he's gotten away with it for so long!"

Chief Kepper smiled. He was happy to at least see his son sober and passionate about something.

He was at least trying.

"Okay, son. You got any evidence to support this, or you're just going off stickers on a map?"

"It's more than that," Tom said. "If you read some of the newspaper articles, a lot of these people disappeared under similar circumstances... I'm telling you, Pop. Something is definitely off about this guy. His past, the way he acts, something is not right."

"Wait, which guy? You have a suspect already?"

"Yeah! Zevon Lang!"

It took the Chief a second to scan through his memory bank until he matched a face with the name. Then, "Oh, for fuck's sake..."

Chief Kepper dropped his fork, balking in a frustrated groan as he stood up and scooped the jacket from the back of his chair. "I just remembered, I have some parking meters to check."

Tom's mouth gaped as his father breezed past him and out of the room, storming off down the hallway. Tom scooped up his pile of evidence and followed, close on his heels, desperate to be heard and believed. They exited the hallway and into the main reception area of the station, where an audience of officers and front desk personnel awaited them.

"*What the hell?* Lang's behavior has been completely suspicious, and I don't think — "

"Enough, Tom!" His father stopped in his stride, turning to face him. "Stop it! Zevon Lang? The nerdy kid you and your friends used to make fun of? Yeah, I'm sure you came to that conclusion through solid police work. Nothing to do with any personal motives or biases, right?"

"No! Pop, I swear! Look..." Tom pulled the folder containing the coroner's report on Charles Lang, holding it out for him to see. "This is the autopsy report the M.E. did on Zevon's father, Charles Lang? It was officially ruled a suicide, but look here! Look at the blood spatter pattern on Zevon in these photos from the crime scene..."

"Wait a minute," Chief Kepper looked down at the documents being handed to him, his ire rising. "Where did you... These are official documents, Tommy!"

"Pop, doesn't any of this sound suspicious to you? Like maybe the kid killed his father and made it look like a suicide? How convenient, I mean..."

"Just go back to your gym, Tommy." His father said, closing the folder and tucking it under his arm. "Fold some towels, wipe down some treadmills. Leave the police work to the police. Okay? ...Nelson! Would you escort my son out, please?"

Tom looked at his father's steely glare and sunk within himself. His work had backfired, the offering he hoped would bring him praise had led to more shame and humiliation. He looked around.

Everyone was watching. People he had once known, once worked with, once been respected by. Officer Nelson strolled up to him, a man he'd once gone on patrol with, had beers with.

"Come on," Nelson said, pity in his voice.

Tom turned as Nelson touched his shoulder, allowing himself to be led towards the front door. Chief Kepper stood like a marble statue, watching his son go.

Tom glanced around the room, noting two of the officers holding back laughter. When he made eye contact, one of them mimed the snorting of cocaine and they both laughed, shaking their heads.

Tom turned his eyes away, unable to look at them. He had dishonored himself years ago and there was no turning back, no redemption. Officer Nelson pushed open the glass front door and Tom trudged out into the street. Nobody would listen to him, he realized.

People are in danger as long as Zevon Lang is on the streets, he thought. And if Claire had become close with him, if that little freak had gone soft on her, Tom didn't want to think of what might happen.

CHAPTER THIRTY-NINE
PRESENT DAY

"YOU THINK you can just leave me?"

Lila's angry reflection glared at Zevon in the pane of his bedroom window as he tossed a large suitcase onto his bed, along with a military-grade duffel bag. Emptying his closet and drawers, stuffing the bags with clothes, he did not look up to meet her eyes.

"Watch me," he said. He spoke through clenched teeth, forgetting his own compulsion to fold everything perfectly as he jammed his clothes into the bags with haste.

"You idiot!" Lila snarled. "You think *she* loves you? She doesn't even like you! She thinks you're a loser and a *freak*, like everyone else!"

"Shut up!"

"You think Claire wants anything to do with you? You're just a tool to her! Look at you! You're pathetic!"

"You're just jealous! You need me; I don't need you! I can be free! I can take Claire far away from here, and we can be free, and we can be happy..."

Zevon's erratic and disjointed motions as he packed his bags were a reflection of his mind. Spinning, sloppy. The memory of Claire kissing him repeated in a scratchy loop as he fought off thoughts of Lila.

Memories of dark alleys, smokey bars and bloody hack saws. Memories of chopping through the flesh of human beings, all to satisfy her... But what about him? What had she ever done for him?

He zipped up his two bags and hauled them off to the front door, carrying them out to the van. He whipped open the tailgate and chucked the bags inside, turning back to the house to get more. With single-minded determination, he stormed up the front steps, quickly searching around for his essentials.

He scooped up his backpack and took it into the bathroom. He stuffed his towels into the bag, followed by soap, shampoo and conditioner, then his toiletry bag. Zipping that bag closed, he tossed it out the bathroom doorway, hearing it clump down the steps into the living room just as he planned. Lila's reflection watched him from the mirror on the medicine cabinet with anguished eyes.

"You swore you'd always take care of me, that you'd never leave. Y-You told me that you loved me..."

Zevon seethed, trying not to look at her. "You used me. You lied to me. You made me do... Horrible things."

He bolted out of the bathroom, back into his bedroom, scooping up his winter coats and his favorite posters he'd rolled into tubes. He carried this new load down the stairs, struggling with his burdened arms to scoop up the backpack when he reached the bottom. Her voice continued to follow him, echoing through the halls of the empty home.

"I love you, Zevon! Nobody could ever love you the way I do!" She pleaded as he crossed into the living room, his face turning red as an unfamiliar pressure built up inside him.

"That's not true!" Zevon stopped, shouting and looking all around. She was everywhere, in the air, in every reflected surface, watching him unravel. "I'm going to find Claire, I'm going to tell her how I feel, and-and..."

"Oh, please!"

"And we're gonna start a new life together! A life *without you!*"

Zevon's words cut deep, and Lila's ensuing scream was so potent as to fracture the glass in the picture frames and windows throughout the house. Zevon winced at the piercing shriek, hurrying out the open front door and once again running out to the van with the rest of his things.

He turned back again, plunging into the house one last time. He crossed back through the living room, flinching as the TV came on by itself, Lila's scorned face taking up the whole screen.

"You're going to fail!" She cried.

"Go to hell!"

"She's going to reject you!"

"I'm going to love her! And she's going to love me! And yes, I'm going to touch her! I'm going touch her and make love to her and do wicked, wicked things! *And I'm going to love it!*"

Lila's eyes squeezed shut on the cracked TV screen, a single tear running down her cheek. There was nothing she could do. Claire could give him more than she ever could, and she knew it. Claire had warmth and she could offer him life, whereas all Lila could offer was death.

She had hoped Zevon would be different, that she could hold his heart, make him stay. But he was the same as all other men, and he too would leave her to wither and die.

"Then go," she whispered. "Be on your own. I don't care. You do what's best for you, Zevon. I'll be fine..."

Zevon stopped at the box on the dining room table loaded with his favorite chisels, sketch pads and art supplies. He could feel the heartbreak in her voice as well as the sting of guilt from his own broken promise.

"This isn't the life I want. I'm sorry..." He turned for the door but suddenly stopped. There was one thing he'd forgotten. Putting the box back down, he hurried off into the den, his eyes glazing over as he looked over his collection of animals. The snakes, the turtles, the frogs, the lizards.

One by one, he picked up the glass cages and opened them up, carrying them out the side door and gently coaxing the captives out onto the free soil. They each slithered, skittered or hopped away.

"Go ahead, you guys. Go on now, you're free..."

Zevon dropped the empty aquariums and terrariums when he was done with each, going back to release the next convict. Tears rolled down his face as he watched them go, back to the woods, back to the lake.

"Goodbye, Randy! Goodbye, Bon!" He returned inside, wiping his eyes and sniffing back his runny nose. Roland and Lemmy were the last to go, and Zevon's face strained and swelled, choking back tears as he released the frog and the turtle, allowing them to be as free as he himself needed to be.

"Goodbye, Lemmy! G-Goodbye Roland! I-I'm sorry!"

Had he abandoned them or had he set them free? And was there any difference? Zevon felt the dam within him break as he watched his two little friends disappear back into the wild forever.

He would never see them again.

Hot tears spilled down his face as he fell against the doorframe, sobbing with abandon. He wept and groaned, struggling to get a hold of himself. Wiping his eyes and nose off on his sleeve, he closed the side door and walked back into the house.

Zevon picked up the box of art supplies on the table and took one last look around. His home, his life, everything he'd known since he was a boy... He was leaving it all behind.

Lila was wrong.

He wasn't pathetic. He could be loved. And Claire felt the same way about him; he knew it. There was a spark in that kiss they shared, a magic, and there was no way she could deny it. What the plan was, he didn't know. He would figure that out later, after he expressed his love and swept her off her feet. He was heading into the great unknown, on an adventure to become a new person, a better person.

Someone he could be proud of.

He carried the box out to the van, placing it in the back and closing the doors. He took a look around at the fading day, the sun beginning to set into a watercolor sky. The air was warm, the trees and grass were a lush green and the bugs zoomed around happily on their own adventures. He nearly climbed into the driver's side, but halted for a moment.

One last thing.

He turned back again, heading around the side of the house. His boots crunched in the grass and gravel and his fingers stroked the side of his work shed as he walked by. He came out into the expanse of the back yard.

Before him, Lake Yakonkwe stretched out into the horizon, peacefully nestled in to the trees of the landscape.

His eyes searched over the water.

And then he saw her.

Over to the left, in the reeds, Lila's head poked out of the water, only her eyes coming up above the surface. Those eyes looked right at him. Their gaze lingered in silence and neither said a word.

Zevon couldn't say goodbye.

He looked down at his feet, let out a sigh, then turned and walked back around the side of the house. Lila watched him every step of the way. He climbed into his van, wiped his eyes clean once again, and started the engine.

CHAPTER FORTY
2009

AT NINETEEN YEARS OLD, Zevon's hair had already begun to thin. A widow's peak was developing at his temples and the bald spot on his dome was in its infancy. He had more hair on his chin at this point. Much more important to him was his physicality, now honed into a high performance machine, as lithe and explosive as a jungle cat.

With his hair and body drenched with sweat and spattered with blood, he finished up his duties in the work shed. He would need to get a raincoat, he decided, unless he wanted to ruin his clothes with blood and gore every time he did this.

He clicked off the light and swung the door open with a gentle *squeak*, carrying the large burlap sack out into the back yard. It was a moonless night and clouds blotted out the stars. An oppressive mist crawled over the land.

At nearly three in the morning, the night was as dark as Zevon's deeds, but he knew his way around at this point, needing no help from a light. With veins straining against his biceps and forearms, he eased the blood-stained bag into the wheelbarrow which sat just outside the door. He then brought out the two-gallon plastic jug filled with blood and loaded that up as well.

Zevon lifted the handles and steered the wheelbarrow down to the lake's edge. He had a chain attached to large cinderblocks waiting on the dock, to make sure nothing of his victims would float to the surface. He reached the dock, strained the wheel over the lip and pushed the cart across the wooden platform with a *clump clump clump*. He reached the end where the floating raft waited tethered, releasing the handles.

"Hey, Lila," he called out in a whisper. "Got something good for ya!" Zevon lifted the gore-stained sack and placed it on the edge of the pier beside the weighted chains. He pulled out the large vessel filled with blood, plopping it down beside the rest of the meal. "This one was a drunk asshole, picking fights at a club. Throwing his weight around. Bully. He got his."

The water rippled in a stream towards the pier and Lila's angelic countenance emerged head and shoulders, smiling up at him from the water.

"Thanks baby," she smiled. "Smells great."

Zevon locked the chains around the sack, edging it closer to the raft. He hefted up the jug and unscrewed the cap with a smile, holding it up over the edge.

"How about an appetizer?"

He poured a spout of blood into the lake for a few moments, the stream splashing beside Lila and dispersing all around. She closed her eyes in ecstasy as the blood flowed all around her. Without needing to drink a drop, she absorbed the life-giving plasma into herself; the lake did the drinking for her. She hummed in pleasure, as if sampling a fine Cabernet.

"Mm, that's delicious. Thank you!"

LADY OF THE LAKE

"You're welcome!" He said, placing the jug onto the raft and squatting down to move the burlap sack there as well. "Plenty more where that came from. He sure didn't make it easy for me, but I think it's worth it. As long as you're happy..."

Zevon's entire body suddenly tensed.

He heard a footstep creak on the boards behind him and felt the glare of a flashlight on the back of his head. He turned slowly as he heard the voice, his heart dropping down into his stomach.

"Who are you talking to, Z?" It was his father.

Zevon stammered. The old man must have stayed up, waiting for him to come home, feeding his worst suspicions with alcohol.

"Dad! I... I..."

"What's in the bag, son? Who are you talking to?"

Charles Lang's eyebrows were crunched under the weight of overwhelming, conflicting emotions. He pointed the flashlight up and down, scanning his son's body, seeing the blood stains with his own eyes. He stepped closer, insistent.

"What's in the bag, Zevon?"

Lila had frozen in place, watching the drama unfold. Zevon could not move, stuttering, clenched and shivering.

"Dad... I-I... What are you doing here...?"

"You want to take my van out late? Okay, fine. You got yourself some friends now? Fine. Hell, you want to do drugs? You're a grown man, you've got to make your own mistakes..." Charles took another step toward his son, teeth grinding and eyes burning. "But my god, Zevon... *What is in the bag?*"

"Dad, please... Please just go back to bed..."

"Open it, son."

"Dad, no. Please..."

Charles pulled a .357 Magnum from his belt with his free hand, letting it hang at his side. Zevon gasped.

"Open it."

"Dad, I-I think you've had too much to drink, and..."

"*Open it!*"

Zevon was cornered, standing at the edge of the pier, nowhere to run or hide. His arsenal of lies and explanations as exhausted as his bloodstained body. He let out a sigh, bent down and loosened the drawstring, spreading open the mouth of the sack. His father took a tentative step forward, angling the beam of light at the opening.

What he saw punched him in the solar plexus and filled his veins with a blast of anti-freeze. A human arm sat atop the pile, severed at the shoulder, its color drained, smeared with its own dried blood. Beside it rested a head, only the very top protruding and visible, a single dead eye staring back at him as if pleading for help.

Charles gasped, staggered, trembled, felt a surge of shock echoing through his bones. He fought against nausea, fought against fainting and desperately grasped for a grip on his own sanity.

"Jesus Christ..." Charles didn't speak the words as much as they just fell out of him on their own.

"Dad, listen... H-He was a bad person, okay? A real bad person... A-And..."

"*This* is what you've been doing all along...?" His eyes overflowed with anguish as he looked upon his son. His *son*.

"Dad, please..."

"You've been going out in my van, and coming back... And committing... And chopping up... Oh my God..." Charles Lang's world spun around him. *How could I have been so stupid?* He thought. *Where did I go wrong?*

"Dad, please believe me... H-He was a bad person! He had it coming... They all did!"

"My god, son... This is all my fault... I'm so sorry..."

"Dad, please don't cry..."

"We're going to get you the help you need, son. I promise..."

Lila's eyes assessed the scene with increasing urgency. She saw Mr. Lang's grip tighten on his gun. She recognized the tone in his voice; he was going to take Zevon away from her.

"You can't let him do it, Zevon." Lila hissed.

"Be quiet..."

"You have to stop him, Zevon!"

"I said be quiet!"

Charles Lang shook his head, witnessing the depth of his son's sickness in full swing as he turned and argued with the empty lake. His trembling hand lifted the pistol, holding it on the disturbed individual before him.

"Who are you *talking* to, son?" Charles cried.

"Her name is Lila, Dad. I-I take care of her! And she takes care of me, a-and—"

"Jesus Christ..."

"Dad, she needs me!"

"Zevon, there is no one *there! No one!*" The boy could not allow himself to hear that. What did he mean, Lila wasn't there? To think she wasn't real, just a construction of his own mind... He couldn't even entertain the thought. She *was* real, and she was the only person who loved him and was there for him.

"Zevon, you have to stop him! Kill him!" Lila commanded.

"No!"

Charles Lang was falling apart, breaking down, the

fabric of reality torn and tattered and collapsing around him. His shaking hands clung to the flashlight and the pistol as if to provide balance.

"What have I done to you...?" Mr. Lang sobbed, fighting back tears, his view of Zevon blurred and fractalized. His son took a step towards him, and his body tensed in response.

"Come on now, son... Come with me... We'll get you the help you need..." Zevon took another step forward.

"I can't do that, Dad. Lila needs me."

"There is no Lila, son."

"Don't say that!" Zevon shouted. Of course she was real. He had felt her fingers in his hair and her breath on his neck.

"Kill him, Zevon!"

"Dad, please put the gun down..."

"Don't... Don't come any closer, son..."

"Kill him!"

Charles Lang extended the gun out further, aiming dead center at his son's chest.

His son.

He pulled back the hammer with an echoing, metal *click*. The firearm spasmed in his grip. Right and wrong were mere academic principles of morality at the moment and the only thought flashing in his head was a resounding *I can't do it.*

Zevon's hands came up, palms out in a defensive position. From here he could shoot in for a double-leg take-down and slap the gun away, or use an arm-drag to take the old man's back; a dozen options from his catalogue of combat flashed through his head. Tried and true methods to easily take down an angry, drunk old man.

But this was *his* old man.

Zevon pressed forward, trying to ignore the pleading voice of Lila in his head —

"Kill him, Zevon!"

"Dad, please... Don't make me..."

"I'm sorry, Zevon..." his father wept.

"Dad, please..."

"Kill him!"

"I'm so sorry!"

Zevon could not lunge for the gun, for in an instant, his father had pulled back his aim, pressing the barrel of the gun into the temple of his own head. Before Zevon could scream in protest, the trigger was squeezed.

The muzzle rang out in an explosion of fire and gunpowder and a small chunk of lead blasted through skull and brain. Charles Lang's eyes flipped open wide and empty. His jaw went slack and his body fell limp to the dock with a meaty thud.

Zevon could not hear his own scream through the ringing in his ears as he dropped to his knees, scooping his father's body into his arms. Gunpowder lingered in the air, the whole world seemed to be *ringing*, and all things in Zevon's perception now moved in slow motion, just like a movie on TV. Zevon shook his father's body, but the life was already gone from it.

Lila was gone.

"Dad! *DAD!*"

Zevon's own voice sounded distant and muffled. This wasn't happening, he thought, it couldn't be. Zevon continued to scream as lights turned on in the neighboring houses.

The police would arrive soon.

CHAPTER FORTY-ONE
PRESENT DAY

THE VAN FLEW DOWN the dark, winding backstreets far beyond the posted speed limit. Zevon had popped in an old mix CD, and Slash's Snake Pit was blasting *Mean Bone* through the feeble speaker system. He drummed along with the beat on the steering wheel as the adrenaline-fueled song propelled his engine like a shot of moonshine. He nodded his head and screamed along with the lyrics, feeling the stew of emotions that accompanied newfound freedom. The world was new and fresh again.

He pulled off the small, unlit country road and onto Route 57, turning right towards town. He would stop at Claire's office, proclaim his undying love and devotion, then they would go back to her place, and she would demonstrate hers. Then they could be together, like normal people.

He could open up a new shop for his work while she prospered in hers. Maybe he could even rent out a neighboring storefront by her office! They could have kids, maybe a little dog... She would love him like a real woman, able to fully accept his love.

Zevon pressed the van faster into town, blowing past a

stop sign and not even noticing he'd almost smashed into an SUV as he flew by. A yellow light turned red, but he could not wait. Nothing would stop or slow this inevitable love, this true romance. He plowed on, speeding through the night. Up ahead on Gower Ave, the strip mall was in sight, and Zevon angled into the parking lot, killing the engine and jumping out onto the pavement.

The light was off in her office and although a handful of cars were parked there for the other stores, he did not see her truck anywhere. Maybe she parked around the corner. Maybe she had the lights off and was working in the back, alone; after all, she had just opened and business wasn't in full swing yet. He had to try. With legs like coiled springs, he bounded the short distance to the front door and pulled on it. Locked.

"Shit!"

He knocked on the glass door, just in case, peering inside and looking around. All lights were off inside and no movement could be detected. He cursed again to himself, turning to run back to his van and continue the search.

His eyes scanned the parking lot again; maybe he'd missed her car and she was indeed there, enjoying one of those fancy, hipster coffee drinks she loved so much in the cafe. Once again, no sign of her. But in his scan, his bold blue eyes locked onto something else and he felt himself being drawn forward.

"What the...?"

Zevon approached the frame that held the signs for each of the businesses in the strip mall. From where he stood behind the signs, the whole display was in shadow, but something about it was off. Something about *his* sign looked different, even from the back. He crossed around to the front where he could see it in the light, and in an instant, the warmth drained from his body. His heart dropped into his feet and his stomach shot up into his throat.

Claire had taken down his sign.

Now hanging in the frame advertising her business was a basic, digitally-printed sign made of a plastic polymer. "Doctor Claire M. Carpenter - Veterinary Clinic." The words were scrawled in a slick, fancy font, each letter a different color, and a cute, cartoon dog on the side smiled in adornment.

"What...?" Zevon's chest heaved. He'd never had the wind knocked out of him without even receiving a blow. He staggered back, his wiry legs reduced to limp rubber. The betrayal burned into his eyes and tears rolled down his cheeks.

His legs gave way and he dropped to his hands and knees on the knoll, staring up at this monument of duplicity. Chemicals and juices and toxins and elixirs pumped and surged through Zevon's brain. His eyes darted from side to side, up and down, on fire. Never before had such a confusion of emotions taken him, leaving him a helpless surfer caught in a crashing wave.

He did recognize some of the antagonists flashing through his psyche as old familiar foes — sorrow, confusion, despair... *Rage.* Yes, rage was a pot sitting on a burner, its broth coming to a simmer. Zevon's teeth clenched, his fists balled, his body trembling. Rage was brewing inside of him, in his eyes, in his chest, in his veins...

His blood boiled with it and Zevon followed its singular pressure, letting it fuel him with strength. He pulled himself back to his feet and his once-scattered and confused mind now focused into a red hot laser beam...

Claire.

TOM SAT IN HIS CAR, a block from Claire's condo. His feast from Cookout Burger was finished and crumpled up in a paper bag on the passenger seat. If he'd still had a gun, it would be sitting there in his lap, rather than a cell phone. Nobody believed him, nobody respected him and he certainly was not a cop anymore.

His clues and suspicions were thin at best, he knew, yet there he was, playing stake-out as if he were some kind of crime fighter. If Claire knew he'd been watching her house for the last couple of weeks, she'd no doubt file a restraining order.

"Leave the police work to the police."

His father's cold words rang in his head like church bells. The image of his former colleagues laughing and taunting him replayed again and again. *This is wrong*, he thought. *Wrong and stupid.* But despite everything, the thought of Zevon Lang kept stabbing into his mind with flashing red lights, and the fear of him coming after Claire and somehow hurting her overwhelmed common sense or reason.

He had considered giving up many times. But giving up was all he had ever done, and just the thought left a bitter taste on his tongue. Claire might need him, so he remained at his self-assigned post.

ONE BLOCK behind Tom's Honda Civic, Zevon Lang's van slid into a parking spot. The lights cut off and the fractured soul got out. He'd parked far enough away so that she couldn't see him coming, and prepared for the hunt. He zipped up his dark denim jacket and tucked his small flashlight into a pocket.

With a light step, he glided up the street like a phantom, well practiced in stealth. He rounded a curve in the road and could see Claire's condo up ahead, her truck parked out front. Zevon continued forward, looking as inconspicuous as possible as he passed an elderly woman walking her Scottish terrier.

Zevon stopped in his tracks up ahead as he saw the back of a very familiar head and shoulders sitting in a parked Honda Civic. Tom Kepper was getting in his way again. With a growl under his breath, Zevon crouched down low, sneaking out around the side of the car.

Keeping his head lower than the windows, he duck-walked slowly along the driver's side panels. He scooped up a small pebble from the ground once he reached position behind the driver's door. With a flick of his finger, Zevon sent the pebble against Tom's window with a faint *rap*.

Tom heard the slight tap against his window and looked out in that direction. Nothing but a faintly-lit suburban street. Darkness and silence hung in the air, as if ready to pounce on him. He looked in his rear-view mirrors, and once again, nothing.

Tom sighed and relaxed back into his seat again. Suddenly, another *rap* startled him, louder this time. Tom jolted to attention, hand clenching his cell phone and ready to dial 911 as he sprung out of the car.

"What the hell?"

Tom looked around, hyper-focused, yet unaware of the crouching figure curled into a compact ball right behind him. Zevon stood up like a shadow, raising his pocket flashlight up over his head and lashing it out like a piston.

Tom felt a *crack* in his left temple, accompanied by

blinding, flashing lights and colors in his eyes. His consciousness rang like a bell, the whole world reverberating as he fell backward onto the pavement. His head throbbed as he looked up, the tree tops and night sky swirling in his vision.

A figure crossed out of the gloom, standing directly above him, towering over. The figure looked down on him as Tom writhed on the concrete, flashing a crooked smile and deranged, icy-blue eyes. Tom's eyes could not focus, but he knew with certainty that Zevon Lang stood over him, relishing in his pain.

"You... You son of a..."

Tom's words were cut short with a short, brutal stomp to the face from Zevon's boot. With Tom out like a light, Zevon smiled, satisfied. If he had time, he would have loved to spend more time inflicting pain on his old high school tormentor, but his laser focus compelled him forward.

Claire.

Wasting no time, Zevon squatted down, gripped under Tom's arms and hoisted him up. With the door of the Civic still open, Zevon tossed Tom's limp body back into his own car. He pulled the keys from the ignition and launched them far into shadows and foliage.

Chuckling to himself, Zevon closed the driver's door, leaving Tom to drool and bleed on himself. Letting out a satisfied sigh, Zevon turned his attention once more to the condo. The light inside. The faint music through the walls. Claire. *She seems to be having a pleasant evening,* he thought.

Time to go say hello.

CHAPTER FORTY-TWO
PRESENT DAY

"WELL, we have to wait for the MRI results, but he may have to have surgery on that knee again," Brenda's voice resonated through the speaker-phone setting on Claire's cell.

"I know, Mom," Claire said, pacing around her new living room in her sweats and a t-shirt with a screen-printed cat cartoon. "It's pretty common. It sucks, but from what I hear, he'd only be off his feet for about a week."

"Telling your father to stay off his feet for a week is like telling a mule not to be an ass."

"I know," Claire laughed, taking a sip of white wine as Fleetwood Mac rubbed against her legs. "Oh, Fleetwood says hi."

"Hi, Puffy!"

Suddenly, a knock came to the door. Three hard, insistent raps. Claire jolted in place, freezing as her eyes trained on the front door. There was no sound but for the soft instrumental playlist she had set up on her Spotify account. She waited a moment, then cautiously stepped forward.

"Honey, what was that?" Brenda asked through the phone's speaker. "Are you expecting someone?"

"No..."

The hard knocks again at the door made her jump. She inched forward, noting that the chain was secured on the latch, as was the dead bolt. Trembling, she drew nearer to the peep-hole to confirm her suspicions.

"Claire? What's going on?"

"Hang on, Mom..."

Claire leaned forward and put her eye up to the peep-hole. Standing outside was the distorted figure of Zevon Lang, warped by the curve of the glass, chest heaving and eyes blazing. He raised a fist and knocked again, this time harder.

"Claire! Claire!"

She cursed to herself. He was steaming-mad and she had a good idea why. She remained at the door, body tensed, trying to think.

"I know you're in there!"

His voice had taken a tone she had not heard before in him. Gone was the meek, sheepish boy who was gentle and kind. Here stood a man on fire, oozing anger, his voice sharp and demanding.

"Sweetie, who is that?" Brenda asked. "What's going on?"

"Mom, just hang on a minute." She placed the phone down and turned back to the door. Taking a deep breath, she decided to try diplomacy. She unlocked the deadbolt and the lock on the handle, but left the chain on. Turning the handle slowly, she pulled the door open and saw half of Zevon's anguished face through the slim crack.

"Hi, Zevon. Sorry, I-I'm just talking to my Mom right

now. Getting ready to go to sleep. This really isn't a good time..."

"What happened to my sign? *Why'd you take down my sign?*"

"Oh, I'm so sorry about that," she said, the gears in her head spinning to concoct a good story. It probably wouldn't go over so well to tell him that he had begun to make her feel uncomfortable, that his nonchalant capacity for violence and his growing obsession with her made her skin crawl. That she'd had her share of abusive relationships, and she had developed a talent for detecting them in advance.

"The uh, the property manager told me it violated the specs they gave me for the sign. Said I had to replace it with one the same size and weight as the others..."

"You're lying! You took it down! Why? You won't answer my calls! Why? *What did I ever do to you?*"

"Zevon..."

The half of his face she could see was locked in a pained grimace, the single blue eye pleading. She realized this was the half she had not seen before, the side he kept hidden from the world.

"All I've ever been is good to you," he pleaded. "I sent you flowers! I put my *heart* into that damn sign! I came here tonight to tell you that *I love you*... And you just treat me like shit!"

"Claire..." Brenda's voice grew increasingly nervous through the phone's speaker as she helplessly listened to the exchange.

"Okay, I think it's time for you to go now," Claire said. "You're making me really nervous."

She began to push the door closed in his face, but an iron hand pushed back from the other side, easily holding it open while he continued to seethe at her.

"You think you're better than me, don't you?" Zevon barked. "I thought you were special! I thought you cared about me! But you're just the same as everybody else! Lila was right about you! You're evil! You're *wicked!*"

"Zevon, let go!"

"I don't know which one of you is worse. At least she's honest! Maybe I should just give her what she wants..." Unhinged, Zevon split open a crooked smile as he peered through the door. Claire pushed back on the door with all her strength, but it was no use.

He was far too strong.

"You're scaring me! Stop it!"

"...And she really, *really* wants to meet you!"

The fingers of Zevon's right hand curled around the edge of the door, clamping down like an animal's claw. He pushed forward, straining the chain to its limit. Claire pulled back from the door, allowing the resistance to go slack for a moment and giving herself space to create momentum.

She then launched her shoulder at it again with desperate force, ramming it closed. She heard the resonating *smash* as wood met bone, and could almost feel the index and middle fingers on Zevon's hand snapping like dry branches.

"Go away!"

She heard an agonized howl from beyond the door as the defeated hand pulled back, throbbing and angry. She slammed the door shut, locking it tight once again. She heard him through the door, groaning in a pain that bordered almost on orgasmic bliss, and she wondered if some sick part of him actually enjoyed it.

"Claire! Are you okay? What is going on?"

Brenda's digitized voice pleaded through the cell phone

speaker again. Claire darted back to the phone and snatched it, wasting no time as she heard Zevon's footsteps moving around the side of her home.

"Mom, I have to call you back!"

She ended the call, feverishly dialing 911. The phone rang. Claire whipped around, her senses piqued. Her eyes darted to every window. All locked. She listened for any foreign sounds outside; any jostling of locks, any snapping of twigs.

Claire paced back and forth as the phone rang and precious seconds felt like hours. Puffy Pants hid under the coffee table, trembling. The phone continued to ring, then finally —

"911 dispatch. What is your emergency?"

"Yes! My name is Claire Carpenter! I live at — "

Her side window suddenly shattered.

Slivers of glass exploded inward as a large potted plant from her patio was launched into the house. Her ears filled with the painful shriek of the glass and the crash of the planter against her living room floor.

Claire screamed but could not hear her own voice. She fell to her knees but could feel no impact. Her cell phone drifted off into space. Shards of shattered window danced throughout the room, bouncing against every surface, lodging in her flesh, her hair.

Her head buzzed, vibrating a frequency of panic as the world slowed down around her. She looked over to the shattered window leading out onto her patio. Her private space, where she liked to drink coffee in the morning and look at cute cat memes on her phone as she woke up.

Out there in the charcoal blackness stood the figure of the man. A stranger she'd thought she knew. He stepped forward, crossing the threshold, his boot crunching down on the fragments of glass inside her house.

Inside her house.

Zevon stepped inside, smiling down at his easy prey.

"No..."

Claire sprang to her feet, fleeing the attacker as the world continued to ring and hum around her. Zevon leaned down, grabbing her arm with his one uninjured hand, yanking her toward the front door.

"Come here!" He ordered.

"No, please! *Please!*"

Her phone lay amidst the broken glass and debris on the floor, the 911 operator's voice still calling out to her:

"Ms. Carpenter, can you hear me? Ms. Carpenter?"

Claire kicked and pulled and shoved and fought to break free from Zevon's sinewy grip. She reached out for the first object she could use as a weapon, a framed photo of her family, and lashed it into Zevon's face. The glass shattered and the photo inside warped, but Zevon's grip did not weaken.

The ruined frame fell to the floor, revealing a collection of fresh wounds on the assailant's face that began to bleed. Zevon's twisted smile did not fade as the blood dripped like hot sauce down his leering features.

"Go ahead, fight back," Zevon grinned.

Claire raged at him, punching him in the chest and the face with her best shots. Zevon smiled. He raised his right hand, front two fingers now swollen and broken, deflecting her strikes with ease. Using every part of his hand besides the two smashed digits, he yanked her around, forcing her back into his chest, and wrapped his arms around her neck.

She kicked and bucked, but his arms slid instinctively into position like two jungle pythons, his left fitting under her chin, hand clasping shut on his right bicep. His wounded right hand wrapped around the back of her head, pushing her head forward while his left arm pulled her back. The old, reliable rear-naked choke sunk in tight.

"*Go to sleeeeep... Go to sleeeeep...*" Zevon mockingly sang.

Claire bucked with all of her might, kicking at his shins, punching his arms, fighting for her life. But she was a worm on a hook. She felt the primordial vice grip tightening around her neck, her head swelling with pressure, her lungs unable to fill.

She was drowning in the open air, as helpless as a baby. It only took five seconds, but she felt everything fade away, her vision going black. Zevon let go, letting her body fall limp into his arms.

He looked down on her in this unnatural sleep, her head hanging back over the nook of his arm. He marveled at her curly, bronze hair, her perfect, caramel skin. So beautiful, and yet... So deadly. Just another vile snake, out to use and betray him.

Another liar, she was impure. Wicked.

Zevon shook his head. There was only one woman who had ever been completely honest with him, loyal and true. And he had left her behind like an unwanted monster in a haunted loch. Lila had been right all along, and he'd broken her heart.

But now, he thought, *I'll make it up to her.*

He scooped up Claire's legs, carrying her off towards the front door. He searched with his left hand until he felt the locks, undoing them one at a time, then swung the door open and walked out into the night, the fresh air meeting the flowing blood on his face.

He felt invigorated, alive, redeemed. Moving with

urgency, he carried Claire's unconscious body off into the murk before anyone could stand in his way.

Once back in the van, he turned the mix CD back on, cranking the volume as he sped away. The next song up was *Beyond The Realms of Death* by Judas Priest. Zevon howled along with the lyrics as Rob Halford cried out to the heavens.

CHAPTER FORTY-THREE
PRESENT DAY

TOM KEPPER BEGAN to emerge from the fog. The first thing he noticed was the pain, his skull throbbing and ringing like a gong. He was twisted on his side, with his face down, smashing into something — His front passenger seat, he realized. The next thing he noticed was the echoing sound of people outside, talking, shouting, running to and fro.

He was in his car, on the street by Claire's house. These realizations came to him slowly as he lay there, immobile, drool puddling up around his mouth and a trickle of blood creeping sideways across his forehead.

Tom began to move.

First his hand, coming up under him to push himself up. Then his head, pulling off the seat while he wanted nothing more than to put it down and go back to sleep. He pushed himself up with a pained groan, his head pulsing. He began to open his eyes, but his right eyelid was sealed closed with some dried substance.

Blood.

He rubbed at it, the flaky crust falling away, then ripped

his eyelids apart. He blinked through the haze, resting on his elbow as he tried to regain his bearings. He noticed outside of the windows were flashing lights, red and blue. Police cars... Cops... A crime scene...

Claire.

Tom bolted up, a double shot of adrenaline blasting through his veins. He looked around, eyes still struggling to focus. Two patrol cars sat on the street, three officers he recognized holding back throngs of agitated civilians. Up ahead, the activity centered around Claire's condo, where several figures stood in heated exchange.

Tom grumbled and opened the driver side door, practically spilling out onto the street. Struggling to get his feet under him, he forced himself up, his equilibrium fried.

He lurched forward, focusing on the figures in the driveway. There was a panicked Steve and Brenda Carpenter, who he recognized from many years ago, and his father, Chief Paul Kepper, officiating the scene. *Claire. What had the bastard done with Claire?* Tom pushed himself forward on woozy legs, shoving through the onlookers as he made his way to the scene.

"Pop...? *Pop!*" Tom belted out, each vocalization like a blade twisting inside his skull. Nelson and a second officer caught sight of Tom as he approached and their eyes went wide.

"Jesus, Tommy! What happened?" Nelson gawked.

"*Pop!*" Tom ignored Nelson, pushing past.

In the driveway, Steve Carpenter held on to his panicked wife's shoulders as she cried, desperately trying to relay the story to the Chief. He held Brenda steady as she shook and trembled, threatening to fall over at any moment.

"A-And then, he-he was pounding on the door, a-and I

heard him screaming, and he sounded so mad! Oh, please god..."

"It's okay, baby. I got you," Steve Carpenter reassured.

"Who was it, Mrs. Carpenter?" Chief Kepper asked. "Who was at the door?"

"I don't know!"

"*Pop!*"

Chief Kepper stopped as he saw his son pushing through the crowd, head caked with dry, burgundy blood, staggering forward on unsteady legs. The chief caught his son by the shoulders, holding him with both hands.

"Jesus, Tom! What are you doing here? What happened to you?"

"Where is she, dad? *Where's Claire?* Is she in there? Is she..." Tom's voice cracked, pleading. Brenda and Steve barely recognized him as the fit, cocky jock their daughter dated back in school whom they didn't approve of. Now, this broken-down, wounded mess was all that was left of him.

"We don't know anything yet," Chief Kepper said. "There was a home invasion. Somebody *took* her..."

Brenda interjected with her shaky recollection.

"She kept saying the name... Ze... Ze-something..."

"Zevon," Tom confirmed.

"Oh, not this again, Tom..."

"*Who?*" Steve Carpenter urged.

"Look Tommy, I want you to go sit in my patrol car and rest, okay? Nelson, take him back to the car and call for an ambulance right away!"

"Let go of me!" Tom shrugged off the help, raging. "You have to listen to me, please Dad..."

"Tom, I'll be right there, I promise. I want you to sit

287

down and rest. You need medical attention. I'll come talk to you in just a minute. I promise. Nelson!"

"Come on, Tommy." Officer Nelson gently touched Tom's shoulder, guiding him back toward the street. Tom turned, allowing himself to be steered back the way he came as his father returned to interviewing the Carpenters.

Tom picked up speed.

"Hey, Tommy! Hold up!"

Nelson followed him the short distance to his Honda, grabbing for his arm, but to no avail. Tom stalked off to the car on a mission, his blood coursing with molten fury. He breezed past his father's idling squad car, pushing his way through the dense crowd.

He whipped open the driver's door of his Civic and jumped in, reaching for the keys. His hand hit empty air in the space where his keys once dangled from the ignition. Now they were nowhere in sight. The bastard had taken them.

"*Fuck!*"

"Tommy, will you just come sit in the car and tell me what happened? Come on, let's get you some help — " Nelson pleaded but Tom wasn't listening.

Tom jumped back out of the car. Wasting no time, he ran the distance from his vehicle over to his father's patrol car, knocking past pedestrians in his path.

"He's got her, Nelson! I need the car!"

"Oh no, you don't!"

Tom jumped into the idling police cruiser, slamming the door behind him and locking the doors before Nelson could catch him. The doughy officer slid into the door with a meaty thump, angrily pulling at the locked handle.

"Don't you even fucking *think* about it Tommy," Nelson

cursed. "Your dad will fucking *have my ass!* You open this door *right now!*"

"He's gonna kill her, man!"

"Tom!"

"Tell my dad... I'm sorry."

Tom shifted the cruiser into reverse and hit the gas pedal. The Chief's squad car shot backward down the street, swerving around, then screamed forward, the light bar still spinning. Nelson watched along with the rest of the crowd as Tom peeled off into the night, hot in pursuit. Nelson hissed.

"*Shitshitshitshitshit...*"

Nelson rubbed his forehead. Two other officers stood behind him in stunned disbelief. The chief, still talking to the Carpenters on the other side of the crowd, hadn't noticed yet. Nelson cursed himself and pushed his way through the crowd as they swarmed around him, wanting answers.

"Watch out! *Watch out!*"

The other two officers helped clear a path for Nelson as he hurried to deliver the news to the chief and get to the remaining patrol car. Precious moments burned away getting to chief Kepper, allowing Tom a sizable head start. The chief turned to see an exasperated and ashen officer Nelson, bounding up the driveway towards him, eyes bulging.

"Nelson... What is it?"

"Uh, sir, it's Tom..." Nelson gulped. "I, uh... I think we have a bit of a problem..."

CHAPTER FORTY-FOUR
PRESENT DAY

DRIFTING in the ether between states of consciousness, Claire's eyes opened to an upside-down landscape of trees and night sky. A full moon shone way down low, a grassy terrain floating high above. She detected a shifting, uneven motion in her conscious moments, noting the sensation of motion. She felt her head swelling with blood and gravity pulling her upwards to the grass and uneven ground.

She was being carried.

She lifted her head, and though still dizzy, the world righted itself, moon and sky shifting back to their proper place above. She saw the side of Zevon's face and bald head accented by cold moonlight. His crooked smile was locked into place, blood drying from the cuts on his cheeks and forehead.

Claire muttered, eyes shifting around to take in the location. She was at Zevon's house, moving along the side and into the back yard. The work shed loomed before them and her sense of dread began to rise into her throat.

She started to move, shifting in his arms as he carried her. Her movements were feeble, still groggy and disoriented, but her survival instinct screamed at her body to catch up. Zevon smiled, letting her legs drop so that he could pull the keys from his pocket and open the padlock on the shed's door. Claire hung suspended by his left arm, limp feet barely touching the ground as he kicked the door open into the musky, black lair.

"Now comes the fun part," he said, dragging her inside. Pulling the chain on the single hanging lightbulb, he dropped her down onto the kill-chair, sighing in relief. He glanced over his tools lining the walls; his chisels, picks and hammers. His knives, axes and saws. Zevon traced his fingers over the tools like a loving father, smiling. "And to think, I almost left you all behind."

"Nnnnoooo..."

Claire struggled to stand up, her wits returning to her by the second. Zevon stepped up to the chair and pushed her back, beginning to tie her down with the leather straps he had at the ready. Working first on strapping her left hand down to the armrest, he smiled at her with an unhinged glare.

"Try to relax, Claire," he said. "You won't even feel the worst part. You'll be dead long before I start cutting you into pieces. That's how she likes it!" All mechanisms of logic had escaped him, all filters and methodologies out the window.

This was someone he knew, someone he'd been seen with. There were living witnesses and authorities that would surely be at his door any minute, but none of these thoughts registered behind his arctic, blue eyes as he tightly secured Claire's left arm to the chair.

"Please, no! Don't hurt me, please!"

"You should be flattered! Lila has requested you specifically! This is a great honor!" Zevon pressed his weight against her, pinning her down as she kicked at the ground.

"Who is Lila? What are you talking about? Please let me go! *Let me go!*"

Zevon moved on to her right hand, pinning it against the arm rest and beginning to secure the strap around her wrist. As he leaned in, his right ear presented itself directly in front of her face. Claire wasted no time and took the invitation, leaning forward and chomping down on the ear with full force.

Zevon's eyes clenched shut in sudden panic and surprise as Claire lashed her head back and forth like an animal, tearing off the top half of his ear. He screamed and stumbled off of her, crashing onto his back as he clutched his now-half ear, oozing thick and red.

Her right hand not tied down yet, Claire reached across and undid the strap holding down her left. With each precious second racing away, she wasted no time and bolted out of the work shed as Zevon got to his knees and grabbed an old 12mm straight-chisel.

Stumbling to his feet, he took off behind her, rapidly closing the distance.

"*HELP ME!!! PLEAASE!!! SOMEBODY HELP ME!!!*"

Claire called out to everyone and anyone as her still-woozy legs carried her across the downward slope of Zevon's back yard. The grass was wet and the ground uneven, and her desperate, unsure footing sent her tumbling into the gloom.

She hit her left hip first, then her left shoulder. She continued to tumble for several yards, the night spinning around her until she crashed to a halt on the shore.

Before she could get her bearings, Zevon was on her in an instant, pinning her down. She looked up at him, his countenance a mask of blood and madness. His eyes were wide and fierce, his foul breath seeping through a psychotic smile.

Claire squirmed beneath his weight hopelessly, watching as he clenched the large chisel in his left hand, training it in front of her eyes with its cold, taunting promise.

"Well, here you go," Zevon hooted. "The two most important ladies in my life finally get to meet!"

"Zevon, stop it! You're crazy!"

Zevon held the chisel over her face as he looked up at the lake, scanning its peacefully rolling surface. His eyes filled with tears as he pondered his own betrayal, his own guilt. He had let down the one woman who had ever cared about him, he realized. He had let her down and broken her heart. He had even questioned her very existence.

But now the time had come to redeem himself.

"You were right," he spoke to Lila, wherever she was out there. "You were right about everything... I'm so sorry... I love you, Lila."

Zevon began to raise the carving tool.

"*ZEVON, NO!!!*"

His hand gripped the wooden handle, the sharp tip of the chisel trembling up high as he strained. In a moment he would release the tension, driving the wood-carving tool through Claire's eye and deep into her brain.

"*FREEZE!*"

Tom Kepper bounded out into the yard, the .12 gauge Remington shotgun from his father's squad car in his hands and trained on the madman before him. Zevon and Claire both turned to see him closing in from behind, the muzzle of the firearm pointed squarely at Zevon's back.

"Tom!" Claire cried.

"Drop that weapon, Lang! Right. Fucking. Now."

Zevon growled, his teeth grinding. "Playing cop again, Tom?" He lowered the tool slightly as he looked back at his old high school nemesis.

"Tom! Help me, please!"

"Do it, Lang! *Now!*"

Zevon lowered the chisel to his side, his eyes on Tom. The burning-blue irises flicked back down to Claire as she squirmed beneath him. With another glance, they looked back up at the lake. The beautiful, mysterious lake, its black water rippling in the light breeze and catching the moonlight.

Everything he was, everything he had done, he owed to her. She had made him strong, confident and efficient. She had taught him about love, loyalty and responsibility. She had given him everything, and he knew he owed her nothing less.

With one sharp movement, he jerked the chisel back up over his head, aiming it straight down at Claire's face. She let out a primal scream, and in the same moment, the scream of Tom's shotgun harmonized with her voice.

Zevon's shoulder exploded with a peppering of lead, knocking him off of Claire and sending his weapon soaring into the lake. She tried to scamper away, but Zevon was on her again, pulling her back down as the two of them rolled to the edge of the water.

"God damn it," Tom snarled.

Unable to shoot without hitting Claire, Tom ran and dove at Zevon, knocking him off of her. The two men collided with the sandy shore, knocking the shotgun from Tom's hands.

Tom reached for it on the ground, but Zevon was on him, delivering vicious head butts. Tom's nose broke from the impact and he pushed against the assault. With his left shoulder shredded with several pellets of .12 gauge shot, and half of his right hand broken, Zevon's ability was greatly diminished.

Claire was on her feet again, watching the two men rolling in and out of the water, her mind racing. She looked around, noticing lights turning on in the neighbors' houses. There was the shotgun, several feet away from the bloody struggle, lying in the grass. She wondered if she should.

If she even could.

Tom threw Zevon to the ground, mounting on top of him and delivering smashing punches to the maniac's face. Zevon bucked his hips, shrimping out of harm's way, and kicked up into Tom's jaw. Tom fell back, landing once again on the edge of the lake and dry land, the water gently lapping against him.

Hot pain shot through his head as the raging Zevon was on him again, lashing down with blows from his right elbow. Tom was taller and heavier, and in his youth would have easily dominated Zevon in a fight. But he was gassed already, lungs straining for oxygen, and the smaller man was far-better trained and in much better physical condition.

Zevon's elbow crunched into Tom's face, viciously lashing down again and again. Shattering his orbital socket. Tom raised his hands in defense, not knowing that Zevon would take that as a friendly invitation to grab one of them and break his arm.

He snatched Tom's left arm and begun to swing his legs into position to perform his favorite arm-bar maneuver, when his wounded shoulder cried out in pain from the motion. Zevon released Tom's arm and fell back, hissing in agony. He rolled over, got to his feet and began to run.

Tom was back on his feet as well, barely letting Zevon get two feet away before jumping on his back and clasping around his body in a vice grip. They struggled for balance, Tom hungrily pulling Zevon down, and Zevon using his well-trained defenses to remain standing.

With feet splashing at the water's edge, yanking and pulling with all their might, balance gave way and they both fell into the water.

"*Tom!*"

Claire gasped as she watched them submerged in the shallows, water splashing around them as they struggled for position. Their faces broke the surface, long enough for each to gasp for air before being pulled back down.

Claire ran to the water's edge as the two men splashed further out, coming up again, punches flying. Zevon smashed his right fist into Tom's face, not even caring about the pain inflicted on his already broken fingers. Tom replied with two blows of his own, staggering Zevon back in the now waist-deep water.

Tom moved in again and Zevon clinched, grabbing the back of Tom's neck with one hand and holding under his arm with the other. Tom pushed back. Zevon pushed harder. Technique and finesse were long gone, both men broken and bleeding and gasping for air.

It had become a sheer struggle of will as they looked into each other's eyes. Who was stronger, and who wanted it more. In Zevon's stare, Tom saw nothing but a monster, an empty, black void.

He would not, could not, allow the monster to win.

"Fuck you," Tom seethed, his blood boiling over. Delivering a vicious head-butt, Tom swept Zevon over his leg, sending him down to the water once again. Zevon went under and Tom was right there to hold him down.

Zevon thrashed as Tom held the back of his neck,

keeping his head submerged. Tom grimaced, intent on finishing the job. "Son of a bitch! You fucking psycho!"

In the distance, Claire could hear the whistling howls of police sirens approaching. Tom held Zevon's head under the water, using his last strength to drown the little weirdo from Mars. Claire waited in anticipation, wishing the nightmare would finally be over.

Zevon thrashed under the water, his hands flailing. They came upon a familiar shape. It was a wooden handle, and at the end, a long metal blade. As his lungs ran out of air, his hand gripped the chisel, but only as his body went limp.

Tom released Zevon's head, letting him float up to the surface, face down. Tom and Claire watched as Zevon floated, motionless. It was done. Tom glanced up at Claire. He did not have any words, and neither did she.

Tom's face was bruised, swollen and bloodied, his head ringing, surely concussed. But he had won, and Claire was safe. They could both hear the sirens getting closer. Within two minutes, the police would be at the house, charging down into the backyard.

Boy, am I going to catch hell from my father, Tom thought. Claire smiled at him, grateful for his heroism.

"You okay?" Tom asked.

"I... I think so."

Their moment lingered peacefully.

Zevon's body lurched in a sudden spasm, startling them both. In the next second, he erupted out of the water in one enraged motion, the chisel firmly in his grasp.

Claire began to scream and Tom barely had a second to flinch and stiffen his muscles before the blade shot forward, slicing between his ribs and deep into the pulsating muscle of his heart.

"NOOOOO!!!"

The desperate shriek came from Claire's mouth, filling every fiber of her being. She watched helpless as Zevon jammed and twisted the chisel deep inside Tom's chest as blood sputtered out of his mouth, filling up his airway.

Tom's shocked eyes locked onto Zevon's in his last seconds of life, the evil, glaring smile of a monster being the last thing he would ever see.

With one final, violent yank, Zevon ripped the instrument from Tom's chest, causing a gushing hemorrhage of deep crimson to flow from the wound. Tom's eyes rolled back and his body went limp, falling forward into the water.

Claire backed away, trembling as Zevon staggered towards her through the waves, his blood-soaked murder weapon dripping, leaving a trail of blood up onto the shore.

He smiled, satisfied.

"Claire," he said. "Time to meet Lila."

CHAPTER FORTY-FIVE
PRESENT DAY

ZEVON STEPPED FORWARD and leered at Claire with rattlesnake eyes. Her body trembled. Tears flowed and she had forgotten to breathe. Zevon's smile split across his blood-streaked face. His left shoulder was shredded, his right hand mangled, and at least two ribs were now broken from Tom's zealous strikes. Still, Zevon limped forward, advancing on Claire.

"Lila is really going to love you," Zevon said. He stopped and turned around, looking back out at the lake, scanning the surface and waiting for her to emerge.

"Lila!... Lila!"

With Zevon's back turned, Claire looked down at the shotgun again. Her hatred of violence was one of the qualities that first led her to become a vet in the first place. She detested the idea of even stepping on an ant or swatting a fly. But now, faced with certain death, she desperately dropped down and scooped the firearm into her hands. She aimed it ahead, holding it the way she'd seen done in the movies.

Zevon turned back around, advancing again. "I take care of her, and she takes care of me."

"P-Please, Zevon. Don't come any closer."

Zevon stopped, turning around again and calling back out to the lake. "Lila! Come on out!"

Claire shook her head in pity as Zevon called out into thin air, as if he expected some woman to magically rise out of the water at his beckoning. *What a sad, lost soul,* she thought, *helpless against his own madness.*

"Zevon, there's nobody out there!"

"Oh, she's out there, trust me. Down at the bottom, watching us. Always watching, always listening..."

"Please, just put it down! You're insane!"

Zevon took another step toward her, shifting his bloody grip on the handle of his weapon. "Oh yeah? What are you gonna do, shoot me? You gonna shoot me, Claire?"

"Zevon, p-please..." She cried.

He continued forward with wild eyes, beginning to raise the carving tool over his head, prepared to scrape the brains from her skull. Claire fought back tears, the shotgun trembling in her hands as her finger wrapped around the trigger. In a few steps, he would be on her.

Whether he lived or died seemed of little importance to him now, she realized. All that mattered to him was to keep moving forward, to go as far as he could until he could go no more.

"Do it. Go ahead. Shoot." It was neither a taunt nor a dare. He was asking. Begging.

He would not stop.

Claire squeezed her eyes closed and held her breath.

She aimed the gun and pulled the trigger.

The muzzle kicked up as the explosive flash blew a pattern of buckshot into Zevon's stomach. He staggered back, glancing down in shock at the hole in his torso. Blood flowed from his body, and Zevon could feel the warmth and life going with it. He did not feel any pain, only cold. A numbing cold began to take him, and with his last effort, he took another step forward in defiance.

Claire pulled the trigger again and another thunderous flash kicked the barrel up. The second shot hit Zevon in the chest, tearing into his lungs and heart. Blasted back off his feet, he landed on his back at the water's edge.

With everything fading into the void, Zevon looked to his side and saw the water. He reached for it, needing to touch it one last time, to touch her. But his hand fell short, unable to reach the water.

What a Metal way to go, he thought.

Zevon Lang exhaled his last breath, dying on the shore.

Claire dropped the shotgun to the ground, sobbing.

The police sirens grew louder. They were probably turning onto the small country backroad at that very moment. Claire wept, looking down at Zevon's body, at the pain she had caused, the death she had caused. Her eyes moved out onto the water, where Tom's body remained face down, floating in the shallows.

"Tom..."

Claire ran for the lake, splashing into it as she made her way for him. She felt the cool water envelope her and slow down her stride as she hurried out to the body, already knowing the answer, but still hoping against hope.

She reached him, turning him over. Tom's lifeless eyes stared up at the moon and stars. She clutched him tight, pulling herself close to him, and wept.

"...Tom."

With her last strength, Claire pulled Tom's body through the water, back to the shore. She strained, placing him on the dry soil and fell to her knees, the water lapping up around her.

Tom's blood spilled into the lake, dissolving and feeding into the water as it dripped down. Zevon's blood also trickled down into the depths. Whatever hunger this body of water had, this offering would at least temporarily satiate it.

But not for long.

Claire sat on the shoreline and cried. Sirens roared as they pulled into the driveway of the Lang house. A trickle ran through the water behind Claire and she could hear something emerging. She heard an unfamiliar voice speak to her from behind; innocent and sweet. A woman's voice:

"Are you okay?"

Claire turned slowly, glancing behind her to see a goddess rising from the beneath the shimmering surface. Her hair was flowing and golden, her eyes blazing blue. She looked at Claire with sympathy and understanding.

Claire gasped at the approaching phantom but was unable to even breathe. A terrified scream strangled itself inside of her throat.

Lila smiled and spoke in a soft, reassuring tone to her new friend.

"Are you going to take care of me now?"

THE END

ABOUT THE AUTHOR

Jesse D'Angelo was born in New York and raised in Los Angeles, working as both a writer and an artist in the film and television industries. His credits include "Sky Captain and the World of Tomorrow," "Species," "Hellboy," "Underworld," "The Cave," "CSI: New York," "Kingdom" and "Ancient Aliens."

He currently lives in Chattanooga, TN, with his lovely fiancée and is focusing his efforts on his book publishing goals. He has a blue belt in Brazilian Jiu-Jitsu, makes pizza from scratch, is the proud father of three feline daughters and gets teary-eyed when he watches cheesy 80's movies.

Made in the USA
Columbia, SC
23 September 2024

42170930R00174